LAST VOTE

EMMA LAST SERIES: BOOK TEN

MARY STONE

MARY
STONE
PUBLISHING

Copyright © 2024 by Mary Stone Publishing

All rights reserved.

No part of this book may be reproduced in any form or by any electronic or mechanical means, including information storage and retrieval systems, without written permission from the author, except for the use of brief quotations in a book review.

❋ Created with Vellum

To Melanie. Thank you for being my friend.

DESCRIPTION

One, two, three. It's a killing spree.

With two team members in the hospital and another traumatized by their last near-fatal case, Special Agent Emma Last and her partner are the only ones left standing—and the only ones available to tackle a gruesome murder in Boston.

If Emma can survive the drive through Salem.

Her increasing encounters with the Other and the terrifying dreams that haunt her are nothing compared to the disturbing pull of her childhood home. But making peace with the Other will have to wait.

The husband of a local politician has been found murdered, his naked body—minus a certain appendage—thrown from the rooftop of a high-class hotel, the Roman numeral one carved in his chest. The case seems cut and dried. The victim's wife is running for mayor, and with all but one of her opponents suspiciously forced out of the race, his murder reeks of a warning message.

Until the prime suspect turns up dead.

With leads piling up as fast as the bodies, the countdown is on. Because if two follows one, then the killer has his sights on victim three. Unless Emma can stop him first.

Last Vote, the tenth book in the Emma Last series by bestselling author Mary Stone, gives new meaning to taking a pound of flesh.

1

Jimmy Conrad trailed his fingers up the long, bare leg extending from beneath the comforter. Brushing the fabric aside, he looked up to meet the girl's beautiful eyes.

So hesitant. Not quite *deer in the headlights* frightened, but…anxious, maybe.

"Hey," Jimmy used his most soothing tone, "it's all right. That was a lot of fun. Maybe I'll ask for you again next time."

He stood, dragging the comforter off her body to reveal her curvaceous form, devouring her with his gaze. Damn. He wished he had time for one more go at her.

The Fallweather Hotel's lush white furnishings set off her dark eyes as she slid to the edge of the bed and rose on shaky legs to join him. She wrapped her arms around his neck and pressed herself against him. Jimmy smiled and returned the embrace, his hands moving lower to cup her buttocks. She stiffened, but only for a moment before relaxing into his arms.

One of her perfect nails ran along the lapel of his bathrobe and the blond hair on his chest, still damp from a shower. "You want something more, sir?"

Her lips, puff-pink and luscious from being bitten, curled into a smile. Yet they were nothing compared to her accent. Jimmy didn't know if she was from Bulgaria or Albania, and he honestly didn't care.

She couldn't have been less like his wife. Dianne had traded sex and pleasure for business suits and fourteen-hour workdays a while ago, but that was working out for Jimmy. The money their investments earned let him do this, and Dianne's devotion to her mayoral campaign kept her from asking too many questions.

He wrapped his fingers around the hair at the back of the minx's neck and tilted her head back, molding her body to his. He kissed her until she was breathless and struggling a little before pushing her away, sending her stumbling in the direction of her clothes.

"Looking for a tip?" He shook his head and pointed to her cheap gold dress on the floor. "Shimmy into that and get out of here in the next two minutes, and I'll give you an extra three hundred."

Her eyes widened a touch, and she all but dove for the dress.

Amused, Jimmy watched her fumble to pull the dress back into form and step into it. She began searching for her heels next, her bare thighs offering another sort of invitation as she knelt on all fours to peer under the bed.

Maybe tomorrow, he really would ask for this girl again.

Whatever her name was.

For Jimmy, tomorrow would be a day like any other. His wife would spend every waking moment campaigning for the mayor's office. Behind closed doors, Dianne would ignore him, keeping her head down over budget sheets and hot-button press releases while fielding a constant stream of phone calls.

In public, she'd kiss him on the cheek, hold his hand high

in the air with hers, smiling big and bright whenever a camera was around. And he did his part, too, schmoozing with the investors he knew the best, the ones he could maneuver into the camera's eye next to Dianne, all but ensuring public acceptance that they were in bed together.

As soon as the cameras left the room, Dianne would drop his hand and turn her attention to one of her staffers or grab the next phone being handed her way. Jimmy would fade into the background, into the obscurity of being married to the current mayoral front-runner in Boston.

He glanced at the girl struggling with the thin ankle straps of her stilettos.

I guess it ain't so bad. If I had a wife who actually gave a fuck where I was at night, I wouldn't be dipping into this kind of honey half as often. Or at all.

Jimmy wondered if there'd be any sounds from the suite down the hall. The girl in there probably knew better than to get too vocal, just like Jimmy's date had known. Not like the last girl. She made so much dang noise, he almost had to smother her with a pillow.

Counting on Fallweather's discretion was no small thing, even though he didn't come here to hide his actions from his wife. She couldn't care less what he did with his time, as long as he kept his extracurricular activities out of the public eye and arrived on time whenever she needed him around.

The discretion was more for Jimmy's protection, and that of the other men who enjoyed what the hotel provided. He didn't need any of these girls learning too much about him. They'd spread word back to their pimps, the guys Jimmy paid to ensure a steady supply of fresh flesh.

If the pimps learned too much about Jimmy, they could make trouble for him, and it would be the kind of trouble that brought his after-hours fun to an abrupt stop.

No way in hell am I letting that happen. I've spent enough time in Dianne's shadow without having any pleasure of my own. I ain't going back to that way of life, no sirree.

Finally, the girl had her shoes on and was standing, ready to leave. As promised, he plucked a trio of folded-up Benjamins from his wallet on the nightstand. He tapped them against her lips. "Quiet time, baby doll, right?"

Wide-eyed, she nodded and kissed the money, then took it and slipped it into her cleavage.

He smacked her on the behind to get her moving to the suite's door, and the way she scampered was flat-out adorable.

Jimmy admired the sway of her hips as she slipped into the hallway and pulled the door closed, leaving him on his own again.

He tried to shake away thoughts of what Dianne might be doing. She was probably at some donor event or on the phone with a staffer. Hell, she might even be screwing one of the interns. If so, more power to her.

Jimmy had his. She could have hers.

And now, I'll have a little bit of something else.

He picked up his pants from the floor and felt in the front pocket. The cigarette case holding his joint was just where he'd left it. He stepped into his slippers and left the room, heading for the rooftop access stairwell at the end of the hallway.

The rooftop lounge area was deserted and had been for a while, judging by the puddles and weather-stained tarps covering the bar and seating.

Just the way Jimmy liked it. This was his ritual. His time.

A trio of Adirondack chairs sat among potted ferns by the bar area to the right. He crunched his way across the rooftop gravel and took the middle chair, wrapping his robe tighter against the chilly air.

With the city spread out before him, he lit up, inhaled, and sat back to enjoy the view.

City's practically mine already. Firmly in hand.

Once Dianne was the mayor, there'd be no stopping him. She'd have her staffers and interns and whatever she liked to do in her free time. Like she'd have any more of that once she was elected.

But the pay would be better, and Jimmy knew that money had a habit of moving uphill. All it needed was a little nudge from the right person.

And Jimmy was definitely that person.

A scuffing sound drew his attention. He rolled his head to the side, casting a look toward the door. Just shadows.

Probably a pigeon taking off to go shit on something. Man, this is some grade A, extra-fine ganja that Rosco dropped on me.

He took the last hit, pinched off the cherry, and popped it back into his cigarette case, which he set on the arm of the chair. Then he stood up to take a piss, undoing his robe sash. He angled so he could water one of the ferns.

A large hand came down on his shoulder, spooking him so that his pee arced across the chair. He moved to turn, but a sharp, pointy object pressed into the middle of his back.

His breath caught. "Who the—"

The person grabbing him and sticking a knife in his ribs shoved him to the side. He fell onto the gravel, shooting little stones up into his face. The weight of his attacker's body landed on top of him, and he was wrenched up to his knees before being slammed forward again.

Jimmy's head cracked against the fern's ceramic pot, stars exploding before his eyes. His vision pinpointed and winked out altogether.

When he came to, the first thing he felt was pressure around his hips, and a cold breeze blowing across his legs.

I'm naked. Why the fuck am I naked?

He blinked and forced the world into focus. All he could see was the backside of whoever had attacked him. The guy was big, wearing all black, and straddled Jimmy with his knees clamped tight around his hips.

The man was pulling on Jimmy's dick.

Jimmy shuddered. "Hey, man. I'm not into guys. Just the ladies."

"Be still. All is over very soon."

Thick voice, with an accent. Sounds like the girl.

"You her boyfriend or something? Shit, man, I didn't think she had anybody—"

"You shut up now."

The guy yanked Jimmy's dick, stretching it out as his other hand rose above his shoulder. In it, he held a shining knife.

This is a joke, right? A warning? It has to be.

Jimmy kicked at the gravel and tried to scurry backward to get out from under the guy, but he was too heavy, and had the advantage. He pounded on the attacker's back, punching at his kidneys, but his gaze fixated on the knife raised above the attacker's head.

He's gonna cut it off. Shit, shit!

"No, man! Don't!"

The guy's hand dropped, bringing the knife down.

Jimmy screamed as an arc of blood shot into the night like a fountain. The heat of pain stabbed through him, radiating from his groin to every part of his body. His brain spun, trying to catch up to the pain.

The psycho cut off my dick. He fuckin' cut it off.

His attacker flung the severed bit of meat off to the side, stood up, and turned to face Jimmy, looming over him.

"Why?" He choked on the words, on the pain, and reached

for what wasn't there anymore. Gaping space and bloodied muscle scared his fingers away, and he dug his hand into gravel, fighting off nausea. "Why?"

The shadowy figure dropped, straddling Jimmy's hips again and crushing his hands against his mangled crotch. "I have nothing to say to you. Only things to do to you."

Jimmy tried to struggle free, squirming side to side as gravel pitted into his back, his ass, and his heels. He kicked and bucked, but the man on top of him must've been solid muscle. He kept fighting, twisting between the man's powerful legs that crushed around his rib cage.

Tears poured down his cheeks as the knife fell again, and a stripe of pain seared along his sternum. He looked down to see a single line of fresh blood beading up from the gash down his chest and stomach.

The attacker followed it with two more perpendicular slashes, at the top and bottom of the first line. The knife went into a sheath on his belt after he wiped Jimmy's blood off on his own pants, and the man stood.

Jimmy rolled over, working to get clear of the guy as blood continued to pour from the stump of his dick. He stole a glance at his chest as he tried to crawl away.

Did he make an I? What the fuck?

He worked himself up to standing. But his attacker's arms wrapped around his waist, spinning him around before the guy backhanded him, sending spit and blood flying out of his mouth. In an instant, he was hefted onto the guy's shoulder. "You are the first man to receive his judgment. Your three friends will get their turn soon."

Through the hot haze of agony, Jimmy understood. The other guys...they needed to be told. But it wouldn't be him doing the telling.

Jimmy cried out when his ravaged groin crushed against

the man's shoulder as he lumbered to the edge of the building. But his cries turned to screams as his attacker launched him over the lip of the ten-story roof. The ground rushed up to meet him all too quickly, and the humiliation of his ordeal vanished with a final, crushing moment of pain.

2

The woods near Emma's hometown of Salem spread out like an angry ocean.

A path swayed before her, undulating side to side. She knew this dream state, had stumbled on the same path before. But something was different this time.

She wasn't alone.

A shadowy figure sped between tree trunks. The woman's skin was dark, her hair curly, flowing down her back.

Each time Emma hurried along the path and called out, the figure darted away. Whoever it was seemed to fear her.

A crack of branches twisted her gaze sideways, and she searched for the source of the sound, but the woods there remained still.

This was outside Salem. She wasn't imagining it. The trees were too familiar.

And this forest existed. It wasn't a product of her imagination.

She spotted the silhouette again as the woman in the trees raced away. Another sound—this one like a heavy boot falling—pulled Emma's attention to the path ahead. And then Denae stood before her, white-eyed and frozen mid-step.

"Denae. Why are you here? You're not supposed to be here.

You're in the hospital, and you're going to wake up. The doctors said you had a good chance of waking up."

Instead of answering, Denae stared at her in silence.

Emma's breath turned to ice, her eyes watering as her friend's white-eyed form flickered in and out of sight. Finally, she evaporated. Tendrils of cold mist were all that remained of Denae, leaving Emma alone with only the haunting woods to keep her company.

Off in the distance, a wolf howled a mournful song.

Monitors beeped an insistent warning, dragging Emma from her dream. She bolted upright. Denae's chest rose and fell with steady, shallow breaths. At least that was a relief.

A nurse slammed into the room, and Emma jerked back from the bedside to give him room. He bent to examine Denae.

"Her heart monitor alarm went off. Have you been with her all night? What happened?"

He wasn't looking at Emma as he spoke and continued to check all the connected tubes and wires that monitored Denae's condition. She'd been comatose since being shot in the heart on their last case.

Emma, Leo, and Denae's family had all taken turns sitting in the room with her, sleeping in the cramped chair, reading to her. Or just being there, holding her hand.

The nurse stood upright and faced Emma. "She seems fine. No changes anyway. Did you see anything happen?"

"No. Nothing." A flush crept up Emma's throat. "I was…I woke up from a dream with the alarm beeping. Denae was still breathing, then you came in."

"I'll update the doctor. If anything happens again, press the call button or pull the emergency cord." He pointed to the dangling red string hanging from an alarm on the wall beside Denae's pillow.

Emma nodded, and the nurse left.

"Oh, Denae." She wrapped her fingers around her friend's hand, comforting herself with the warmth of Denae's skin. "Please don't scare me like that again. Please."

Her breath came out choppy as she glanced around her at the hospital room.

Vases of flowers decorated the small table to Emma's left. A sketchbook full of Jamaal's drawings, and some stuffed toys her parents had brought, sat beside the vase.

Everything was just like it had been.

"People with severe heart injuries, or who experience cardiac arrest, often go into comas. Approximately eighty percent of the time, in fact. Ms. Monroe's case mirrors others that have resulted in a successful recovery."

That's what the doctor had said. But that didn't mean she'd recover for certain.

If Emma was seeing her as a ghost in her dreams…she might've been moving between life and the Other right then.

Emma banished her dark thoughts and squeezed Denae's hand.

She fought the impulse to think about her dream, but the images came to her like a flood. Denae's ghost…that had to be what she'd seen in the woods. She'd been dead or almost dead.

That explained the heart alarm going off. And it wasn't the first time Emma had looked into her friend's face and seen empty, white eyes.

She'd been screaming at Denae's ghost after she was shot. With Leo right next to her. He knew, but she still hadn't spoken a word to him since that day.

Because she hadn't just been screaming for Denae to stay with them, to come back. Her friend's ghost told her something that Emma still didn't understand.

"Tell Scruffy I'll keep the wolf quiet for a while."

Emma had collapsed to her knees beside Leo as he and a

team of paramedics frantically tried to control the bleeding and keep Denae from death's door. Her ghost wavered and vanished in front of Emma, coming and going as if struggling to choose a destination while uttering that confusing request.

"Tell Scruffy I'll keep the wolf quiet for a while."

Emma demanded an answer from her friend's ghost that flickered in and out of view above her body, as if it were deciding whether to stay and fight or die and be trapped in the Other forever.

And presumably, Leo's terror at the thought of losing the woman he loved had kept him from asking any questions beyond the obvious ones.

"What the fuck are you talking about? Emma? What the hell—"

The paramedics took over. They kept her alive, but just barely. She'd coded twice on the way to the hospital and required immediate open-heart surgery to remove bullet fragments that perforated her left ventricle.

The trip to the hospital was one Emma wished never to repeat. Along the way, she'd continually had to fight the urge to yell at Denae's ghost, demanding she stay in her body instead of flickering in and out of an Otherly existence in the seat between Emma and Leo.

And the whole time, all she'd said was that same thing about the wolf and someone named Scruffy.

If Emma was seeing Denae's ghost in her dreams now, and the heart monitor alarm had been triggered, then her friend was still fighting that battle between life and the Other.

She gripped Denae's hand with both of her own. "Hold on to me. You hold on, and you stay with us. Please."

The door opened, and Emma expected the nurse to be back with a doctor. Instead, Leo stood there, his face a mask of warped sorrow. The corners of his mouth pulled down, but his eyes swam with confusion or anger, maybe both.

"Why are you holding her hand like that? Is she okay?"

Emma released her grip and stood. She explained about the alarm, and the nurse coming in.

"He didn't say anything had changed. Leo, we...I need to explain about what I said. About the wolf—"

"Not now." Leo brushed past her. "Just let me sit with her. Jacinda's waiting for you downstairs."

Of course. If Leo's here, that means she is too. They've been coming in together every day to check on Denae, Mia, and Vance.

With perfunctory nods to each other, Emma and Leo traded places. She left the room and closed the door quietly behind her.

Leo would want to talk sometime, and soon. Glancing through the window in the door, Emma saw him lowering his forehead over Denae's hand, the same one Emma had been holding. He sat there, hunched over, his body shuddering with sobs.

Spinning on her heel, Emma left the ICU and headed for the waiting room.

She considered stopping in Vance's room, but headed for the elevator instead, punching the button for the first floor. Her other colleague's condition required more regular attention from nursing staff, to treat the second-degree burns he'd received and to monitor his recovery from a traumatic brain injury.

Both had been caused by an explosion he'd run into headlong, believing he would be rescuing Mia.

But it had been a trap, set with the intent of killing all of them at once.

The elevator doors opened, and Emma stepped out, nearly bumping into her Supervisory Special Agent. The two of them stepped to the side, making room for a patient in a wheelchair and her nurse to enter.

When the doors closed, Emma reached out and gave Jacinda a hug, which the SSA returned. They both, and even Leo, had found comfort in the gesture after the events of their last case. After nearly losing two of their teammates, and with Mia suffering the trauma of being abducted and force-fed pure methamphetamine…human touch counted for a lot more than it had before.

Standing back and releasing the other woman, Emma smoothed her shirtsleeves. "Hey, Jacinda."

"Emma, hi." She gestured to a pair of empty chairs in the waiting area. They sat, and Jacinda withdrew a file folder from her bag.

"Is that what you wanted to talk about? Leo said you were waiting for me."

Jacinda sighed. "I'll understand if you're reluctant to take this assignment, temporary as it may be." She held up the file. "Our colleagues in Boston are shorthanded. A politician's husband was found dead, apparently with signs of gruesome premortem knife work."

Emma blinked. She knew what "shorthanded" could mean. "The Boston team, they haven't…"

"No." The SSA's tone was firm. "They're not dealing with…anything like what we've been through. They have one agent tied up in a court case and another on paternity leave. Travel information is in the file, with case notes from SSA Tibble. You'll meet him at their Bureau offices."

Her chest a touch lighter, Emma nodded. "Thanks. This is just what we need." She looked at the elevator. "I don't want to leave, and I know Leo's going to hate the idea of being away from her. But…"

"It'll be good for you both to get back to work."

"What about you? Are you joining us?"

Jacinda shook her head. "I'll be tied up dealing with the review from what happened, so I won't be available except for the occasional text." She leaned forward and touched Emma's arm. "I will, however, keep you updated on everyone's status here. I believe Mia's due to be released soon. If anything changes with Vance or Denae, I'll let you know as soon as I can."

Before Emma could stop herself, the words came tumbling out. "Jacinda...we don't think you did anything wrong. You know that, right? This whole review thing is bullshit."

Jacinda huffed a sad-sounding chuckle. "I appreciate that. I do. It's just policy. The file has your assignment details. Get home and get packing. Leo already has a bag ready. He got prepped when I picked him up this morning."

Emma nodded and collected the file from Jacinda, giving her one last short hug before standing and marching from the waiting room.

The quicker she got on the road and to her apartment, the quicker she'd be back into her work mindset, focused on a case.

On a problem you can solve, instead of the ones you're helpless to affect. And this time with Leo...you can explain yourself and hope he understands.

Before speeding home, she looked up the weather in Boston. A few degrees colder than D.C., only with the wind blowing through the next couple of days.

At her apartment, she whipped through the door and immediately battled with her old Keurig, swapping out pods twice before giving up and deciding her morning fuel would come in the form of a bagel instead.

This'll be an interesting trip. What with Leo not knowing what to think of me and how close we'll be to Salem. Heaven help us both if my dreams get worse.

By the time she'd scarfed down her bagel and added a few more days' worth of clothing to her go bag, Emma's phone had chimed with an email from Jacinda, confirming their travel arrangements. Flights into Boston Logan were all booked, so they'd be flying into Beverly, a suburb north of the city, and renting a car to get to Boston.

Emma stared at the email and reread the plans a few times more. If she remembered right, the route from Beverly to Boston would be putting her right in Salem's backyard.

Looks like it's time to go home, or near enough to it. Whether I'm ready or not.

3

Leo fidgeted as he waited for the person ahead of him to stuff a carry-on into the overhead compartment. Jacinda'd picked up two commuter fares for them on the short hop to Beverly. The narrow plane had two rows of five seats across, one a double and the other a set of three. Leo was happy to see his and Emma's tickets had them on the double side of the aisle.

He came to their seats and hoisted his bag into the bin above. Emma did the same, and Leo stepped aside, allowing her to slide in first. Once she got settled in the window seat, he drew a deep breath and edged his way into the aisle seat beside her.

Now or never, pal. Say what you need to say.

"Emma, I need to ask you something, and this is probably the best time to clear the air."

She sat up a little straighter. "About Denae, I know."

Around them, other passengers continued to shuffle and squeeze their way down the aisle and into seats. The mild commotion was enough to obscure quiet conversation, but that wouldn't last for long.

"How did you know about the wolf, and about her nickname for me?" He coughed, suppressing a laugh. "'Scruffy.' I never mentioned either of those things to you."

Emma stared at the seat in front of her. She took a deep breath. "I was at my high school graduation party the first time I saw a ghost. In life, he'd been a bully, some jerk who thought his strength and social status granted him access to women's bodies."

Leo froze. The commotion in the aisle faded until all he heard in his head was white noise. Whatever he'd been expecting from her, that certainly wasn't it.

Emma's hand settled over his on the armrest. "I know I sound like a crazy person, Leo. Like I'm making something up to put you off the scent, so you'll ignore how weird I am and stop asking questions. But I swear I'm telling the truth."

Leo swallowed. *Keep an open mind, Scruffy.* "Okay, but I'm failing to make a connection between a high school bully and—"

"The bully was killed in a car accident hours after our graduation ceremony. I saw it on the news the next morning. Only, I'd seen him at the grad party that night, dressed in his varsity jacket and wearing one of those super-styled ball caps." She gestured at her neck and shoulder. "He had some kind of stain on him. I thought it was puke at the time, but after seeing the news, I knew it had to have been blood. Because he'd died an hour and a half before that. He was my first ghost."

First?

"And this relates to Denae how?" He shook his head. "I'm sorry, I'm still not seeing—"

"Denae's ghost talked to me, before going back into her body. I saw her again on the way to the hospital." Emma's cheeks were pale. "Each time she coded in the ambulance, and they revived her, she would flicker into the space between you and me in the SUV and say the same thing. 'Tell Scruffy I'll keep the wolf quiet for a while.' I'm sorry, and I know it looks like I'm using Denae to—"

"I believe you." His voice broke. He shifted in his seat to keep his back to the passengers still moving down the aisle. His head bobbed, ever so slightly, as he fought back tears. "I don't think you're using her. I don't know why I believe you. I shouldn't, but…"

"And again this morning, right before you came in. She was in my dream, and then a wolf was howling. I woke up, and her heart monitor alarm was going off." She looked him in the eye. "What do you know about the wolf? What is it to you?"

"Only that I've been hearing howls since our second case together. I had a nightmare about my grandfather. Wolves were chasing him. Then on that bomber case, when you almost jumped off the balcony that night…"

She gave a fast nod. "Yes. The wolf was in my dream that night, and I heard it outside and wanted to go to it for some reason I cannot explain."

"Is that why you flew out of the old pastor's trailer, back in Little Clementine? Because of the wolf?" Recollections tumbled through Leo's brain, making connections at rapid speed. "Or on our first case, where you were talking to the perpetrator like you knew things you shouldn't have known, distracting him with talk about needing 'hand powder.' Did the wolf howl them at you, or was it a ghost?" He searched her face. "I'm sorry for all the questions, but this is a lot, Emma."

"I know. I get it. On our first case, that was a ghost. Penelope, the trapeze artist who was killed first. She was telling me over and over that she needed hand powder, just like you remember. I had no idea what it meant, just like I didn't know why Denae told me what she did." She closed her eyes and shook herself, like she wanted to forget something traumatic. "I don't know how the wolf is connected, only that it is, and that I can't seem to escape it. I still have nightmares about it sometimes."

"But it wasn't in the trailer that day at the circus, or in Little Clementine."

"No." She shook herself again, and her grip on his hand tightened painfully. "That was the elder Pastor Darl's ghost. He was taunting me, and…you remember what his body looked like, right? After being cut apart with an axe? Imagine that, but all the pieces are coming back together and still dripping blood everywhere. Plus, he's shouting at you."

Leo shivered. "The man was a literal holy terror when he was alive."

The last of the passengers had boarded, and the flight attendants were checking seat belts and closing overhead bins.

Leo patted Emma's hand. They'd finish the conversation later. "I still have questions, but they can wait. Baby steps, okay?"

She nodded and smiled. He returned the gesture, then faced forward in his seat, closing his eyes and waiting for the plane to move.

Denae's face had barely left his mind since he'd last seen her, lying in her hospital bed, connected to monitors and IVs. Her parents had come to sit with her since he would be leaving. They'd each hugged him, even Jamaal, who gave him a solid, brotherly slap on the back.

"We'll keep watch, Leo. We know you got your duty out there. She'll be here when you get back, and…she'll be awake too. Big sis ain't staying out of the fight."

Exchanging sympathy and words of comfort with the Monroes, being so close to them and in those conditions… he'd felt so awkward.

But Noah Monroe, Denae's father, was quick to welcome him and express his gratitude.

"I heard you helped save our daughter's life. You need anything, just ask. Anytime you get hungry, there'll be a place at our table. I mean it. You're family, as far as I'm concerned."

Denae's mother, Carrie, wrapped him in a hug and told him she knew her daughter would come back to them.

"Because she loves you. I know it in my bones, Denae loves you and that's why she's going to wake up."

Leo wanted so badly to believe Denae would come out of the coma and be the same woman she'd been before. They'd pick up their relationship, and he'd start visiting her family for dinners, maybe for Jamaal's next birthday. His college graduation, which would happen someday, he knew it.

Or the next time I see the Monroe family again, we might be standing together at a grave side service.

Leo clenched and unclenched his hands, then rubbed his fingers against his pants. Subtly, but enough to remind himself his hands were clean of Denae's blood now. Had been for days. And she was alive.

Beside him, Emma tucked her phone away and gazed out the window at the ground crew signaling the pilot to begin taxiing.

She looked so normal. Not like a woman who talked to ghosts.

Maybe Denae had told her about the wolf Leo kept hearing and shared her nickname for him. But he doubted it. They'd kept their intimate talk where it belonged, strictly between the two of them. And in his mind, that had made their moments spent together all the more special.

All the more real and separate from the job.

But those moments and memories were haunting him now.

Early in their relationship, he and Denae had woken

together after one of their sleepovers at his place. She'd done most of the sleeping, while he'd fought with nightmares about howling wolves.

The next morning, he'd told her that the howls felt like a sound he could never escape. She'd promised to do what she could to help him, confused as she'd been by the recurring nightmares. And he'd felt better, just from her earnest promise.

After that, he'd made her his special veggie omelets and black beans with *pico de gallo* and cheese, a breakfast that had become her favorite. The two of them had eaten together and ridden to work together and been more of a couple than he'd ever imagined possible. An ideal he'd only dreamed of in the past.

He'd tried to make the same meal for himself yesterday and had broken down in tears. The whole mess of eggs and vegetables went right into the trash.

Now he blinked hard. He'd already broken down once at Denae's bedside, and he wouldn't do it again so soon. Let alone on an airplane surrounded by people he didn't know.

Forcing Denae out of mind, Leo considered Emma's claim about ghosts instead. It was far less painful than dwelling on his fear that Denae might never wake up.

Talking to ghosts. He wondered what his yaya would have said to that. While bizarre and otherworldly, the idea that Emma could see and communicate with spirits of the dead would explain plenty about her odd behavior. He'd chalked up her curious insights to a fantastic instinct or intuition, whatever they wanted to call it. That was an easy answer, a waved hand that Leo had never been ready to accept.

But ghosts weren't an easier answer. Were they?

Emma shifted, and he glanced at her now that the flight attendants had finished their spiel.

Small talk. He'd start with small talk and work his way

back up to ghosts. Once they were fully airborne, other passengers would have headphones in or be occupied with their own conversations. He'd be careful to keep his voice low, anyway, just to be safe.

"You know if we're getting help from the D.C. BAU on this case?"

She shook her head but kept quiet. A few awkward seconds ticked by, and she added, "I talked to Jacinda about making sure we got back when Denae wakes up. She guaranteed it."

"That's Jacinda in a nutshell."

Emma *mm-hmm*ed. "But she didn't say anything about other D.C. agents heading to Boston. This one's on us."

She turned back to the window, seeming to consider the conversation over. Maybe guessing Leo needed some space. As much as could be had on a commuter hop anyway.

There'd been a moment where he'd wanted to elaborate. To tell her his real reason for continuing to work. He had no choice, really. Stopping for any length of time would mean admitting defeat.

Giving up and accepting the terrible fact that he couldn't actually protect the people he cared for, that he couldn't guarantee their safety and ensure they were free to live their lives.

He hadn't been able to save his grandfather. And he hadn't really been able to save Denae.

Tears nipped at his eyes again, and he faced forward once more. Now wasn't the time to get caught in those thoughts, real or not.

Carefully, he stole another glance at the agent beside him, who was the one thing—person—able to offer him any sort of distraction.

What would working with her look like, going forward? That was the real question weighing on him as they approached another case for the first time since her revelation. If he chose not to believe her, he couldn't imagine how they'd trust each other after this. But convenience and comfort weren't good reasons to believe something so crazy. And, hell, *pretending* to believe Emma could be the worst betrayal of all.

Even if I choose to accept what she says, leaving belief aside for the moment, there'll be a part of me that doubts what she tells me. No matter how hard I try to believe her.

To trust her.

When it came right down to it, neither option was ideal.

And all he could do, it occurred to him, was tell her that. If they were going to trust each other ever again, he had to start with honesty. Not some fake lie that might placate her and churn in his gut for the foreseeable future.

"Emma…" She shifted to meet his gaze, and the purse to her lips told him she sensed what was coming. "I'm struggling with…what you told me. I can't help believing you, and I do. But I'm still confused about why, and I don't know where that leaves us."

She stretched in her seat, moving so that her back rested on the wall of the plane as the pilot announced they were fifth in line for takeoff. "I'm not lying, but I get it. I understand. Hell, if you'd told me the same thing years ago…" She let out half a chuckle, even though the squint in her eyes looked sad. "I'd have thought you were crazy. So yeah, I get it. It's hard to accept."

Leo's chest went a touch lighter. That was the best response he could have hoped for. "Does anyone else on the team know? Did Denae?" His throat closed on her name, but Emma was already shaking her head.

"Mia, but Denae doesn't. I'd planned to keep it a secret, but Ned, Mia's brother, came to me and…" Emma cut herself off, glancing around as if they might be overheard. He could understand why. "When he *came to me*, I couldn't keep it from Mia. I had no choice but to tell her."

He knew he was staring. Waiting for a third eye to pop out of her forehead, or for her to tell him it had all been a stupid joke, but she only held his gaze and waited for him to say something. "So...you'll tell me? If they come to you. Or if...if you see Denae while we're in Boston."

She paled. "Of course I will. But that's not going to happen. She's alive, and she's going to stay that way. We're getting her back, and Vance and Mia too. We're not losing anyone."

You can't know that. Or can you?

Knowing how bad it would sound to ask if a ghost had given her inside information, Leo quietly nodded and smiled. "Okay, then. Just keep me in the loop if any...friends of yours show up."

"That's the plan." She tapped her palm against the armrest. "No more secrets. I'll be telling you. And when you get a chance, I hope you'll talk to Mia about it. Maybe that'll help too."

"Yeah, it'll be good when she's ready to talk." He caught her eye. "Thank you for trusting me. I know it took guts."

Because whatever this is, she believes it. I can see it in her face. That means, at least, she deserves this much.

Emma nodded, her smile easing a little. "No more secrets, Leo. I promise. If you don't always believe what I tell you, that's okay. I get it, and hopefully it'll change, but I get it. But no matter what, I'm not going to lie to you or hide anything else."

She went quiet on that note and resumed gazing out the window. Leo stared past her at the rolling patches of grass alongside the runway as the plane built up speed.

All he could see were blurry patterns of green and gray, broken up by the runway light posts standing sentinel. As the aircraft left the ground and Leo watched the grass and pavement disappear from view, he felt as if he were climbing into a future that might not include Denae.

He caught a glimpse of Emma's mouth curled into a smile as she settled into her seat. Maybe what Emma had seen out the window included the hope and conviction she'd expressed before—that Denae would wake up and the whole team would come back together.

And maybe that was a good thing. Wherever that hope came from.

4

Emma had wanted to drive, but Leo grabbed the keys for their rental car while she was in the bathroom. So now she sat in the passenger seat, while Grandpa Ambrose merged into traffic going from the airport toward the highway.

When they reached the junction, Leo slowed for the cloverleaf, looping them around and onto the highway. Emma rolled her eyes as he hugged the shoulder to allow a semitrailer to rumble by.

She held in a scoff when Leo allowed another car, the one that had been behind them, to pass them.

He eventually slid into the lane and had them cruising at a steady fifty-five. Emma wanted to applaud but figured that would undo whatever goodwill she'd earned during their conversation before takeoff.

Leo set the cruise control, and she released the tiniest groan.

"I'm driving, so you may as well get used to it. Besides, neither of us knows this area particularly well, so going a little slower than *bat out of hell* can't hurt, can it?"

She let his joke slide and gazed out the window at the

view of what had once been her old stomping grounds. "I grew up not far from here."

"Salem, right?"

"Yeah. We're going to pass through, but you can't see my neighborhood from the highway."

"Want to make a quick stop?"

She wondered if seeing the streets she'd played on as a child might help her understand anything about the Other or the wolf howls she—and apparently Leo—had been hearing.

But they'd come here to assist with a case, not take a trip down memory lane.

Or any lane. There's nothing of my family left in Salem except our home and all its ghosts.

She didn't think the Last family home was haunted. At least, she'd never suspected it when she was a child.

Doesn't mean the old homestead is empty of secrets. You still haven't cleared out all the furniture or decor, Emma girl.

They continued on the highway for a while, with Leo making chitchat about the scenery. Emma listened with half an ear, her mind drifting to thoughts of what going back to Salem might be like.

She spotted the sign announcing the city up ahead. "Here we go. Back to where it all—" She caught a sudden chill and wrapped her arms around herself. "Can we turn up the heat?"

Leo glanced sideways at her. "If you need to, yeah. I'm fine."

"I swear it feels like the temperature dropped ten degrees just now." She reached over and raised the setting to seventy-four.

Outside the car, the trees and buildings of Salem stood like quiet sentinels. Even though Emma had grown up in this city, none of it felt familiar or welcoming. If anything, the trees along the highway formed an imposing fence while the buildings towered like ominous fortresses.

They were halfway through Salem when the chill came back with a vengeance, sending fingers of ice across her skin.

Emma jerked and grabbed at the shoulder belt before wrapping her arms around herself. Leo was talking to her, yelling something, but all she could think of was the freezing grip that had wormed its way over every inch of her body.

"Emma! What's happening? What's the matter?"

A shiver racked her, snapping her head back against the seat. Her teeth clacked together, and her hands clenched over her biceps as she gripped herself.

"Emma, what the hell?"

"C-c-c-cold. I-I-I can't…so c-c-c-cold."

"The heater's still on." He reached out to cover a vent with his hand. "I can feel the airflow. What's going on?"

Her whole form was racked with shivers, and she pulled her legs up, setting her boots on the seat edge. "Keep…keep driving. Faster, please." Emma curled into herself, burying her head forward between her knees. "I-I'm gonna be…sick."

She moved to wrap one arm around her stomach, one around her knees, and remained curled in the seat, rocking against a wave of nausea that rose against the constricting chills racing up and down her body.

"Do I need to find an ER?"

"I…I don't know." Another shiver racked her. She flinched when his hand briefly touched her shoulder.

Signs littered the highway ahead. He nudged the car over the speed limit, taking it off cruise control. "I can take us to—"

"No!" Emma shot her head upward to focus on the signs, then spun toward him. She knew her face had to be ghostly pale. She shook her head and gripped his forearm. "Don't stop. Not…not in Salem. Please. We have t-t-to…" She swallowed and forced the words out of her mouth by sheer will. "Have to get p-past…Salem. Don't…s-stop."

Focusing on the road, he nodded. "Okay. Gimme my arm back."

Emma released him on command, pulling back into herself as she kept shivering. Leo brought both hands to the wheel, and she made a silent promise never to joke about him driving like a grandpa again.

He swerved around a slower vehicle, getting them into the fast lane. Emma watched him check the mirrors before pushing down on the gas pedal.

The vehicle surged again. In seconds, they'd shot up to ten miles over the speed limit, then fifteen. He moved into the middle lane to pass a pickup and wove back into the fast lane as soon as it was clear.

Emma forced herself to laugh against the painful chill that kept clutching at her. "Y-you're spee...speeding f-for me."

"Tell me if you change your mind and want me to pull off for a rest stop or hospital."

"Just...j-just g-get past Sa...Salem."

It's like I have hypothermia. What the hell is happening to me?

A hospital would've been the smart thing. The rational thing.

But this cold wasn't anything a doctor could diagnose. It wasn't natural.

It was Other.

Something like a high-pitched whimper bubbled out of Emma's throat, and Leo's hand moved back to her shoulder. "If you need to get sick—"

"G-go faster. Please."

Head up, she took deep breaths. One of her legs slipped back down until her boot landed on the floorboard. She stared out the window at a sign that thanked them for visiting Salem.

The chills receded. The sense of being gripped inside a

glacier, crushing her in the seat...it was passing. With every foot of roadway added between them and Salem, she found it easier to breathe.

"You okay now?" Leo moved the car back to the travel lane, easing off the gas until they were back at the speed limit. "What the hell was that?"

"I'm okay." Her breath shuddered, but she'd stopped clenching herself. She smoothed back her hair and then combed her fingers through it. "Thanks for speeding up. I know that can't have been easy for you."

"You're welcome." He clenched his fingers around the steering wheel. "But you didn't answer my question. What the hell was that?"

She shook her head, licking her lips. "I don't know, Leo. I don't. I just...all of a sudden, I felt like I was freezing to death."

"You looked like it, too, but when you grabbed my arm... your hands felt warm. You said we had to get past Salem."

"Yeah." She shifted in her seat, forcing herself to sit up straighter.

"Yeah? Something you want to tell me? I thought we'd crossed over. No more secrets, right?"

Emma sighed, pinched the bridge of her nose, and gave a series of rapid nods. "You're right. No more secrets. I...I've been having these dreams. About Salem. The woods around the city, and people my mom knew. That's where I was in my dream this morning, when I saw Denae again."

"Did you see her just now?"

The intense—almost commanding—tone of his question put her back in her seat. "No. I swear, I'll tell you if I do. Whatever that was, it had nothing to do with her."

Leo gave her a sideways glance. "Okay. So what happens now? Do we go back and figure it out, or..."

"We can't go back right now." She shook her head so

vigorously, her hair fell into her eyes. "I'm not sure I want to. I've been wondering if I should, but it hasn't been possible. And just then? I don't know. It was like…like I was being pulled. Like something wanted me to stay and refused to let me go until I'd crossed some boundary. It started and stopped so suddenly."

"So why didn't we stop? We could have at least pulled over until whatever was going on passed."

"If we'd stopped, I don't think I'd have been able to leave until I dealt with whatever that was, and we don't have time for that. I need to come back, but…not now."

Even as she said the words, Emma knew, like it or not, she'd have to make her peace with the city of her childhood soon, if she truly wanted to understand her relationship with the Other.

5

Monique Varley sat back suddenly, nearly crushing a lemongrass plant in her small greenhouse garden. Her hands dug down into the soil at her sides, finding purchase in the carefully tended ground and holding on with everything she had.

For almost thirty years, she'd found refuge in her little hideaway outside Salem. Shelter from the one woman who would end her at the drop of a hat.

It's been like living in a tomb full of memories. Memories of what I chose to risk for Gina Last, and why I made that choice.

Despite the warmth of her tiny, hand-built greenhouse and the pleasant spring day outside, she'd been overcome by a withering chill. As if an icy wind had stolen in through the cracks in the greenhouse door to pierce her skin to the bone.

Like an accusation, like she knows what I've done.

But the soil around her hands was warm against her freezing fingers, and none of the plants around her showed the terror of frost.

Only Monique felt the cold.

This has happened before, Moni, and you know it. If you're being honest with yourself, you know why.

She closed her eyes, dug her hands deeper into the soil, and thought about her promises. The one she'd made with Gina when they were alone.

And the ones she made with Gina when they weren't so alone.

Slowly, ever so slowly, Monique's breath banished the unnatural freeze that'd overcome her without warning just moments before.

She gazed beyond the glass of her greenhouse to her little shack. A tiny front porch, just large enough for her century-old rocking chair. Plants hanging from the eaves, some that she'd only just brought outside to enjoy the spring sunshine. The home was clean and safe—all she could ask for—and she'd lived there for years without anything like this happening until a month ago.

The freezing numbness burned away any sense of safety. Wherever it came from, whoever was doing it, they meant her harm.

And I'm probably not the only one they have their eye on.

Thinking about the way her fingers felt trapped in ice, the way her blood seemed to slow, and how her heartbeat sank to a dangerously slow pace, Monique finally had to ask the question she'd been putting off.

Turning to her mirror, she did what she'd always done. Asked the person most likely to know the answer.

"Is this because of what I told Gina I would do? Or is this the other promise, the one the three of us made together?"

She wouldn't even think the third woman's name. Doing so might be all that was needed to reveal her hiding place, and that would bring her face-to-face with an enemy she knew not to underestimate.

Her foe had failed to find Monique for over two decades, while Gina's daughter grew ever stronger.

Dread rose in her, and she pushed herself to her feet. She was no good to the plants this way. *I'm no good to myself.*

She brushed the dirt from her hands, already beginning to catalog a list of supplies she would need to restock. Just in case. And once she did that, she'd turn her eyes forward.

It was time to call upon the Other and see exactly what was going on around Salem.

6

Emma breathed a deep sigh as Leo pulled into the Boston Bureau's parking garage. He drove them past lines of private and official vehicles searching for a space to park their rental.

The garage's low concrete ceiling and dim lighting conspired to give Emma the same constricting chill that had gripped her earlier. She resisted the reflex to curl in on herself and instead sat up in her seat, watchful and alert as Leo maneuvered into a narrow space near the stairwell door.

They were here, finally, and far enough away from Salem that she was ready to get to work, whatever that might entail.

Jacinda still hadn't sent any new information about the case, except to let them know who to talk to once they arrived.

"Jacinda says SSA Walter Tibble is our contact here. VCU offices are on the fifth floor."

When the elevator opened to the fifth floor, they found a stocky man with a buzz cut leaning on the wall across from the stairwell. He straightened up and adjusted his glasses as he greeted them. "Agents Ambrose and Last. Thanks for coming. Follow me."

Leo shot Emma a look as they followed the man down a short hall.

She only shrugged in return. SSA Tibble had been told to expect them, and if he had a murderer on his hands, she couldn't blame the man for being blunt.

The Boston VCU's bullpen was smaller than theirs back in D.C. Tibble beelined through it to a conference room. Two agents sat hunched over their laptops inside. The SSA pointed to the woman, a petite thirtysomething with dark hair worn in a tight bun. "Special Agent Midori Nishioka."

She rose to standing and extended a hand. "Pleased to meet you both. Thanks for joining our little party."

"And I'm Special Agent Paul Branner." The barrel-chested man stood up beside her. "The older veteran, but none the wiser. Welcome."

Emma and Leo exchanged handshakes with the agents, and the four of them took their seats.

"Do you need anything?" Tibble's gaze raked between them. "I should've asked, but the afternoon's wasting."

"We're good." Leo nodded at the screen at the front of the office, which showed the driver's license of a blond-haired man whose crinkled skin suggested a lot of years in the sun. "Fill us in."

Emma pulled out her iPad, her eyes focused on Tibble as he lifted a remote from the table and turned back to the screen. "Meet Jimmy Conrad, husband of local politician Dianne Conrad. He was thrown naked from the top of our downtown's Fallweather Hotel last night. He had a small knife wound in his back, a set of three slash marks, forming a capital letter *I* or Roman numeral one on his chest, and—"

Paul grunted. "Someone John Bobbitted the poor bastard before throwing him off the roof."

A whistle slipped from Leo's lips, but he waved Tibble on.

"Right. Thank you, Paul. Not an everyday murder." Tibble changed displays on his screen, and a gruesome, battered body came up. Unrecognizable, bloody, and misshapen. A second image took its place as Tibble thumbed his remote again. A blood-spattered taxi sat alongside a curb. "Victim landed on the sidewalk beside this vehicle and died on impact. It's a narrow sidewalk right there, so we're lucky the passenger being dropped off hadn't exited the car yet. They'd have been a landing pad, and we'd be dealing with two bodies."

"I'm sorry." Emma held a hand up, stopping him. "Died on impact? He wasn't—"

"As Paul said, our M.E. confirmed Conrad was likely alive when he was tossed off the rooftop. The mutilation certainly occurred premortem, and witnesses have described hearing screams before the moment of impact."

Emma kept her gaze on the screen, examining the photo. "We're sure he was thrown from the roof? He could've jumped, perhaps to escape an attacker that was torturing him."

Tibble reached toward the screen and drew an imaginary line between the nearest building and the body. "The angle at which he hit the sidewalk brought him here," he indicated the area next to the taxi, "where the cab driver was letting out a passenger. If Conrad had jumped, with the sidewalk as narrow as it is right there, he would have impacted on the cab itself."

Across the table, Paul squirmed in his chair, shifting his bulk side to side. "Not like he'd cut his own dick off either. Somebody had to be up there with him doing that, unless there's some new kink going around."

Midori elbowed him before looking up and across the table. "He didn't leap to avoid some other fate." She spoke firmly. "He was helped by someone…or someones…strong enough to force him off the roof."

Emma jotted down what they'd already been told, then looked back to Tibble. "I take it forensics hasn't come to any conclusions about suspects?"

"The rooftop lounge area is pretty clean, other than the blood and the, uh…the remains."

"Remains?" The facts hit her even as she asked the question. "Oh, Mr. Conrad's severed penis. Gotcha."

Tibble nodded nervously and squirmed in his seat. "They also collected a monogrammed cigarette case containing the remains of a joint, which autopsy results reveal Jimmy Conrad smoked before he was attacked."

Leo glanced up from his notes. "He's known for that?"

"No, but trace residue was also found in his pants pocket. His clothes were in his top-floor suite, room ten twenty-three."

"So he got high, then got naked and went up to the roof?" Leo held up his finger and circled it. "Or the other way around?"

Tibble pressed another button, showing a photo of a torn hotel robe lying on some gravel. "We're assuming he had the robe on while he was getting high on the roof. At some point, the robe was forcibly removed." Nearby, a pool of blood glared bright in the artificial light set up for photographing. "No weapon was found."

"We have a suspect." Midori cleared her throat. "Mark Wilhelm."

Tibble shifted over to a new driver's license, this one of a man who looked slightly older than their victim. He had gray hair, perfect teeth, and was clean-shaven.

Leo leaned closer to the screen. "Wilhelm doesn't look like someone who could heft another guy off a roof. Fit, sure, but he's a little old for that."

Tibble grunted and straightened his glasses again. "He's a little older than me, and I'd be able to do it, but the fact is that this isn't a man who'd do his own dirty work. Midori, go ahead."

"Wilhelm is a candidate for mayor running against Dianne Conrad, Jimmy's widow." Midori clasped her hands on the table in front of her. "The election's later this year, and Wilhelm's opponents have been disappearing one by one."

Emma frowned at the picture. "Disappearing, as in you have active missing persons cases that we need to be looking at alongside this murder?"

"Uh-uh, disappearing out of the mayoral race is what she means." Paul motioned to Tibble, who changed screens again, then waved at the new photos of two similarly put-together individuals, one man and one woman. "Meet Peggy Brauer and Robert Saylor, both previously candidates for the mayor's office. Peggy dropped out after her kids were expelled from a private school, supposedly for vandalism. Brauer claimed she received threats directed at herself and her children but wouldn't release them to us. Idiot destroyed—"

"Paul!" Tibble glowered at him, leaning against the table. "Could we refrain from name-calling? Or at least reserve the name-calling for our unsub?"

The agent scowled, and Midori took over. "She claimed she destroyed the threats. Robert Saylor's house was burned down. Nobody died, but it was a close thing. The working theory is that Wilhelm's been hiring people to take out his competition in very real, physical ways." She jerked her chin at the screen where the faces of the two former candidates smiled down at them. "Conrad's murder would make this the most severe attempt at swinging the election, but Dianne Conrad is the front-runner by a wide margin. He could be getting desperate."

Emma scribbled down the developments before looking up to meet Tibble's gaze. "We're sure the mayoral race is worth that much to him?"

"It is." Tibble gave a short, definitive nod. "By his own admission. Wilhelm has been quoted, repeatedly, as describing the mayor's office as the last step in his career. This is his 'make or break campaign.'"

"Okay, but scaring off competition through threats and arson is a long way from mutilating a man and throwing him off a roof."

Leo shifted in his seat. "Not much finesse to what happened to Conrad. And I hate to be the one to say it, but is Wilhelm really that stupid? His name would be the first on any cop's lips, and he has to know that."

"We've been trying to make a case against Wilhelm for a while now." Tibble shifted the screen to the remains of a large, burned-down house. "However, his money and connections are making things difficult."

Emma could only imagine. "What makes you so sure he's behind all this? Leo's point stands."

"Man's been strong-arming his way into positions of power for years." Paul's voice had gone a touch more serious, maybe a bit chastened, but his dislike of the politician still rang through the words."

"How so?"

"Both Peggy Brauer and Robert Saylor refused to press charges or testify, despite claiming to know, for certain, that their difficulties were Wilhelm's doing. There's obvious intimidation at play, especially considering that we couldn't even get Peggy to hand over the threats she'd received."

Tibble's gaze was fixated on Robert Saylor's ruined house. "Damaging property is one thing. Who would've expected mutilation and murder?"

Emma waited, and when Tibble didn't go on, she asked the obvious. "Why not go after Dianne instead of Jimmy?"

"Wilhelm thinks he's invincible, but he's also old-school. Sexist." Tibble shrugged. "Maybe he couldn't stomach the idea of sending his goons after a woman? It was a man's house that was burned down, after all…a single man's, not even a dog inside…and in the case of the Conrads, the adult kids live out of state. Hard to get to the wife through them, so maybe he went after the husband. Polls are getting worse for him, so maybe he told his folks to go all out."

"No offense," Emma leaned forward, drawing Tibble's gaze, "but that's quite a few maybes."

For a moment, she thought the SSA would bristle, but he wilted instead. Leaning his hands against the conference table, he nodded before answering. "And not a lot of evidence, I know."

Midori coughed gently. "Not any evidence yet, but it's what we've got."

Tibble sighed. "Which is why we called in reinforcements."

"We're glad to be fresh eyes." Leo shut down his iPad.

"That's what we need, fresh eyes." Tibble straightened. "Last thing I want is for any of us to get tunnel vision. Even if it looks like Wilhelm is behind this, in person or otherwise, we need to be open to other possibilities. Putting aside the fact that he wouldn't likely have gotten his own hands dirty in all this."

"You want us at the hotel?" Emma shut down her own iPad, already antsy to get moving.

"I'm going to ask you to go over there with Paul, yes." Tibble pulled out business cards and pushed them across the table to Emma and Leo. "That's my number. Text me yours, and I'll send you what we have. Namely, of note right now, the full log of all guests who were staying at the hotel last night. We're already running background checks, but you should have the names, and we'll let you know if anything suspicious comes up."

"Sir?" Midori raised one hand. "What about—"

"You get some rest." Tibble held up his hand when it looked like she was about to argue. "No buts, Midori. You were on call last night and showed up to that crime scene, and you haven't stopped since. Leo and Emma can help Paul investigate the hotel while you get a few hours of shut-eye, and then the two of you can trade off later. Understood?"

She sighed, but nodded and began packing up her things.

"I'll be reviewing autopsy results and call you if anything else comes in." Tibble shifted his gaze toward Paul. "Try to act civilized, yeah? No yelling at politicians or knocking in heads that don't belong to murderers?"

Emma raised one eyebrow but couldn't quite force down a smile as Paul gave an exaggerated salute to his SSA. The agent might be a touch abrasive, but she'd dealt with worse.

Having another agent tag along with her and Leo was a bit of a relief. The tension between them might have calmed as they'd traveled from Salem to Boston, but another party being present could only mean they'd stay all the more focused on the investigation.

And if they came across some ghosts, she'd give Leo the chance to play interference and distraction. Until then, three heads would be better than one.

7

Emma settled into the back seat of the Bureau SUV with her tablet on her lap. Neither she nor Leo knew the area, and she welcomed the extra time to review her notes.

Eyes on her tablet, she raised her voice over the local rock station. "Can you give us more about Mark Wilhelm? He's a public figure, most likely to be accused of offing the competition. What else?"

"Old money in Boston." Paul reached forward and spun the radio dial until the volume went down to just above normal levels. "I'm just the other side of fifty, spent my whole life here, and his family's been around for as long as I remember. Longer. Man's dad was a Massachusetts senator, and his grandfather was a wicked smart shipping tycoon who practically ran the wharf. Most of the public criticizes the family, but he's found his way onto a popular mayoral ticket anyway."

"You don't think much of him." Emma set her tablet aside and rested her elbows on her knees, resigned to leaning forward to hear him over the radio.

"Hard to think otherwise. Seems like there's never any

new blood in our elections. Same old, same old. Just like Congress."

Emma waited for the man to go on, but when he didn't, she decided to settle back for the ride. They didn't have long to go before Paul pulled into a circular drive in front of the historic Fallweather Hotel.

A valet in a vest and bow tie waved them toward a parking space, only betraying a small grimace of annoyance when Paul flashed his badge.

Lifting a hand to wave at the valet, Leo snorted. "He looks happy to see us."

Paul laughed. "Nah, just the average Masshole's way of saying he likes you." He wheeled them into the spot, and they got out, heading to the hotel entrance three abreast. Paul stood aside, letting them precede him past the young man holding the door open "I'm gonna let you two lead. I was here this morning."

Waiting for Paul to get inside, Emma examined the gleaming marble columns and polished brass fixtures of the lobby.

"This is some hotel. You sure they'll be up for talking to outsiders?"

"Maybe they'll take kindly to new faces. Concierge desk is a good place to start. Guy on duty this morning said last night's man would be here by two, so he oughta be here now."

Leo led the way across the marble floor, his shoes clicking a steady beat beside Emma's. At the concierge desk, a skinny young man with curly red hair and prominent freckles stood staring at them. Emma half expected him to sneer like the valet had, but he offered a comically large smile and a wave as they walked up. "Hey, how are you? Don't supposed you're looking for symphony tickets?"

Leo flashed his badge. "Special Agents Leo Ambrose and Emma Last and, no, afraid not. You were here last night?"

The young man's smile wilted a touch. "Yeah, I was on. I'm Elliot. Elliot Patten."

He flashed a glance over Emma's shoulder, toward the front desk, and she could easily imagine a manager staring their way. "Maybe we could talk later. I can take a break… meet ya at O'Brian's Cafe across the street?" He aimed a thumb over his shoulder. "Say around five?"

Leo passed Elliot his card, and the man pocketed it in the blink of an eye. "I'll be there as close to five as I can."

Emma waited for Leo to jot down the name of the place, then met Elliot's gaze again. "So for now, if we could just—"

"Agents! Agents!" A bulky man with a slight accent pushed himself in front of Elliot's lectern, forcing her and Leo a full step back. At a glance, Emma imagined he made a habit of such behavior. Gym-bought muscles bulged under his too-tight button-up.

Behind them, a curse slipped from Paul. The muscled man went bright red but talked as if he hadn't even noticed the slight.

"I am the manager on duty, Dirk Bency. I am sure I can be of more help than our dear Elliot here. Let me show you upstairs, away from the, uh, guests?"

Emma glanced over her shoulder to a small group of tourists gesturing their way. One had a phone out to record. "All right. Show us upstairs, Mr. Bency."

"Splendid!" He turned on his heel and all but ran toward the elevator.

"Frickin' Chippendales wannabe, this guy." Paul followed along regardless.

Leo and Emma hung back a few steps. "Muscleman seem nervous to you?" Leo kept his voice low.

"Could just be paranoid about the hotel's reputation."

Emma shrugged, slowing her steps toward the elevator. "Can't be easy to balance hospitality with an investigation."

"He was nervous about us talking to Elliot, though."

Ahead of them, Bency adjusted his glasses while he waited for them to catch up. Emma clocked him pressing the already lit elevator button twice.

Nervous as an informant. Question is, why?

On the way up, Bency began a well-rehearsed speech about the Fallweather's history. The longer he spoke, the more Emma was certain his accent was either Russian or from somewhere in Eastern Europe.

The man made a special point of addressing the hotel's respect for Boston's law enforcement. He patted Leo and Paul on the arm, in turn, and gestured to Emma. "We always love you guys, too, do not get me wrong. Feds, cops. You are all in the same club, and it is a good one."

By the time they reached the tenth floor, Emma wondered how his nose hadn't turned brown. She let him keep talking as they walked down an ornate hall toward a luxury suite.

Bency used a house key to open the last room on the right and waved them inside. "As requested, we have not sent the housekeeping up. Let us know when we can? Leaving it empty, uh, you know, this costs the hotel money." He forced a smile, but Paul stepped closer to loom over him.

"Give us the room?" Paul put a hand on Bency's shoulder to usher him out. "We know how to get to the roof from here."

"The roof access is still taped off." Bency backed out of the doorway. "Nobody has been up there but you and the cops. Please, you know, tell me if you have to take the hotel's property for evidence."

With that, he let the door click shut. Emma surveyed the well-appointed suite as she pulled out a pair of gloves. A huge flat-screen TV took up most of the wall by the door, across from a king-size bed. A wet bar stood in one corner with an assortment of sample-size liquor bottles from brands that Emma had only ever seen on the top shelf at a bar.

"Empty or otherwise, this room cost money. A lot of it." She caught Paul's eye as he hummed his agreement and waved at her to put the gloves away.

"Jimmy Conrad had a lot of money, so no surprise he'd use a spot like this."

"Use? And why no gloves?"

"Forensics was already here, and up on the roof. They found evidence of various bodily fluids on the bed. Conrad shared this suite with someone other than his wife."

Emma kept the gloves out. "They already took his luggage? Get fingerprints and all that?"

"Wasn't any luggage to take. Only prints found were either Conrad's or possibly a housekeeper's. We're still waiting for results."

Leo gestured to the bed. "He have a known mistress? That would explain why the hotel's being cagey, wanting to protect a scandal."

The local agent shrugged. "Doesn't every politician have either a mistress, a pimp, or a favorite prostitute on speed dial?"

Ignoring the snark, Emma moved over to the window and looked out. "Ten floors is a long way down. Next stop, roof?"

Paul nodded and led the way. At the end of the hall, a door had been propped open. The stairwell inside had loosely wrapped crime scene tape blocking the way up the final flight of stairs. He untied it, gestured them up, and tied it again behind them before following Emma and Leo.

Emma emerged onto the roof and stepped just far enough

out to take a good look around. The space was designed for rooftop parties, with a sheltered bar area to the right and seating arranged around a firepit. All of that was currently draped in heavy, padded tarps to protect against the elements during the offseason. Stains and puddles of muddy water made it clear the furniture had been covered for quite a while.

Potted plants against the roof edge framed a trio of Adirondack chairs.

Paul pointed in that direction. "That's where Jimmy went over."

Leo led the way to the nearest chair.

A short trail of drag marks and blood droplets revealed Jimmy's final moments. Emma knelt and examined them. "Looks like he struggled. Lots of scuffing and shifted gravel along this trail, and here's where he got cut." She aimed a finger at a patch of rust-colored gravel. Leo joined her, but Paul stayed near the chair.

"Two sets of footprints here. That was him standing up, maybe lighting up. Then the attacker comes up behind him, and it's go time."

Careful not to disturb the marks, Emma stood and moved to join Paul. "Did he sit down, or was he attacked on his feet?"

Leo called from where he was still examining the gravel. "I'd say he was on his feet, and either stumbled or got pushed down. A body could've made this imprint, by the bloody patch."

The dip in gravel surrounding the blood circle might not have been recognizable as the shape of a body if they hadn't known to look for it. Taking it in, even from her position a few feet away, Emma could see the impressions where elbows and knees sank into the gravel with force.

"The attacker went down with him. On top of him. There

are two sets of depressions where their knees landed. But then it looks like Conrad was rolled over. More depressions here, and here." Emma pointed at the marks. "Could be our attacker's feet, or his knees if he's straddling Conrad while he mutilates him."

Leo had his phone out and was snapping photos of the impressions and blood marks. "I'd say you're right." He eyed the door they'd just come through. "Could be Conrad was on his way back downstairs. Do we have the attacker's approach anywhere? I'm not seeing anything except the marks by the chair."

"Could've been somebody he knew, so their tracks aren't as clear until the fight starts. It's hard to make out the path Conrad took to reach this point." Emma cast a look along their route from the door. Their own tracks were difficult to pick out on the gravel surface. "I can barely see our trail."

"Fair point, and who knows how many people have walked through the evidence without even knowing it? Paul, you and Midori were up here, but Boston PD got here first, right?"

"Yeah, but they know better than to go traipsing through a crime scene."

"Sorry." Leo waved his hand. "Didn't mean to imply otherwise. Just noting we have a lot of feet to consider in addition to Conrad's and his killer's."

Emma moved back to join Leo, holding out her tablet for size comparison with the marks in the gravel while he took photos. "The largest blood mark is at the bottom of this wide impression. Was he still face down?"

"Looks like the killer flipped him over to do the messy part. See that smear in the gravel?" Leo aimed his phone at a long mark. "Could've been made by his hand coming down and sliding. We know how he was mutilated, and that implies he was face up toward his attacker."

Paul gave a curt nod. "Color me impressed. That's what our forensic team guessed." He pointed to a couple of flagstones marked as having contained evidence. "That's where his robe was. His johnson was found in that fern over there. Wallet and keys were found with the rest of his clothing still in the room."

Emma rose and surveyed the whole of the roof. From this vantage, she spotted a structure that looked like a shed over toward the other end. The outline of a door stood out against the sunlight. "Is that our killer's exit and entry point?"

Leading the way toward the door she'd singled out, Paul shrugged. "Our guess is the killer used the same door as Conrad. Either snuck up on him or was waiting for him. We looked at this door earlier, but it's locked from the inside. Manager said it hasn't been opened in ages. Mostly serves as an extra fire exit when there are events up here. Maybe to get supplies up and down from the kitchen."

Emma eyed the slightly rusted door, then jiggled the handle. Solid metal. "Weird place for a fire door, but you need a second exit, like Bency said. You could fit a few hundred people up here for a party."

Paul confirmed that two exits matched the state's fire code. "But since this door's locked and Bency says it mostly stays that way, I'm guessing their parties never get that big if they happen at all. From the looks of things, the bar area's been under wraps for a while, maybe a year."

Moving off to look around the abandoned bar area, Emma shoved the second fire door to the back of her mind for now. Someone had to have a key, but it didn't look like it had been used anytime recently. The bar area was bare except for the covered furniture, some of it stacked and held down with chains connected to a steel ring mounted on the rooftop.

Leo came over and collected photos of the area. "Killer

might've used the bar as a hiding place. If he came up before Conrad, he could've lingered here, waiting for the right moment or building up his courage. In which case, he knew Conrad was coming. He knew his habits."

Thinking about the bloody fight that took place only a few feet away and the gruesome act of mutilation that had occurred there, Emma shook her head.

"Whoever did this, he's not afraid of killing." She swept her gaze from the bar area to the edge of the roof where Conrad went over. "He struck with purpose and intent and probably had all the courage he needed before Jimmy Conrad took his first toke."

8

Downstairs, on the second floor, Emma followed Bency along a hallway of offices, glancing into each glass-walled space as she went.

Flat-screens the size of my kitchen in the upstairs suites, with modular offices. The exterior screams old money and history, but this is a twenty-first-century operation.

Leo and Paul followed behind her as she did her best to keep up with Bency's speed-walking. The relief on his face when they'd come down from the roof had been almost comical.

Bency gestured the three of them into a long room that looked more like a sound booth than a security office. Plenty of dials and knobs on fancy machinery, and six monitors all focused on various public spaces in the hotel. "This is Steven Nassar, head of security for the Fallweather. We all like to joke he should be playing for the Celtics."

Behind the desk sat a man whose lanky frame dwarfed the swivel chair he was occupying. He nodded at Bency, who gave him a wave and a laugh in reply.

"Steven will show you what you need."

"Agents." Nassar gave a long look to all three of their badges while Paul grumbled that he'd seen his earlier that day. "Just being thorough." He folded himself back into the chair and smirked at Paul, as if to say he'd earned some payback.

Guessing these two butted heads this morning.

"Mr. Nassar, could you show us any footage you have for Conrad?" Without being invited, Emma took the seat beside him and waited for him to work the monitors. "Entering the lobby, entering his room, and heading up to the roof? Anything else you have of him also."

"Nothing else available." Nassar punched some buttons and pointed to two views of the lobby. "Conrad checked in at just before seven yesterday evening and headed upstairs."

Emma watched as their victim, in a dark suit and light-colored, striped button-down shirt, turned from the front desk, where Bency greeted him and shook his hand while leaning in to say something. "Pause that, please." Nassar did so, and Emma turned to the hotel manager. "Mr. Bency, do you recall what you said there?"

The man's mouth curled in a smile that didn't reach his eyes. "Uh, I might've been telling him we had his room ready just the way he likes it."

"How did Mr. Conrad like his room?"

"He, well…sometimes it was champagne on ice. When it was cold out, he wanted freshly warmed towels and robes."

"You knew his routine pretty well then?"

Bency's jaw tightened. "I knew him as a regular guest of the Fallweather." He aimed a finger at the monitor. "I don't remember exactly what I said there, but it was probably something to do with his room being ready to his specifications."

Emma waved for the security manager to start the footage again. They watched Conrad cross the lobby and move out of screen. Nassar punched a few more buttons and showed him by the lobby elevators, then, in another view, exiting on the tenth floor and moving down the hall.

"Few hours later, he came out in his robe, right around a quarter to midnight." Nassar pointed to the time stamp on the monitor and used two monitors to show Conrad first exiting his room and bypassing the elevator, then moving down the hallway to the stairwell, which led to the rooftop. "That's all we got. He didn't order room service, didn't have any guests, and nobody else passed him or interacted with him."

"Didn't have any guests, or didn't have any who were captured on camera?" Before he or Bency could get a word out, Emma added, "Forensics took the sheets. Trace DNA will likely show a second or even third person was present. So why are we certain he was alone last night?" She glanced back at the manager, whose frown had grown deeper legs, his neck another tense vein.

Nasser only lowered his eyebrows at the monitor, as if doubting his own eyes. "I mean...the footage is right here. They wouldn't be invisible, so—"

"*They?*"

"You said it could be more than one person." Nassar gestured at the monitor. "I'm just going off what I can see from the footage. If Jimmy had someone with him, they'd be here. They're not, so I'd say he was alone."

Paul barked a laugh that cut off the stumbling security guard. "What are we saying, the man came in for a catnap, got high, then got dead? Gimme a break."

Leo leaned in for a closer look at the footage, and Nassar edged back to give him space. "Would that be unusual? That he'd just come in by himself for a few hours and go up to the roof to smoke a joint?"

Bency bristled behind them. "We do not allow smoking at the Fallweather. That is absolutely not—"

Nassar waved his hand at the manager, cutting him off. "Guest privacy comes first, that's what you get at the Fallweather. If he smoked on the roof, he smoked on the roof, but we don't have footage for up there."

The manager huffed. "I was about to say the same thing."

"What about for events?" Emma glanced between the two hotel employees. "Even if the events are rare, you must have security?"

"Well, yeah." Nassar's pale face flushed, barely noticeably. "For parties, they get turned on. Otherwise, we keep 'em covered for the weather and leave 'em off rather than distracting from the areas of the hotel that are actually in use. More data storage and video feeds and all that, ya know?"

"All right." She pointed to the monitor frozen on Conrad entering his room. "We've seen him go in and out. Can you show us the activity on the floor between seven p.m. and when he left?"

Nassar nodded amiably and leaned over the keyboard before him. Within moments, he was fast-forwarding over footage of an empty hallway. He stopped at around the nine p.m. mark so that they could take note of a couple walking together with their faces obscured by hats and scarves. The two of them went into a room near the elevators, and then the fast-forwarding began again.

Leo shut down his iPad. "Is it always this dead on a Wednesday night?"

Bency drew himself straighter. "The tenth floor is reserved for wealthier clientele, who have more presence on weekends. Having only four or five rooms occupied midweek is not abnormal."

Emma imagined they did like to keep public figures separate, so that much made sense. She stood up and stretched, then refocused on Bency. "I'd like a copy of this footage, as well as the contact information for all your guests who stayed on the tenth floor last night."

The manager looked at the security guard and then to Paul, mouth agape, before glaring at her. "You must be joking."

Leo stood up beside her. "Mr. Bency, we're not joking. Jimmy Conrad, the husband of a prominent local political figure, was killed here last night."

Paul tucked his phone away and stood straighter, hands on his belt. "I think you'll find none of the agents on this case are kidding about anything. Do we need to have this discussion downtown?"

Sweat broke out on Bency's forehead. He swept one hand over his brow before turning his focus to his security guard. "Steven, get these agents copies of all requested security footage from last night. However…" He took a deep breath before meeting Emma's eyes. "I have to talk to the corporate headquarters before I can give you the private information for guests. That is a matter for—"

"Yada yada yada." Paul waved his hand, shutting the man up in a single stroke. "Privacy first. 'That's what you get at the Fallweather.' We heard the sales pitch. Call your damn lawyers and get back to us, *capisce?*"

The manager went red in the face but nodded. Scratching his chin, he stepped out in the hall, striking a square-shouldered pose. "We are done here? I am sure Mr. Nassar and I both have other things to deal with."

Emma fought a smile at Paul and Nassar sharing an annoyed look between them. Any earlier rivalry between them was now safely defused in the face of Bency's efforts at theatrics.

After confirming Nassar had sent her and Leo the footage, Emma and the others headed to the elevator.

Downstairs, the lobby doors opened as Paul was telling them about a club across town where the "political bigwigs" supposedly hung out.

But a sharp spike of Other cold stole Emma's attention.

She stepped out of the elevator and zeroed in on a spindly young ghost near the bar. She stood barefoot in a flimsy negligee that looked designed for an older woman as she stared at Emma. Her mouth moved like she was muttering something, but Emma couldn't make it out.

Emma shot Leo a quick smile. "I'm gonna get a sip from that water fountain. Be right back."

Before he could respond, she headed over toward the Fallweather's bar entrance. The ghost had changed focus, and her white-eyed gaze seemed to follow Bency as he made his way from the elevator to the front desk. Emma nearly held her breath, working to make out the ghost's words…but they were gibberish.

She bent over the water fountain, shivering in the cold of the Other, listening.

As best she could, she committed the syllables to memory. It was another language, and she didn't have a clue.

"Mao pack a lee. Mao follow seet. Mao ru-een-a. Mao pack a lee. Mao follow seet. Mao ru-een-a."

Last word sounds a little like "ruin," Emma girl. Maybe a place to start.

The woman whimpered, shuddering in her negligee and bare feet and turning away from Emma.

It had to be a foreign language, either Russian or maybe a Slavic tongue. Emma tried to commit the young woman's image to memory, as well, but aside from having pale skin and dark hair, she didn't feel she could hazard even a guess at the woman's heritage.

Emma looked over to see Leo and Paul lost in conversation across the lobby. She tried catching the ghost's eye, but the young woman's focus remained on the hotel manager, who now stood beside the concierge's lectern greeting a guest.

Before she left the ghost behind, Emma ducked into the women's restroom, checked that she was alone, and then set her phone to record, reciting the syllables she'd heard as best she could. "Mao pack a lee. Mao follow seet. Mao ru-een-a."

She stood still for a long moment, her phone in hand, before shaking herself back to the present. Elliot Patten was waiting for them across the street and clearly had something he needed to share outside the hotel walls.

9

Emma spotted Elliot Patten immediately. He'd commandeered a booth in the back of the little café and sat against the wall slumped inside his jacket. His red hair stood out all by itself, broadcasting the anxiety that appeared to be consuming him as he clutched a steaming coffee mug. Around him, the café bustled with early evening meetups and creative types hunched over their laptops.

She offered him a wave as they made their way over, and she slid into the wooden booth across from him. Leo sat beside her, and Paul pulled up a chair.

Elliot sipped from his coffee. "I don't have much time."

Emma projected as much calm as she could in responding. "Whatever you can tell us, we're listening."

Elliot nodded, seeming to refocus on her rather than the larger space. "It's just, Dirk isn't giving you the full story about Jimmy Conrad. He…Jimmy, I mean…stays on the top floor at least a few times a month. He comes in alone, but he always ends up in a woman's company. They just don't come in with him."

Leo opened his iPad. "You're saying he has a mistress?"

"No. I mean, maybe?" Elliot sighed. "Look, I was filling in for someone in room service a week ago, and I brought up two plates of oysters, caviar and crackers, and champagne. I had to leave it all outside Jimmy's room because I could hear him having sex inside."

"You mentioned a woman." Paul leaned on his elbows at the edge of the table. "Can you be certain you heard a woman's voice in addition to Jimmy's?"

Elliot shrank even deeper into his jacket, like he wanted to be anywhere but on the business end of Paul's question. "It was a woman. She was loud, like she really—"

Waving a hand so Elliot would keep the details to a minimum, Leo prompted him to continue his earlier train of thought. "He was inside having sex with a woman, and you delivered room service but left it outside the door. What happened next?"

"I headed downstairs and asked Dirk about it. I mean, that's a lot of expensive stuff to just leave in a hallway, right? Dirk told me to stop asking questions."

Emma shared a glance with Leo before following up. "Did you hear the woman speak, by chance? Did she sound American? Have an accent?"

Elliot's cheeks reddened. "I didn't hear her...say any actual words."

Emma could feel Leo's eyes on her but ignored it. "And you didn't see her? With Jimmy in his room? Not coming or going?"

Elliot shook his head fast, eyes darting around the room. "No, and if Dirk even knew I was saying this much, he'd fire me. Guest privacy and all, ya know? And it's not like Jimmy was a low profile guest." He took another sip of coffee. "But one of the other room service guys heard me talking and told me the same thing's happened to him *repeatedly*. So I'm thinking his main reason for coming around was to have a place to bring women. It's Dirk being so up in arms about me asking that really bugs me."

Leo nodded. "He's protecting the hotel. But your conclusion about Jimmy makes sense. He's got a mansion in town, so why else stay there?"

Why else indeed? Whether we're talking about a girlfriend, or multiple girlfriends, or sex workers.

"Strangest thing about the interaction with Dirk?" Elliot sighed, wrapping his hands tighter around his coffee mug. "Guy's only been working here six months after moving here from somewhere in Europe. And for the first couple of months, all he did was shit-talk Jimmy. Got all pissy when the guy commented on Dirk's shirt being two sizes too small and rode him ever after, to whoever'd listen." His brow furrowed. "Then, about a month ago, he shut his mouth. Wouldn't say one word against Jimmy. Just stopped. And it happened out of the blue."

Emma shared a glance with Paul, whose brow was knit in thought. "Anything happen a month ago that you'd see changing things?"

Paul frowned and shook his head. "Nothing in terms of what's come up in the investigation so far." He looked at Elliot. "You see any change in Conrad around the same time? Or notice anything that might've changed your manager's attitude about the man? Maybe he got spanked by a higher-up for having loose lips?"

Elliot shrugged. "Could be, but I don't have a clue. Nothing changed in how Jimmy acted, though. Not that I saw. And Dirk kept on as usual, spilling dirt about all the other guests, ya know? Like knowing some dirt made him better than them."

Leo caught Emma's eye. "So much for privacy being 'what you get at the Fallweather.'"

She returned the focus to their interviewee. "You were

working room service the one night, but you're usually stationed as the concierge?"

Elliot nodded.

"Have you seen a woman coming in alone on the same nights Jimmy came around? Or women, plural?"

The red in Elliot's cheeks crept up to his hairline. "I mean, I was curious, you know? What kind of woman he'd be cheating with. I think maybe it's, uh…pro…you know?"

"Sex workers?" Emma supplied the phrase, and Elliot nodded gratefully.

"But the problem is, they kinda stand out too. Even the classy ones. Hired escorts." His gaze went a little past her shoulder, as if he were losing himself in thought. "Seems like I woulda noticed them. They'd be wicked pretty, right? Standouts?"

Paul pressed his lips into a thin line. "Think you could tell? I can't half the time."

Elliot hunched his shoulders. "Either way, I haven't noticed anybody I could say for sure was a…a sex worker, and I try to pay attention. I guess they could come through the garage, but I haven't seen any girls who look like that in the lobby on Jimmy's nights."

"Could the hotel have been paid to turn a blind eye?" Emma kept her voice quiet. "Maybe Conrad was paying for silence, and that's why Dirk was forced or bribed to deflect from talking about him?" She shot a glance at Paul, who didn't seem remotely surprised by any of their discussion.

Elliot downed the last of his coffee. "Honestly, I don't know. I don't know Dirk well, and I didn't know Jimmy well. Dirk doesn't flash money around, but I don't think it'd be beneath him to take a kickback."

Leo waved his hand in acknowledgment. "We get your point."

"Listen, I gotta get back to work." Elliot shifted in his seat, looking between them. "You need anything else? You can always find me at the hotel, and we can meet here if we need to, but honestly, I don't think there's anything more I could say."

Emma passed him her card and waved him off. Paul stood and pulled his chair back to make it easier for the young concierge to escape.

When he'd left, Paul resumed his seat. "Can't say I'm surprised."

"You didn't look it." Emma pursed her lips. "Any thoughts on how to go forward? This is your town."

"Finding a particular sex worker who was with the good candidate's husband last night?" Paul snorted. "Her existing wouldn't surprise me. But unless he's using the same girl over and over again, which it sounds like Elliot was on the lookout for, the best we could hope for would be to nail down how he's contacting them."

"Thoughts on how to do that?"

"Conrad's phone is with our office. I'll let Tibble know to be on the lookout for information once they crack the device, but knowing the SSA, he probably already is."

Emma reclined against the booth, leaving the table in silence for a moment as Leo hammered notes into his iPad. "Maybe Bency clammed up because he was being paid to keep quiet. Or maybe he clammed up because he was planning to murder him." She waved off Paul's raised eyebrow. "Yeah, yeah, I know. Hear me out. It is possible he clammed up a month ago because he was planning on murdering Jimmy and didn't want to be seen passing around dirt on a victim."

Leo nodded as he continued to type on his iPad. "I've heard weirder things than a manager protecting a high-class hotel's reputation by trying to find a way to get rid of a headache. Especially if he didn't like the guy to begin with."

"It would explain his nervousness." Paul drummed his fingers on the table. "And I guess he could even be faking his nerves to hide the possibility he'd have committed such a bold crime."

"I get it." Emma looked back and forth between the other agents. "None of us make him for a murderer, but he's behaving oddly. We have to keep him in mind and figure out what the hell happened to change his behavior a month ago."

Paul's phone buzzed, and he held it up to show Tibble's name before answering. "I'm here with our friends from D.C., Walter."

The SSA's voice crackled through the phone, but Emma could only make out Paul's side of the conversation.

"Not yet. Just working up more lines of inquiry and trying to figure out what we're looking at." Paul raised an eyebrow at Emma and Leo, both of whom shook their heads in the negative. "I'll write up notes for you when we're back in the car."

Tibble said something in reply, and Emma caught Midori's name.

"Yes, sir." Paul ended the call. "Boss wants you to wait for Midori. She'll take over while I get some sleep. Sounds like you'll be interviewing Conrad's widow next. You get to give her the good news."

"The what?"

"Her husband's dead, but he was killed after screwing around with another woman. Forensics pulled DNA from the bed sheets."

With that, he lumbered off without a backward glance, and Leo shifted over to the other side of the table before waving over a server.

Emma took the menu with a smile and hurried to glance over it while keeping Paul in the corner of her vision.

As soon as the agent left, Leo turned to face her. "Emma?"

She pivoted toward him. "Yes, to answer your question, I saw a ghost. She sounded Slavic, maybe Russian. I don't know much about Eastern European languages, but that's my best guess."

He sat with what she told him, seeming to mull it over.

"And I have what she said right here," she patted her phone, "in a voice memo."

"You made a recording of what you heard, so we might be able to figure out which language she was speaking. Good thinking." Leo sat against the booth back and stared straight ahead. "You, um…you haven't seen anyone else, have you?"

"No. Nothing at all, except the girl in the hotel. I promise."

With a sigh of relief, Leo picked up the menu and ran his finger down the list of sandwiches. "Let's make this quick, yeah? We still have to tell the good candidate that her husband died after a night of adultery."

10

Emma eyed the quiet street full of mansions. Massive shade trees leaned over both sides of the road, which was split by a perfectly manicured median dotted with shrubs and the occasional cherry tree.

Leo whistled at a house that looked more like a European castle than a Boston home. Midori laughed. The deeper they went into the luxurious neighborhood, the grander and more ostentatious the houses became.

Emma felt her eyes go a size larger as Midori pulled up to the wrought iron gate of a home with a regal plaque proclaiming it *The Conrad Manor*. She reached out the window and depressed the intercom button.

"FBI Special Agents Nishioka, Ambrose, and Last, here to see Mrs. Dianne Conrad." Midori sat back and raised her window as a metallic voice replied through the intercom in the affirmative. She shot a glance at Leo beside her as they waited for the gate to pull back. "These folks are so rich, I wouldn't put it past them to have some AI robot controlling the gate, intercoms, you name it."

Emma cringed. "As long as you don't tell me we're

hunting down a robot killer. You do that, I'm catching the first flight back to D.C., no offense."

Midori shot her a grin as she finally passed through the gate. They faced a long driveway that led to a gigantic stone home. The structure loomed over a pristinely manicured front yard. A four-car garage stood off to the side, firmly shut and no doubt containing at least a few luxury cars.

By the time Midori stopped the SUV, Emma thought she'd just about managed to lift her jaw up to normal range. "And this woman is *running* for mayor? Not there already?"

"These campaigns are high stakes, for high rollers only. Gotta have money to play the game." Midori opened her door and hopped out. "Unlike us mere peons."

A man met them at the doorway, dressed as if for a business meeting, and waved them into a large, marble-tiled entryway. Passing by, Emma clocked a slight bulge at his waist, as well as an earbud. Maybe the guy was a high-priced butler, but he was also private security.

Not that she was surprised, based on the home's interior.

Their footsteps echoed off the marble and ornate, solid-wood paneling. He led them past a spiral staircase and into a large sitting room arranged around a central grand piano. "May I get the three of you anything? Coffee, perhaps? Mrs. Conrad will be a few minutes more. Ten, at most."

Power move of the rich, Emma girl. Keep the peasants waiting.

Leo glanced around the room before sitting awkwardly in what looked to be an antique armchair from the Victorian era. Emma half expected there to be a silken rope with a little *Do Not Sit* sign on it, like at a museum. "Coffee would be great."

The stiff attendant accepted nods from Leo and Midori before turning on his heel. He disappeared as the two women sat down diagonally from Leo. Emma glanced at their

Boston colleague. They'd barely exchanged names earlier, but they had time now.

Emma leaned in just slightly and did her best to recap what they'd learned with Paul that morning. Midori nodded along. "That fits what I saw when I was at the crime scene with the techs. This is not going to be an easy conversation."

When she didn't offer anything else, Emma changed tracks. It wouldn't hurt to build more rapport with Midori, and so far, she was easier to stomach than her crasser partner.

"So what brought you to the Boston FBI? You couldn't be less like Paul, and he's a bit more of what I expected."

Midori raised an eyebrow.

Emma put her hand up. "No offense meant." She flushed. "You know what I mean."

"I'm not what people expect, no." Midori pressed her jacket down along her arms and glanced at the door they'd come through. "Not at all what Dianne Conrad would expect. The fact is, my father got caught up with the yakuza when we lived in Japan, and my family had to flee to escape them."

Emma blinked. She'd never even considered that Midori could be an immigrant.

"No accent anymore, right? That's what you're thinking?" At Emma's surprised nod, Midori smoothed her hand over her impeccable bun. "I worked hard on that in school. But, yes, that's why I joined the FBI. I knew too much about the horrible things the yakuza did, and the Bureau seemed like the best way, in my new country, to fight back against that sort of evil."

Leo leaned forward, hands on elbows. "If you don't mind me asking…how old were you when you made that decision?"

Midori laughed. "I was ten. A bit young for life-changing decisions, I know, but I have no regrets."

Leo simply nodded, but Emma glimpsed the thought behind the expression. He hadn't been far from that age when his parents died. When his grandfather died afterward, he'd been pushed along the same path. Knowingly or not.

I like her. And if she's anything like Leo, we have a good team here. We'll figure this out, one way or another.

Leo opened his mouth as if he might be about to offer his own history, but an exaggerated wail sounded from the foyer. Just as Emma turned that way, a middle-aged woman came in with a silk handkerchief held to one eye, rubbing it hard. She continued to wail as the three agents stood to greet her.

But as much as the woman *sounded* like she was choking back the end of a tearing jag, Emma saw not a drip of moisture.

Dianne Conrad kept the handkerchief to her face as she shook hands with Leo and pulled Emma and then Midori into overly familiar hugs. Emma tensed in her arms and fought to keep a straight face as she drew back. The woman switched her handkerchief to her other eye, the finely embroidered cloth still bone-dry.

"Anderson, why haven't you brought these agents any refreshments?" She dropped onto the couch near the armchairs, not even looking at the man who'd greeted them at the door. He once again disappeared without a sound.

"Mrs. Conrad." Midori spoke up, catching the widow's attention, "We're sorry to bother you at this difficult time, and sorry for your loss. But we do have some questions."

"Call me Dianne." The woman twitched one salt-and-pepper chunk of hair behind her ear.

The expensive silk shawl around her shoulders hung loose over her pantsuit, and Emma couldn't help noticing that the whole ensemble appeared built for a night out. Dark, muted colors suggested—if you thought about it—a woman in mourning, but there was no crease suggesting she'd been lying in bed crying or curled in a chair, thinking of her husband.

"Ask what you have to ask, please. Whatever you need. You must find justice for my dear, departed husband."

Emma didn't think she'd heard that phrasing outside of an old-time Hallmark movie.

But okay. Let's roll with it and see what you can tell us, oh, grieving widow.

Leo opened his iPad. "Dianne, can you tell us who you think might've wanted to hurt your husband?"

"Jimmy!" A little whimper bubble escaped her throat, and Emma wondered if she'd had any acting experience. "He was a sweetheart. So caring. I don't know how anybody could do this to him. Who'd be so horrible? Such a monster?"

Midori made a valiant attempt at getting the interview back on track. "Any enemies—"

"Enemies!" Dianne blotted her dry eyes again as the attendant hurried in with a large tray carrying little silver platters of coffee cups, one for each of them.

Emma took a platter as if it contained a serpent rather than a cup, feeling like she'd stepped into another century as she did. Who served coffee on silver platters complete with spoons anymore? The butler put a spread of sugar and cream on a nearby table before exiting the room.

Dianne went on. "None! Everyone loved Jimmy."

Leo sipped from his coffee. "With all due respect, somebody didn't."

For a moment, Dianne's eyes widened just a touch, annoyance bleeding through the grief act.

Unused to being contradicted, but I guess it's no wonder.

"Maybe it's my fault, then." Dianne simpered, making eyes

at Leo. "I'm the political one. The one stepping on toes. But Jimmy…he was a good man. A sweet man. And so capable."

Emma was ready to mention the adultery, but Midori coughed. "Ma'am, forgive me for saying so, but the fashion in which he was murdered. The brutality—"

"Stop!" Dianne sat straight, glaring at her, all but hissing. "There's absolutely no need for the details. I was subjected to the gore earlier by a cop, a man who may well have brought a seasonal flu bug into my home. I complained to the police chief and learned that officer is now on sick leave. He should be fired. I do not wish to hear again how Jimmy died."

Silence did reign for a few seconds, none of them knowing what to say. Emma couldn't even imagine the reaction some poor detective had gotten that morning when he'd shared those details.

Finally, Leo broke the silence. "Ma'am, we appreciate that. But whatever you can tell us could be of help to the investigation. Business rivals, perhaps? Of yours or Jimmy's?"

Vaguely, Dianne began running on about Jimmy's business ventures and how well he knew how to work a room. How he knew a joke for every occasion and just the right drink to offer, the right baby to kiss.

The whole thing was absurd, and Emma's ears quickly went numb to the litany of posturing and attempts at convincing them Jimmy Conrad was anything but a powerful man who liked his position in society.

"I was at a brunch this morning." Dianne sniffled. "It was so difficult without him. He was *supposed* to be there."

Emma met Midori's eyes ever so briefly, just keeping her expression in line. The woman spoke like Jimmy Conrad had inconvenienced her by dying versus having been murdered. The bit of Emma that wondered if this couple had ever been in love shut its mouth and backed into a corner.

If there'd been love between them, it hadn't been romantic...not anymore, at least.

Midori set her coffee aside, somehow managing not to rattle the cup, which was all Emma had been doing. "Mrs. Conrad, can you tell us why he was at the hotel last night? When he lives this close to downtown?"

"The hotel?" Dianne blinked. "Perhaps for a business meeting? Maybe the wind was up?"

Emma waited for something more and asked when the woman instead focused on her coffee. "The wind? What do you mean?"

"Oh, he was supposed to be on Shane's yacht." Dianne waved her hand, as if the change in plans was of less concern than the weather. "They're always yachting about, those two. I find boats so boring, don't you? Perhaps off the coast of Italy, where there's actually a *view*, but here?"

Leo's sympathetic smile became more forced each minute as he picked up the thread of Midori's earlier question. "And you have no idea why he would be at the Fallweather, with a luxury suite in his name? I'm sorry, Mrs. Conrad, I know this isn't an easy question to hear. Did you have any reason to believe your husband was having an affair?"

The politician came out in full force, replacing the grieving widow like she'd never even been in the room. "Agent Ambrose, I have no knowledge of my husband's activities ever involving another woman, or man, in any way that might be considered adulterous."

Leaving a whole pile of things unsaid. I would not want to go up against her in a debate.

"Let's go back to your husband's friend if you don't mind. Shane who?"

"Hmm? Oh, Field. Shane Field..."

Dianne kept going, but a glimmer of movement from near the front staircase drew Emma's attention instead. A long-haired young woman in torn jeans paced near the bottom stair, her arms gesturing wildly. For a moment, Emma thought she was real, but then the butler passed directly through her without reacting.

Emma set aside her coffee—little platter rattling as she did—and broke into Dianne's running commentary on her husband's interest in yachts. "Dianne, I'm sorry, but is there a restroom I could use?"

"What? Of course. Right out there." She waved back toward the stairs, just as Emma had hoped she would. "You'll take a left at the stairs and go a little way down the hall to our powder room. You'll see it across from the large bay window with vintage cushions. But, please, don't sit down. The window seat is just for show."

Because, of course, even the cushions are worth more of your attention than your dead husband.

Emma stood up with a fast, apologetic glance at her colleagues and made her way back out to the entrance. Halfway there, her flesh grew goose bumps, and her lungs worked a touch harder as the atmosphere thickened around her. Like in the car, the Other seemed to want to trap her… but she forced herself forward.

As she approached the young woman, the chill grew deeper. The ghost's frantic words were audible now but not yet intelligible. Emma passed her by, since she was in Midori's sight line. She turned left and moved just far enough ahead of the stairs that she'd no longer be seen from the piano room.

The young woman had tears streaming down her face from her empty, white eyes, broadcasting emotion that was far more authentic than Dianne Conrad's.

"Mao pack a lee. Mao follow seet. Mao ru-een-a. Tot chay soon-tee-estay sex."

Pacing, the woman repeated the words over and over

again, gesturing wildly but never looking at Emma, who remained still and listened as hard as she could, despite her skin growing tight from the cold.

The ghost was a different girl than the one she'd seen at the hotel but the first three sentences echoed those of the other ghost. The fourth sentence was new.

Emma followed the ghost's line of sight to the opposite side of the foyer, where a framed painting of Jimmy and Dianne Conrad hung above an antique entry table.

"Mao pack a lee. Mao follow seet. Mao ru-een-a. Tot chay soon-tee-estay sex."

Emma did her best to catch the statement and trap it in her memory. The final words sounded like *"este,"* which Emma knew was Spanish for "this." But it had been tacked onto another word and followed by "sex" in English.

The original three phrases didn't sound Spanish. And although college was far behind her, and she'd never been close to fluent, Emma still felt like she'd have recognized more of the words if the ghost were speaking Spanish.

The woman gesticulated more wildly toward the portrait, and the words came faster and faster without variation. Emma hurried to find the restroom, leaving the cold behind her.

She usually appreciated that the Other always brought along a distinct chill, that thickening of the atmosphere she'd very nearly grown used to. But after that freezing episode in the car, she couldn't help being anxious to escape it. Warning or not, some part of her expected to be forced to the ground shivering.

And try explaining that to the "grieving widow," especially if said widow were involved in her husband's unfortunate fate. The way the ghost had been targeting her remarks at the couple's portrait sent shudders through Emma.

She circled her thoughts around the foreign words she'd heard the ghost speaking. She needed to get them down before they escaped her memory. In the marble-tiled bathroom, complete with sculptures of fauns and nymphs set in niches around the vanity mirror, she pulled out her phone and repeated that last phrase as well as she could.

"Tot chay, soon-tee-estay sex."

One more thing to translate, assuming she could figure out what language was being spoken.

When she made her way back toward Leo and Midori, the cold of the Other had dissipated, and there was no sign of the ghost. Her emotions seemed to have soaked into the whole of the entry, though, and Emma couldn't help shivering again as she passed through.

Midori and Leo were rising as Emma reentered the room, and Dianne took their business cards without glancing at them. "Yes, of course, I'll call if I think of anything." Her gaze moved to Emma. "Did you see the pieces in the powder room? Originals by Dylan Pontieche. We bought them last year. They bring the room together, don't they just?"

Emma forced herself to nod, noting that the woman no longer bothered to fake her grief for their benefit. She jutted her chin back toward the home's grand entrance, and Leo was by her side an instant later.

Midori came up behind them as they approached the door and leaned closer to Emma. "I'm also going to hit the washroom. See you outside?"

"We can wai—"

"We'll see you outside," Emma cut Leo off, one hand already on the door.

When they'd made it down the front steps, Leo narrowed his eyes at her. "What gives? In a rush to get rid of Midori?"

"More like to give us a second without her." Emma closed the door and then lowered her voice. "I saw another ghost just now, speaking the same foreign language as the other one."

Leo's lips pursed, and Emma could practically see the disbelief radiating from him. Her heartbeat pitched in reaction. "How do you know you didn't see a housekeeper? At the hotel *and* here?"

"I can feel the Other when I'm near it, Leo. It's a freezing cold, not like what happened in the car, but similar." His eyes went hooded. She'd just as soon forget that part of the day, so she pressed on. "Housekeepers don't wear negligees in a hotel lobby without causing a stir. The butler walked right through the one I saw inside the house."

Leo frowned and tore his gaze away from hers.

"And they don't have any pupils or irises. It's just all white."

That turned Leo back around. He looked sickened by the thought, but Emma pressed on.

"I still don't know the language they were speaking, but they used some of the same phrases." She paused, allowing him to soak that in. "The one inside here was aiming her accusing words at the portrait of Jimmy and Dianne, the one hanging right inside the entrance."

He put his hands on his hips and lowered his eyes. "I said I believe you, and I do. What I'm stuck on is understanding how any of this helps us, since we can't exactly call your witnesses in for an interview, much less to testify."

Emma held her phone up. "If we can figure out what they're saying, we might have something to point us toward the killer, whether that turns out to be Dianne Conrad, Dirk Bency, or someone else. Maybe this friend of Jimmy's did it, the guy with the yacht." When he remained unmoved, Emma went for the most straightforward thing she could. "I think this is a lead we can follow, and I could use your help."

He remained silent for another moment but finally gave the tiniest of nods. "I'll try to help. I can do that."

Midori came out the door a moment later, her phone to her ear. She walked down the stairs with the device held up, listening rather than speaking. She dropped the phone into her bag and gestured toward their SUV. "That was Tibble. He's been on the phone with Wilhelm's campaign office but hasn't been able to get ahold of the man. We'll try the residence tomorrow if we don't have anything else before then.

"Back to the Bureau, then?" Leo opened Emma's door for her, then opened his own.

Midori nodded. "Yup. Maybe just for a debrief and then call it a night. We'll see if anything changes before we get there, I guess. Tibble wants us all fresh for tomorrow."

Emma met Leo's gaze through the rearview mirror as she buckled her seat belt. He nodded, ever so slightly.

A break in the case would've been nice, but a rare early night would give them some time to translate her ghosts' desperate messages.

11

I watched the ship glide into the Conley Terminal, its passage guided by shore lights as a tug pulled it through the dark water, slow and steady. From where I hid in the shadows of shipping containers, I waited for the vessel to moor. I dreaded its arrival, as I had each time before, since coming to this country.

Ever since Daniela alerted me to what had happened to her and my sister, Cristina.

Her letter, secretly sent one night from a hotel she never knew the name of, told me everything I needed to know about these ships.

And everything I would need to do to stop their passage.

Three more men required an education in suffering. As I watched the ship grow larger against the night sky, I thought of the one who would receive my next mark, the number-two man who'd helped pay for the operation that stole my sister's life before she had a chance to live.

In the darkness, the outline of the ship alone felt like a death sentence for everyone involved.

How many women are on board this time?

Whatever they'd been through in the guts of that ship, traveling while drugged or starved or dehydrated—or all the above—they would be in for worse now.

Some of them would stay in Boston, and some would only be here for a night before being moved somewhere else.

They've taken these girls all up and down the seaboard. All of them lost now, never to see their families or know comfort again. Like Cristina.

A pair of shore cops wandered through the maze of containers around me. I could hear their footsteps and voices echoing around me, gradually fading into the distance.

I imagined they were being paid by the bastards bringing the girls in. They should feel my knife just like that son of a bitch Jimmy Conrad, the one who started the whole thing.

He had paid a criminal to collect young women from my home country so they could be sold and imported like fabric and furniture. And the cops let him do it.

But killing two police officers who were taking bribes would alert America's federal agents to the reason for the killings. They were still in the dark, and I wanted to keep it that way.

I had seen one of the dirty cops talking to Wilhelm, shaking his hand as the "cargo" was unloaded in a long line into a caravan of limousines. The girls were so eager to be transported in such luxury, they never asked questions.

Wilhelm and the cop watched with greedy, lecherous smiles on their faces, knowing the girls would soon be delivered to another location and loaded into the back of a moving van at gunpoint.

All pretense of safe harbor and comfort would be removed, and any questions the girls dared ask, or any protest they might make, would be met with a swift slap or the crack of a gunstock against their heads.

I should kill those two cops right now. They deserve it for what they have allowed to happen to so many. To Cristina.

I would have liked to ask them if they ever met my sister. If they were present when she arrived in Boston. If she'd begged for help, and they ignored her or laughed or slapped her across the face and shoved her into a van with the others.

Unlikely they would remember her name. As if they'd ever known she had one. But if I pressed my knife into the right places…

Not tonight.

My closest ally, Daniela, was suffering while my mission unfolded. I would not insult my sister's memory and assure her best friend's continued torture by allowing myself to get sidetracked.

The ship edged closer to shore, its dirty containers glistening beneath the stars. The port scene was far too pretty for its ugly deeds. I pictured girls like my sister hidden in one of those hot, rusty containers, terrified.

They would have been loaded in under the pretense of being "snuck into America." Some might have suspected the lie, but at that point, they would have been far from home and had their passports stolen, along with any money or identification they had.

Some of them probably did not survive the voyage, not given enough attention over the course of the travel.

It mattered not that I had already killed Conrad. His crimes would live on. He and Wilhelm were often at the hotel on the same night. They traded jokes about the mayor's office while they stood on the rooftop after desecrating the girls.

Daniela had witnessed this herself, on the night Wilhelm had paid for her to join him.

The FBI agents who had come to the hotel were clueless about what their dead man had been engineering within their precious city—assuming they also were not being paid off by Conrad's cohort of abusers. The longer they chased other leads, the more time I had to enact my plan.

I had seen with my own eyes, in Europe, what happened when a justice system was left to care for young women's lives and the injustices that befell them. I had no doubt these agents would, too, be useless.

Cristina probably wished for justice, even begged for it. Maybe even from people like those FBI agents. Maybe from Conrad himself.

For a moment, I pictured my sweet sister falling to her knees in front of those agents I had seen earlier. Begging, crying. Her body too thin from drugs and malnutrition. Wearing that old plaid shirt of Tata's, the one I last saw her in.

She would be as tattered as the shirt. As in need of care.

I tore myself from the horrors of my imagination and stared instead at the ship. At its containers. At its evildoers.

This must be my focus.

I would continue to mourn Cristina, but this night, I must remember the promise I made myself to stop others from facing her same fate.

Once I had learned of the inner workings of the Fallweather, I made it my duty. Any good man would do the same. And I would not fail Cristina or those girls in this mission.

The people behind this arm of the sex trade had to be stopped. Forever.

The sound of the parking gate lifting finally broke over the port. That meant my next target had arrived. I pulled my gloves on as I watched the ship. "Time to make them pay."

And if I could do anything to throw off the FBI as I dispensed real justice, to make sure I had the time to finish this work, all the better.

Listening to the creaking of the gate, I hurried down the row of containers toward the private vehicle parking lot. A sleek black car pulled into the space closest to the harbormaster's office. The driver got out and opened the rear door, standing aside as Conrad's partner in crime emerged. I could hear Wilhelm's distinctive growl, yelling at the driver as he emerged.

Wilhelm, you filthy shit. Your time has come.

So arrogant, he did not even thank the driver, who glared at Wilhelm's back as he moved off toward the dock and the approaching ship.

I kept to the shadows as I moved toward the car. The chauffeur nudged the back door closed with his ass, got into the front seat, and pulled out his phone. He had his head down, probably focused on some game or social media.

I hid behind a pallet of fuel barrels between the containers and the car and watched the scene at the dock unfold.

The two cops I had seen earlier were there. Wilhelm handed them something—money, I guessed—and a string of curses built on my tongue.

Without waiting any longer, I sprinted through the dark and into the shadows beside the very car my next victim had traveled in. The chauffeur only bothered to look up from his phone when my hand lifted the driver's side door handle and popped it open.

He tried to pull the door closed. "Hey, pal, I'm—"

My knife pierced his chest, navigating the slice of muscle and organ between ribs and stabbing deep in a single, heavy push. Blood pulsed around my gloved hand, heavy and thick, but the man was already done. He spasmed once, gurgled, and clutched at the knife I had sunk into his heart.

I knocked his hat off so that it stayed in the front seat, then dragged him to the ground beside the car. "Shh." I put my free hand to his brow, covering his eyes. "It will be over soon. I am sorry."

He jerked once more and went still. I lifted my hand, saw his lifeless eyes, and relaxed. With a gentle motion, I closed his eyelids, regretting what I had been forced to do but knowing it was my only choice.

The military had trained me to view an enemy as merely a target for my aggression and my skill at arms, and perhaps butchering the monsters I hunted was no different. Being forced to kill an innocent was another matter.

He should not have suffered at all, but the least I can do is make it quick and clean.

Still holding the knife in his chest, I used my free hand to draw a large bandanna from within my jacket. This, I wrapped around the blade, withdrawing my knife and pressing the bandanna over the wound.

With the blood kept mostly to his body, I would be safe from discovery later. Nothing had sprayed out to mark the car or my clothing. I'd learned a valuable lesson after the mess I had to deal with after killing Conrad.

Nobody would know I had killed this man, or Wilhelm. Carefully keeping the bandanna pressed over the dead man's heart, I worked him underneath the back of the car.

Several boulders marked the edge of the parking area. Anyone in the harbormaster's office would have to walk into the parking lot to find the body before daylight.

If someone did find him, so be it. For now, I was safe to proceed as planned.

I hurried back to take the dead man's place behind the wheel, snatching up his cap from where it had fallen. I slipped the cap onto my head and rested my gloved hands on the wheel. I would sit and wait for Wilhelm, and if he yelled at me to get out and open his door, I would pretend not to hear.

Let the man do something for himself at the end of his life. He could open his own damn door.

And then my work will commence.

12
———

Mark Wilhelm's hands shook. They wouldn't stop shaking all the way back to his car.

He didn't like being the one to hand off money. Hadn't liked it the first time he'd done it and liked it even less now. Even with that envelope now in the cops' hands instead of his own, he could already feel the eyes on him—as if a single glance from anyone would broadcast the amount of money he'd just paid or where it was going.

He'd feel safe once he got home, but his damn dumb chauffeur was apparently deaf now too.

"Harold, you lazy ass, open the door. Harold."

Great, now I can add "hire a new chauffeur" to my long list of shit for the week.

He yanked open the back door, got in, and slammed it shut. Fumbling for his seat belt with one hand, he slapped another against the driver's seat headrest. "Get us out of here. Faster the better, and then you can hand in that driver's uniform. After you deliver me home, you're fired."

Without a word in reply, his chauffeur started the engine, circling away a few seconds later.

Jimmy's dead. This whole thing could fall apart without him, and that's not even the worst of it. People might find out I'm involved. There goes the mayor's office or any hope of breathing free air again.

Mark laid his head back, loosening his tie. His nose twinged at an odd smell in the air—fish and oil and garbage, he assumed, along with everything else that came through this port. He tugged a stick of gum from his pocket, popped it into his mouth, and breathed deep while he chewed.

That was better.

At least something was.

Even the cops were asking him who killed Jimmy. He didn't have a clue. He only knew one thing.

The FBI would try to pin it on him.

One hundred percent, they're going to think I did it. That harpy wife of his will aim them my way, basically securing the election in her favor.

Dammit, but Boston needed new blood at the top, and he'd been so certain he could pull it off. He hadn't told Jimmy that, of course, even when they'd joked about it at the Fallweather.

If the Feds hadn't been called in, maybe Mark and his people could've put enough money into the right hands and turned Jimmy's killer into the nearest random hobo they could find. Case closed.

Harold was moving at a snail's pace toward the exit, which was irritating enough, but then he pulled to the side to give more room to a tractor trailer lumbering by with two shipping containers in tow.

A grunt of disgust escaped Mark's chest. "You can keep the lane, Harold. We have places to be."

Two weeks on the job, and he's already worthless. I should have fired his ass after the flat tire he got last week.

The truck cleared the lane, and Harold got them moving

slowly along. Mark closed his eyes and waited for the tedium to end.

The drive across the city was long. He could possibly get some sleep along the way. They just had to leave the damn parking lot, and it'd be a straight shot to I-90. But right before the gate, the car swerved, and Mark's eyes shot open.

"What the fuck are you doing?"

They'd turned into a dark lane between stacked containers and come to a sudden stop.

Harold turned the car off and got out. He stood in the darkness beside the driver's side door like he was losing his mind. After a moment, he stalked around the front and down the right-side passenger door.

Then he pivoted, facing the shipping containers with his back to the car.

What the hell's he doing? Taking a piss?

Mark unbuckled, leaned way over, and popped the door open. "Finish up quick and get back in the damn car. I don't want to be out all night dealing with this shit."

His chauffeur rolled his shoulders, and Mark noticed both his hands were by his sides.

If he's pissing, it's got to be running down his leg.

With a sudden rush of movement, Harold spun around and surged forward, into the back seat, pushing Mark against the door behind him.

He looked into his chauffeur's eyes and froze.

Shit! Fuck! That's not Harold!

Mark put his hands up, trying to shove the attacker away, but he was too heavy, too strong.

Thick, muscular legs pinned him against the seat as he tried in vain to force the man backward.

"What are you doing? What do—"

The man held up a knife, which already appeared slick with blood.

Pieces fell into place in Mark's mind in rapid succession. *He killed Harold. Oh shit, it's the guy who did Jimmy. Shit!*

The knife was up a moment later, at his throat.

Mark opened his mouth, forming words, but the heat of the blade stopped him. An arc of blood shot out his throat. He felt his head canting back at an odd angle, loose on its usually solid foundation. His vision went gray, obscuring his sight.

Blazing pain shot from his neck down, his arms and legs going numb. The animal ripped open his shirt, and then two lances of sharp heat shot down his chest. Those cuts were followed by two more sideways slashes.

Mark felt the weight of his attacker leave him. But before he could slump down in the seat, the man took hold of his legs and tugged him out of the car and into the night. Blood welled from his throat. His limbs were numb, cold, heavy, and dead. He hit the pavement hard, his head bouncing off the metal of the doorframe, gravel biting into his back.

"Mark Wilhelm, you are the second man to earn a place in hell for what you have done. And I am the one who will deliver you to the devil."

Wilhelm swore he knew the voice, or one like it. *But it couldn't be Rosco. He got his envelope earlier and sounded happy when he confirmed.*

Blood bubbled up through his mouth and nose. Mark tried to cough, but only a wet whimper escaped his lips. Death encircled him in its grasp, he knew that, but if only the killer would turn him over so he could breathe one last time…or just finish him.

Then he felt the knife tear at his pants. Blazing heat erupted from his groin, and another shot of blood arced up from his body, one final torrent of agony.

He only wished he could scream.

13

Leo and Emma had been huddled at the desk in her hotel room for about an hour, playing with Google Translate in every way they could think of. Trying different ways to spell the words she'd recorded, trying different languages, trying everything.

So far, they'd gotten little more than gibberish from any spelling or language. Leo went out to the vending machine in the hall, grabbed two sodas, and headed back to the room.

"Thanks." Emma took one and popped it open. "Smart thinking, grabbing fizz without the caffeine."

Leo downed a quarter of his own drink in one gulp. "Say that in two hours when we're still at this and falling asleep."

Her smile caught the corner of his eye as he stared at various spellings they'd tried, and he turned. "Listen, Leo, thanks. For believing me enough to try to work through this. You could have said it was useless and given up or just not believed me enough to be here. This means a lot."

The honest gratitude in her voice stilled him for a second, enough that the soda pooled on his tongue before he finally swallowed. Her sky-blue eyes shined with honesty. It was hard not to believe her.

Ghosts or not. She heard something, or we wouldn't be doing this.

"You're welcome." His words came out choked. He cleared his throat and looked back at the screen. "Let's go over what we have, on top of your recordings. Number one, if that last word is 'sex' just like it sounds, then it's the same in English as whatever language we're looking at."

"Which means we're probably looking at a Slavic language." Emma glanced at more of the notes they'd made, written out on a hotel stationery pad. "Most of the Slavic languages seem to share the word 'sex' with English."

"And it sounds Slavic, to my ear." Leo pointed to where Emma had written *soon tee-es-tay* on a hotel-branded notepad. "We've been connecting these last three syllables, but like you said, the *es-tay* sounds like *este* in Spanish. *Este sex.*"

Emma circled the word again and again on the pad. "And *este* is 'this' in Spanish. We've established that, but how can we be looking at both a Slavic and a Latin language?"

Leo took another sip of his soda. Something niggled at the edge of his brain. "Say that again?"

"Huh?"

Leo spiraled his finger, signaling her to go on. "Just say what you said again. I feel like it's getting my brain somewhere. Humor me."

She shrugged. "Okay. How can we be looking at one language that's both Slavic and Latin? Those are two different influences. Two different groups, so—"

"The ghost is Romanian!" Leo nearly spilled his soda all over the computer, the thought hit him so fast. Emma's eyes went wide.

Getting excited about the ghosts? Calm down, man. You sound as crazy as her.

"Look." Leo pulled up the Wikipedia page for Romania and pointed to the map. "When I was young, Yaya would talk about a cousin who'd moved away from home. He went north to Romania, for a girl he'd met in a foreign exchange program in school. He had to learn the language and had an easy time of it because he already knew Italian and had studied French as well. They're all Romance languages."

Emma scrolled down the page, reading the sidebar information. "I guess that fits with *este*, but—"

"Romanian is a Romance-influenced language, yes, but look at their neighbors. Mostly Slavic except for Hungary. If you put a bunch of Slavic influences onto a Romance language-speaking people…"

Emma was already nodding. "Let's see if we can use Romanian to translate the ghost messages."

In another moment, she'd begun playing with spellings for the first sentence, translating them into Romanian. The first three tries produced gibberish.

And then, *mau* produced the word "they."

"Not exactly a silver bullet, but it's a start." Emma shot Leo a grin, and he pointed her back to the screen.

"Next word. You said it sounded like 'pack a lee' but as one word. I doubt we're looking for a 'k' in this language, so start with p-a-c-a—"

"Then *l*." Emma typed in what they had so far. "Let's say that's our base." After that, she tried *ee* and then *i*.

With a few more attempts, they landed on the final syllable as "it."

Mau păcălit.

Leo breathed out at the sight of the sentence. "They tricked me." Although the translator added a hyphen to "m-au."

Emma jotted the words down, eyes bright, and went back to experimenting, but Leo felt the air leave his chest as he sat heavily back in his seat. Watching her.

He hadn't believed her. He truly hadn't believed her.

This whole night had felt like an exercise in random sounds and word play. Pointless.

Just because you found the language doesn't mean there are dang ghosts. Slow down. Just slow the hell down here.

Emma let out a little squeak of excitement. "Leo, look! Second sentence. *They used me.*"

M-au folosit.

They used me. Holy shit.

Leo spoke before he even considered what he was about to say. "Third sentence. Your ru-een-a sounds like 'ruin a.' You said it yourself. Add an *a* or an *at* and see what happens."

M-au ruinat.

Emma sat back staring at the screen. "They tricked me. They used me. They ruined me." She gulped what was left of her soda and then dropped the can into the nearby bin. "One girl's speech down. One more sentence to go."

And it didn't take long. With their new confidence in which language Emma had heard, the final sentence from the ghost at the Conrad Manor sat staring at them within another few minutes.

Sunt bun numai pentru sex.

"'I'm only good for sex." Leo read the translation out loud, making it real, and then scribbled it onto the stationery pad, even as Emma added it to the full translation in the document on her laptop. "A woman saying she's been tricked, used, ruined…"

"That all she's good for is sex." Emma's lips flattened with the chill of the words in the room. "We thought Jimmy might have had a sex worker in his room, but this doesn't sound like a sex worker. And the ghosts I saw were *young*. Early twenties or even late teens."

Heaviness settled in Leo's chest. "Girls, then. Sent over from Romania via sex traffickers. That's what we're talking about. The girls are probably teenagers." Rage seethed through him, the same fury he'd felt on their first case together, when he'd suspected a fifty-something circus ringleader of molesting a prepubescent girl.

He stood up so quickly that Emma jumped in her seat beside him, but he waved her back down. "I'll be right back. I'm gonna grab a real drink from the minibar. You want a beer?"

"White wine." Emma went back to staring at the screen.

Leo made a beeline for the door, pretending not to hear Emma's offer that he could just raid the minibar in her room. He needed a breather.

When he reached his room, right next to Emma's, he got inside and simply leaned back against the door, quelling the anger that had boiled up in him.

After several deep breaths, he realized his emotions weren't strictly due to what they'd discovered.

It's how we got there. We translated a bunch of gibberish Emma says she heard from ghosts.

His gaze went to the wall between their rooms. On the other side, Emma was probably still at her desk, considering the words they'd translated...

From two ghosts. Who she described as "girls."

He stumbled to the minibar and pulled out two beers, along with a mini bottle of wine for Emma. But instead of heading back to her room, he opened one of the beers and took a pull. The beer hit his tongue, but he barely tasted it.

Realistically, this didn't prove the existence of ghosts... but it sure felt like it. The implications of what had just unfolded in Emma's room couldn't be ignored.

Romanian was a real language, and Emma hadn't recognized it. Leo had no doubt of that in his mind. They'd wasted too much time playing with Google Translate, fighting for the right meanings and teasing out different spellings.

She simply hadn't recognized the language, and he wasn't even sure she'd have found it tonight without his help.

Unless she was lying about not knowing it was Romanian —and he was fairly positive she wasn't—then that meant the ghosts she'd seen were real. Right? He couldn't think of any other explanation.

But if ghosts *were* real…

He swallowed. The beer in his hand sat propped on his knee, all but forgotten, as he gazed around his hotel room. If Denae had died that day, or if she'd died in the hospital while he'd been in Boston…would she be sitting beside him? Lying in his hotel bed right now, even though it looked empty?

Jacinda said she would call. She would let us know the minute Denae's condition changed. We'll know as soon as she does.

But if Denae's dead, and Jacinda doesn't know yet…

No, he wasn't going to head down that road. Emma said she would tell him, and so far, she'd had nothing to say about Denae. He'd been watching her, too, looking for signs she was staring at something that wasn't here.

Or talking to someone who wasn't there.

But he'd seen nothing from Emma to suggest she'd seen Denae and held back from telling him.

Taking another sip of beer, he lay back on the bed for a minute. Emma was intuitive. She'd figure out he just needed a minute. And he really, really did.

What if there'd been a whole group of ghosts standing around and watching him during all his most private moments over the years? Had his mother and father actually made it to his school play, watching from this Other place

Emma talked about? The thought made him choke on the very air coming into his lungs, but he pushed forward with it anyway.

Maybe I should talk to Yaya about it. About Mom and Dad and Papu. Ghosts in general.

He remembered his grandmother talking about spirits. They were vague memories, but he had them, just the same. He'd just never thought about them.

Questioning Emma further would maybe make sense… but he wasn't ready to admit the truth. That he was actually starting to believe her.

He'd told her as much and been firm about it. And that had felt honest.

But if he'd been asked to stand on one side of a line, dividing belief from disbelief…until they'd worked through the translations, he would've been ready to jump back to the side of that line that felt normal.

Because it was normal, but now "normal" has changed. Normal is something you've never seen before, but you need to get used to it, and fast.

"I could just ask Emma why she doesn't ask the ghosts who killed them. That would make our lives a hell of a lot easier." A nervous laugh broke from his lips, but the thought lingered in the room.

He sat up, staring at the doorway into the hall that led to his colleague. There'd come a time when he needed to talk to her about how all this worked and why asking that question wouldn't work—he sensed that her world of ghosts wasn't that simple, or else she'd have been practical enough to have asked the gold star questions already. But he couldn't have that conversation, not just yet.

Right now, when he could barely bring himself to believe her, the question would come out venomous. Full of doubt and snark and distrust. Better to hold his tongue.

But maybe he could talk to Yaya before Emma. That was something to consider.

When he felt a touch more present, he downed the rest of his first beer and picked up the second, along with Emma's wine. At the door, he glanced around his room. No sign of Denae, and no sign that his world had just changed.

Or maybe it hadn't…but it felt like it had.

When he got to Emma's room, he gave a single knock, and she opened the door almost immediately, meeting his eyes briefly.

He could swear she'd been crying. "Everything okay?"

"Yeah." She stepped aside to let him in. "Thinking about those girls…got to me."

He passed her the wine as he stepped in, then opened his second beer.

She twisted off the top, looking out the open door and talking to him over her shoulder. "You took off like a rocket back there. You good now?"

He watched her, noticing that she had one hand on the door, holding it open. She slowly closed it, as if ushering someone out. "You're sure I didn't miss anything? Anyone who might've come by while I was gone?"

Tilting the little bottle to her lips, she grimaced at the taste. "No…nothing you could've seen."

She still hadn't met his eyes.

"Emma. Was…shit, was Denae here?"

A single tear traced down her cheek, and she finally looked him in the eye. "Briefly, just now. I told her we're not done yet, and she needs to stay where she is. In the hospital, with her family."

Leo staggered to the bed and sat down hard. "I was just thinking about her, wondering if you'd seen her and hadn't told me."

"I promised, and I have told you." She sat next to him on

the bed. "No more secrets. I meant that, and nothing's changed."

"I know. And I said I believe you. I still do." He threw back another swallow of beer. "I'd hoped to get through this without…without her showing up."

They sat in silence for a while, sipping at their drinks. Leo stood and went to the desk again, looking at the notes they'd made of the translated Romanian. "I was thinking…the Fallweather felt *off*. Like something was just wrong in terms of what was happening there."

He grimaced and returned to his seat by the desk. In a moment, he had the security footage pulled up on his iPad. "I don't know how long it'll take to get the hotel to loosen their grip on guest records. It could be weeks. But something about the videos is bugging me."

Emma joined him at the desk and watched over his shoulder as the video played out. Leo watched with her, narrating what they saw.

"Jimmy Conrad coming into the hotel, checking in. Goes off camera, then he's at the elevator. Jimmy on the top floor now, going into his room—"

"Wait!" Emma slammed down into her seat and began typing at her laptop. "The crime scene photos. Look."

She opened up the photos and angled the screen toward Leo. The pile of clothes sitting beside the bed in Jimmy Conrad's hotel suite. A nice pair of dress pants and a button-down.

And then he saw it.

Leo's gaze shot back to the security footage, frozen on his screen. The video was paused on Conrad striding down the hallway toward his suite, wearing a suit and a light-colored, striped button-down. But in the hotel suite picture, clear as day, the button-down was a dark color, interwoven with light thread in a paisley pattern.

He scrolled back to the footage of Conrad entering the lobby where he met Bency at the front desk. "Paisley patterned shirt, just like the photo."

Emma looked up at him, her eyes triumphant. "The footage from the hallway is fake, or it's been switched out."

"I'm gonna text Tibble. We need to talk to that security guard again." Leo punched out the text and took another sip of his beer. His head hadn't stopped spinning since they'd stumbled on the correct translations.

Even as he focused on their new lead, on this discrepancy that most definitely meant something—because someone had to have hidden the real footage on purpose, given that the date and time on the feed were correct—his heart kept on going back to the Romanian translations still visible on the hotel stationery beside him.

Those translations were based on the words of Romanian ghosts. And as much as his head wanted to focus on the case, his heart was pulling in a very different direction.

Not to mention one other pressing question. If ghosts were real, and Emma really knew the truth of them...how many other people in this world did too?

14

Monique Varley finished drying herself with a towel and hurried back to her small bedroom. She'd used spell work to cleanse one of her favorite outfits over the course of the night, and now she herself was newly cleansed. Maybe something would come of it.

She dressed carefully, attentive to every drape of cloth as she added crystal-studded jewelry for protection and power, just as she'd done so long ago, with Emma Last's mother.

All yesterday and late into last night, she'd done her best to get in touch with the Other, to see if Gina Last herself might be responsible for the chills that had been chipping into her bones like coffin nails.

Every bit of spell work she'd tried had left her drained and no closer to an answer.

The Other isn't talking, Moni, at least not to the likes of you.

When she'd finally given up and gone to bed, it had been with the knowledge that she'd need a much stronger incantation.

In the kitchen, she began boiling a pot of water and placed hematite stones all around the periphery of the appliance. Calling back to her memories of doing this very same spell with Gina at her side, Monique slowly added in the herbal mixture she'd left chilling in the refrigerator overnight.

By now, the herbs and water she'd pooled would be well and truly muddled.

Maybe, just maybe, that'll be what it takes to give me clarity around what's happening. And learn whether or not Emma will be able to take care of herself when the time comes.

After a few stirs, she covered the pot and headed out to her garden. The mix boiling on her stove, along with her crystals, should keep any observer from being able to understand exactly what she was harvesting or for what purpose. Still, she moved quickly.

Her little greenhouse, normally a refuge, felt insignificant around her. Like a glass house awaiting a boulder.

And this is only the first step. Even if I gather what I need and get inside without being revealed, I'll still have to get the magic just right if I want to hold on to everything I've worked so hard for.

Not to mention surviving her...

Monique cut off the thought, nearly biting her tongue in the process. It wouldn't do to think the woman's name. Especially not now, while she frantically worked against the clock to keep herself—and her life and endeavors—safe from view.

She had no other choice.

Pausing to catch her breath after collecting all the ginseng and rosemary she could spare—without killing her plants anyway—Monique gazed out the clear glass window of her greenhouse. The woods had begun to seem darker and darker with each passing day.

Was she being watched?

Was it possible her home had been discovered?

A flock of birds shot from brush outside the greenhouse,

and Monique nearly dropped everything she'd been gathering.

This wasn't the time to wonder about that woman.

One way or another, she had to figure out what was going on, what it might mean about Emma's connection to the Other.

Whatever she learned, Monique knew she would have to act before it became too late.

15

Emma's phone buzzed ten minutes before she'd set her alarm to go off, and she reached for it on instinct. Her eyes had barely opened when she brought it up in front of her face.

Mark Wilhelm and his chauffeur murdered at Port of Boston. Get there ASAP.

SSA Walter Tibble's text woke her up in an instant.

"Shit." Emma shoved herself out of bed, knowing Leo would be doing the same next door. With the team's prime suspect dead and two more bodies added to the case, they needed to be moving yesterday.

She was in and out of a mostly cold shower, dressed, and ready to go in under five minutes. Leo was waiting by the elevator as she exited her room, tablet and phone in hand. "Almost texted you." He tucked his phone away. "I'm ready if you are."

"As ever."

The elevator doors opened, and they both slid inside. She thumbed the ground floor button and glanced at Leo, gauging the way his eyes remained focused on the door. Whether he was avoiding her gaze or simply ready to move, she had no idea. "If you're okay with me driving, can you text Tibble again about that discrepancy on the security footage just in case he's not at the port? Maybe he can work on tracking down our cover-up."

Leo gave a quick nod. "Sounds like a plan."

The GPS helped them avoid the worst of the traffic, and Emma sped their rental through the port's front gate right around the time Leo was wrapping up his conversation with Tibble.

"Midori and Paul are following up with the other candidates, the ones who'd exited the mayoral race."

"So it's on us to get after that footage problem at the Fallweather?"

"Looks like it, but that may be for the best, since we're the ones who spotted it. We'll have more energy to get answers, you know?"

At the port entry, a large sign reminded drivers the area wasn't open to the general public except by prearranged appointments and special conditions. Emma pointed to it as they flashed their badges to a cop in the gate kiosk. He hit a button and waved them through once the gate opened.

"Killer and victims got in somehow."

"It seems that Wilhelm flew first class even when he was walking, so he probably had pull to get his car in here."

"Or he benefited from an arrangement that wasn't on anybody's books."

The scene of the crime was tucked between two towering stacks of shipping containers. One cop stood bent over at the waist, vomiting on the pavement behind Wilhelm's car. Others stood pointedly looking away from the crime scene they'd cordoned off with yellow tape.

Emma parked behind a forensic van. Once she'd stepped out of the vehicle, she pulled on a pair of gloves as she moved on to the main attraction.

Splayed on his back between his car and the shipping containers, Mark Wilhelm's naked body lay bare in the Boston morning. His mouth hung open as if to emit an agonized scream. Dried blood covered his lips, chin, and teeth. Wilhelm's neck had been slashed open. But a mess of gore in his groin made it evident they were dealing with the same killer.

And slices on his chest made a clear Roman numeral two.

A tech crouched beside the body, measuring each of the slash marks. When he was done, he stood up with a grimace and waved to Emma and Leo. They approached with their badges out.

"Special Agent Emma Last and Special Agent Leo Ambrose." Emma glanced at the mangled mess that had once been Mark Wilhelm and forced a smile for the tech. "What can you tell us?"

"Not much." He swept one hand through the air, over the body. "You have a very dead mayoral candidate whose, ah...*penis* was cut off with something sharp. It was left beside the body, and we've bagged it for evidence."

Leo bent to one knee beside the body, leaning over the marks on the chest. "These postmortem?"

The tech pursed his lips, eyeing them. "I'll tell you, it was close, one way or another, but you'll have to get the M.E.'s final word on that. Obviously, they aren't the killing wounds. Not enough blood. The M.E. got called to another early morning meeting, but I imagine these bodies'll be his first priority once they get to the morgue."

Emma snapped her attention to the tech. "'These,' as in plural. The chauffeur isn't here, though."

The tech jerked a thumb over his shoulder. "Back beside the harbormaster's office. Body was left in the parking lot. I'm headed there after I get Wilhelm processed and loaded."

Emma gave another glance to Wilhelm's pale, naked

corpse and a quick nod to the nearby pile of his clothes marked as evidence. Even from where she stood, they appeared covered in blood and left in a heap, not like they'd been rifled through. "Anything missing? Out of sorts?"

"Not that I've seen. Wallet and keys are present. Same for the driver."

Leo gave one glance back to the gate, as if to prod the transportation vehicle to show, but Emma only shrugged.

"Rush hour traffic and a lot going on for a Friday morning, I guess. Shall we?" She gestured in the direction the tech had indicated for the harbormaster's office.

The walk to the parking lot took a few minutes, and they passed another group of cops, some wearing Massport badges. The second stretch of crime scene tape became visible as soon as they got to the lot, which was bordered by a row of large boulders. A pair of Massport cops stood beside a body covered with a sheet.

Emma and Leo showed the cops their badges, and the officers stepped aside to give them room to examine the body.

"Anything we should know?" Emma asked as Leo lifted the sheet aside, revealing a thin white male wearing a black jacket and slacks. His formerly white shirt was now a mess of light- and dark-red stains from a wound directly above his heart.

A wadded-up bandanna sat above the wound.

One of the cops aimed a finger at the messy piece of fabric. "Found him like you see him, but that bandanna was stuffed against the wound. Must've stuck to the sheet and moved when you uncovered him."

Carefully, she glanced around, waiting for some signal from the Other. The only sense of cold that came her way was the coastal breeze blowing in across the water. "Collateral damage, you think?"

Leo stood and stepped around the body, as if eyeing the dead man's position. "I don't see any wounds other than the obvious one. Right over the heart, from the look of it. For some reason, this guy didn't earn a Roman numeral, like he didn't 'count.'"

Emma signaled at a cop watching them idly from the side of a patrol car. "Who found the bodies?"

"Graveyard shift, fittingly." He guffawed at his own joke but straightened up when Emma stared at him without smiling. The cop pointed across the lot. "Fontaine and Darrow. The two guys in the middle." Emma followed his finger to the group of officers she and Leo had passed coming from Mark Wilhelm's crime scene.

Pulling her badge, she approached the group, sensing Leo do the same beside her. The cops paused as she drew closer, and she plastered a smile on her face, waving for the two on either side to continue on.

Once they'd moved back to the chauffeur's body, she sized up the officers in front of her. A lanky, black-haired one returned her smile fast, maybe by reflex. Beside him, a stockier one with a beard beyond regulation length only deepened his scowl and stood a touch straighter. He pointed to his name tag. "Port Officer Bill Fontaine. This here's Port Officer Jack Darrow. Guess you heard we found the dumps."

"What time did you find the bodies?"

"We spotted Mr. Wannabe Mayor as we were getting off shift, making our last rounds. That was about five in the morning." Officer Fontaine tugged at his beard as if to nurse his frown. "Then, when we were coming back to clock out with the harbormaster, we spotted the driver."

Emma gazed beyond the confines of the parking lot and the road running up to it. Shipping containers towered as far as the eye could see, and although there was something of a straight path from the parking lot down to the dock and the ships, it was lined by still more containers.

Anybody coming from either direction shouldn't have had trouble spotting the chauffeur's body, with only those boulders ringing the lot.

And the killer would've had plenty of places to hide and avenues for escape.

16

Leo gestured back to where Wilhelm had been found. "Any idea what he was doing here last night?"

Darrow shrugged, his tongue darting out to lick his lips. "Don't know. This part of Conley isn't usually active at night. We patrol around, but mostly we're near the harbormaster's office."

"Any ships come in last night?" Leo eyed the dock and the surrounding vessels, all of them giant and full of containers. Things looked quiet now, but until the M.E. had examined the corpses, there was no telling when the men had been killed.

Fontaine turned his head and spit to the side. "Only one. The *Yamurgi* brought in a shipment of industrial goods that started in Istanbul. We musta been down there on the dock or in the harbormaster's office whenever these guys were killed."

"The driver's body was lying in plain view from 'whenever these guys were killed' until 'about five in the morning.'" Leo narrowed his gaze at Fontaine. "You don't ever check the parking lot on your rounds? It's adjacent to the office."

"And the door's on the other side of the building. We got cameras on the lot anyway. Me and Darrow, we spend our shifts with our eyes on what counts. The cargo."

Emma pointed down toward the dock. "You mind taking us down there to see the *Yamurgi* and 'what counts?'"

Darrow started walking, speaking over his shoulder before his partner had even turned. "Captain should be on his ship. Haven't seen him leave it."

Emma and Leo followed a few paces behind Darrow, with Fontaine trailing after them. Leo tapped a hand against Emma's shoulder. "Their casual attitudes don't sit too well with me."

"Join the club." She glanced over her shoulder at Fontaine. "A local politician and his chauffeur are killed on their watch nearby, and they lead with 'we didn't see it happen?'"

The *Yamurgi* appeared two-thirds full, with the middle range of the cargo area mostly empty. Darrow nodded to it and spoke as they climbed aboard. "They unloaded in Amsterdam before coming across the Atlantic."

A man with crackled, sunburned skin appeared from the ship's bridge, waving to them from above as Fontaine joined them from the gangway.

The captain came down a staircase and met them on the deck, a clipboard held loosely in his hand. His squint became more prominent as he approached, but Leo noted the easy handshake he offered.

"Captain Tanan Mariz, at your service."

Leo tucked his badge into his pocket and nodded. "Thanks for speaking with us, Captain Mariz. Sounds like your ship was the only one that came in last night?"

The man's lips pursed, and his intense gaze never left

Emma. Leo wasn't sure if he was flirting or trying to threaten her when he spoke. "Whatever you need, just ask."

"Can we see your manifest?"

"Be my guest." He held out the clipboard, meeting Leo's eyes briefly before turning back to Emma.

Leo reviewed the pages on the clipboard. He felt Emma startle beside him and glanced up. She wore a look of wonderment, eyes wide and a smirk curling her lips as she stared at him. "You know how to read a ship's manifest?"

Leo chuckled. "I was on and off ships almost weekly in Miami. This all looks in order."

He handed the clipboard back to Captain Mariz.

"Always is." The captain glared at the port cops, and Darrow shrank back a touch. "Or I wouldn't be allowed here, would I?"

Fontaine growled. "Just let 'em look around and lay off the attitude."

They moved among the containers and then up to the bridge, where Leo took lead in examining further paperwork. When he picked a container at random, the captain led them back into the maze of containers on deck. They stopped at a rusted blue container.

Two crew members appeared and opened it up to display large crates that were then opened up themselves. Huge rolls of brightly colored fabric came into view, and the captain nodded.

"Most of what we're carrying right now is likely clothing and textiles. Generally, that's what we carry. Sometimes, shipments of grain." He gestured to the dense array of crates filling the rest of the shipping container. "You want us to unpack all this for you?"

Leo glanced to Emma, who nodded. "We'll need every container opened and checked against the manifest."

Both cops and the captain rolled their eyes, and Officer

Fontaine in particular seemed about ready to punch something. "You gotta be kidding me. I just worked a graveyard, third time this week."

Leo planted his hands on his hips. "And two men were murdered on your shift. Their killer could be hiding inside any one of the containers on this ship, since it arrived at some point late last night, possibly around the time of the murders."

Officer Fontaine lifted a hand to his mouth and dragged it down his beard, looking off to the side. Leo stepped forward, closing the space between them.

"Hey, we're on the same team as you, just with different badges. How about you get word to the harbormaster to conduct a full inspection of this ship first? We'll need warrants before we can open any more of the containers, because they're owned by the companies who have goods inside them. Meanwhile, you can show us that surveillance footage of the parking lot you mentioned."

Fontaine turned on his heel and stalked across the ship, leading them and Darrow back onto dry land.

Inside the harbormaster's office, Fontaine sat before an ancient desk and keyboard with an array of six monitors behind it. He punched in a few commands and stabbed a finger on the enter key, then pointed up to the far-left monitor. "This is Mariz's ship, the *Yamurgi*, soon as it came into view."

Leo leaned toward the monitor, seeing the ship as a large blip on a dark screen marked ten thirty p.m.

The Massport officer fast-forwarded until they passed through about two hours of footage. "There's the *Yamurgi* again. She came in on schedule and moored where instructed. Captain Mariz handed over the manifest, and me and Darrow checked him out just like you did. And just like you, I felt everything was in order. Because it was."

Emma straightened to look at Fontaine. "Except for two murders that had occurred, were occurring, or were about to occur."

"Hey, I got two eyes, same as Darrow. I can only put 'em in one place at a time. Right here." He stabbed a finger at the screen. "I'm showing you my eyes were on my job. Making sure Mariz's ship came in right."

"What about the gate?" Leo gestured to the surrounding monitors. "You have cameras all over the port, like extra sets of eyes. Let's see what they caught."

Fontaine hit some more buttons. "Okay, wise guy. I got my extra eyes coming up for you."

Ignoring the jab, Leo took a breath and rested a hand on Emma's shoulder, as if to encourage her to let Fontaine's attitude slide. The guy had been up all night long and was about to end his shift when he found two dead bodies.

He's running on fumes and shreds of patience. We know the feeling.

With a click of his mouse, Fontaine brought a new camera view up for them. The gate they'd come through appeared on a central screen. At approximately eleven p.m., Mark Wilhelm's car arrived.

"That's about when Mariz's ship came into port."

The car parked by the harbormaster's office, and the driver exited. He opened Wilhelm's door, closing it after the man stepped away. Wilhelm headed toward the front of the harbormaster's office and was out of camera view.

Leo scanned the monitors, looking for one that showed the front of the building they were in. The lower left screen showed where Wilhelm should have appeared. After close to a minute, he hadn't, and Leo tapped a finger on the monitor. "Looped footage maybe? What's going on here, Fontaine?"

"I don't have a fucking clue."

Darrow moved closer, from where he'd been leaning on a

wall across the room. "Fontaine, show 'em the footage already. I wanna get home before the next shift starts."

"Shut your hole." Fontaine began hitting various buttons while staring back and forth between the monitors and his computer. The lower-left monitor continued to show an empty roadway in front of the building. Leo looked at the other screens and saw the same thing. Empty roadways, aisles between shipping containers, and the parking lot where, just minutes before, Wilhelm's car had pulled up.

"It's been wiped or looped, just like the Fallweather."

Fontaine jerked in his chair and slammed his mouse down on the desk. "Dammit. Gimme a few minutes to figure this out, will ya?"

He backed out of the system he'd been using and began hitting more keys as he pulled up the settings on the security footage, then a different set of cameras that showed still shots of container towers.

Another series of mouse clicks and keyboarding brought up more of the same. When another minute had passed, the Massport officer cursed under his breath and turned to face Emma and Leo.

They'd already guessed what was coming, though. Leo's eyes went back to the lower-left monitor showing nothing but an empty roadway. "Somebody tampered with the system."

Shoving back from the desk, Fontaine stood up. "Don't ask me who, because I don't know." He tugged at his beard before he shook his head in apology. "I'm sorry, but we've got nothing. Whoever's responsible for the murders must have accessed the security feed or interfered with the footage somehow. After eleven last night, we got nothing this side of the port. Dock, container stacks, and the parking lot where the driver got killed."

Leo scanned over the security setup. "All right. We'll get our people out here to see what they can find out."

Fontaine pushed the chair in hard enough to jar the desk. "You two need anything else? I gotta make some calls and get this shit fixed. Then after that, maybe I can go home and get some sleep. Thank fuck it's my weekend coming up tomorrow. Pardon my language, but I've been up close to eighteen hours here."

"I wish it were that simple." Leo already had his phone up, calling Tibble. "Now that we know the security footage was interfered with, we need our people on this. And we still need Mariz's ship inspected."

"You think *I'm* gonna do that?" Fontaine jabbed his finger into his chest.

"Just let your superiors know it needs to happen and that we'll need to examine the security equipment before anyone tries to fix it. If your sergeant wants to speak with me, I'll be available."

The man's eyes went dark and shaded, his lips opening to argue, but Tibble had answered.

"SSA Tibble, sorry, I'm at the port with Agent Last. Just a second, please." Leo held up a finger and stepped to the side as Emma pulled out a business card and handed it to Fontaine.

He took the card, stared at it, and finally pocketed it. With little more than an annoyed look between the two of them, he lifted a thumb for his partner to follow him and stalked out of the office. "Ain't gonna be our asses if city hall gets up in arms about port traffic being screwed up for two weeks' wortha Sundays, I'll tell ya what."

With that, the two port officers disappeared, and Leo wandered over to the window as he filled in Tibble.

The call was quick and to the point, just as Leo had hoped it would be. When he finished with Tibble, he noticed Emma staring out the window to his left, looking at the containers just like he'd been doing.

"Tibble's gonna talk to the port sergeant and get some Cyber folks over here to look at the camera setup. He'll also liaise with Massport Police on that ship inspection and getting warrants for its cargo. Ready?"

Emma shifted toward the door by way of an answer.

Has she seen another ghost out there? Or in here?

He'd have to ask her later. Right now, they had forensic data to review and the hope of finding anything that might point them toward a suspect for the grisly murders of two prominent and wealthy men.

If it weren't for the mutilation, Leo could come up with any number of possible motives. As he stepped back out into the cold sunlight, he looked back to where Wilhem's body had been found.

But there is something else in play here, and we need to find out what it is before more blood is spilled.

17

Emma sat back in her seat at the Boston Bureau's conference table, glad to finally be off her feet. Around her, the Boston agents were just settling in from their own day of work, and none of them looked entirely comfortable with the newest developments. Emma supposed she'd have felt the same if she were in their shoes. It was never a good thing when your primary suspect was the next body to drop.

She and Leo had spent the whole of the day at Conley Terminal, supervising and helping to process the scene. At some point in the proceedings, Jacinda texted to update them on Denae and Vance.

Neither of their colleagues had improved or changed. Emma supposed that was good news. It meant they were still in the fight. Mia, at least, had shown improvement, recovering from her dehydration and the worst withdrawal symptoms.

Jacinda said she'll be released within a day or two.

Their day in Boston had ended with little more than a hiccup of progress for the investigation. Massport officers completed their inspection of the *Yamurgi* and found nothing out of order. The security system was still being tested to determine how and when the footage was tampered with.

And that leaves us back at square one, but with two more bodies in the morgue and a killer still on the loose.

"I still can't believe it wasn't Wilhelm who killed Conrad." Paul flipped through the crime scene images on his laptop. He pulled out a chair beside Emma and sat, all but dropping his laptop onto the table.

Midori frowned up at the map of the port. Tibble had the image projected on the screen at the head of the table. "And from what the Cyber folks said, whoever messed with the security footage there had to have gone into the building to do it. The fact that nobody saw them means they knew the place, but we don't have a single fingerprint that doesn't match up to port personnel, or, so far, any record of someone logging into the system outside of normal hours."

"Agents Last and Ambrose, what was your read on the personnel you interviewed?" Tibble leaned back in his chair at the head of the table. "Any red flags?"

Leo powered up his iPad, reading the cops' names out for the others' benefit. "Officers Fontaine and Darrow found the bodies. They were a little nonplussed for our taste, but that's also at the end of a graveyard shift that got extended into nearly another six hours of work. I'm surprised Fontaine didn't bite through his own teeth, to be honest."

"Exhaustion can put us all on our worst behavior, so by way of red flags, that's not a big one."

Emma tapped a pen on the table. "Still wouldn't be a bad idea to look into their backgrounds. They were at the dock when the footage went funny."

"Fair point, but do we have any reason to suspect their involvement beyond that?" Tibble clasped his hands behind his head. "You'd think they'd have hidden the bodies if either of them knew the killings would occur or witnessed them."

"That place is a maze." Leo gestured at the map. "They know it inside and out. Wouldn't make sense for them to kill those men and leave them out in the open like that unless they wanted to draw attention to the bodies—"

"And that'd take balls." Paul barked a laugh. "No pun intended. Even if they did take Conrad's and Wilhelm's sacks, I don't know if it'd be enough."

Midori rolled her eyes and shifted her chair toward Emma's. "We heard what you and Leo discovered with the hotel security footage last night. That's a good catch. Me and frat boy over there," she thumbed at Paul, "got stuck in traffic and couldn't make it to the hotel this afternoon, but it feels like that's the next step."

Paul grimaced. "Fuckin' tunnels in this city."

Tibble nodded, ignoring Paul's griping, and brought up stills of the two shots of Jimmy Conrad that Emma and Leo had focused in on last night. The picture of him walking down the hallway to his suite showed the striped button-down shirt. But the picture of him entering the hotel, and of the clothing left in his suite on the night of his murder, showed the paisley shirt.

If Emma squinted, she thought she could even determine a different level of five o'clock shadow between the hotel lobby footage and the hotel hallway footage.

"It's Jimmy Conrad in both shots." Tibble pointed back and forth between them. "But I agree with Emma and Leo. The footage may be from two different nights."

Paul grunted, then shifted to stare at Emma and then Leo behind her. "What about it, D.C. whiz kids? Any suspicions as to who our new prime suspect should be?"

Tibble gazed pointedly at Paul. "I'd settle with a guess from *anyone* who made that first trip to the hotel as to who might've been the one to tamper with the security footage."

"I've been thinking about our manager, Dirk Bency."

Emma opened up her iPad, going back to her notes from the day before. "He seemed nervous the whole time we were there, and the concierge we spoke to didn't trust him. It seems the concierge, Elliot Patten, suspected Conrad of having sex workers in his room."

Paul slapped the table. "I agree. High rollers like Conrad usually have a few tagalongs. Hired escorts maybe, or just the latest intern to fall under the spell of money and power. We thinking the girl did him like that? Because that'd be a strong woman to heave a guy off a building."

Emma shook her head. "I'm thinking the particular sex workers Conrad hired were actually sex slaves. Women who'd been trafficked for the purpose." She tapped her iPad. "We like Bency for being involved in some capacity, either as procurer or, perhaps, as an enforcer for whoever is behind the trafficking."

Midori straightened her notebook in front of her. "What puts Bency in the hot seat?"

Leo lifted his hand, and she nodded for him to go ahead. "Patten reported that Bency went from gossiping about Conrad to clamming up completely just a month ago. Something changed."

At the head of the room, Tibble started pacing. He recited what they'd discussed about Bency so far. "Anything else that gets us looking at him?"

Emma piped up. "The security manager at the Fallweather, Steven Nassar, had a less-than-favorable opinion of Bency. Seems there's some kind of beef there."

Paul nodded. "He looks like a gym rat too. Don't know if he got the muscles from working out or steroids, but I bet he could toss a dick off a roof." He smirked at his own pun.

Emma fought down a laugh. Paul needed no encouragement from her.

Tibble rolled his finger to get them back on track. "Okay,

so Bency's just another suit, got it. What motive would he have, exactly?" He jabbed his keyboard, and Bency's driver's license came up on the screen. "Leo, Emma, what are your ideas here?"

"Could be he was being paid by Conrad to keep his mouth shut." Leo aimed a pen at the screen. "I don't know why that would lead him to killing either Conrad or Wilhelm, especially with the added mutilation. But if it's a big enough cover-up, and there's enough money involved, I'd guess it's possible."

"And as a manager, he'd have access to the security footage." Emma stared at the bald man up on their screen, who she couldn't help thinking was hiding behind his glasses. "But the hotel maintains security staff who monitor the hotel's footage. They certainly know the system as well."

Tibble turned to stare at the image of Bency. "Same could be said of Massport Police. You said the two men you talked with were exhausted and 'nonplussed.' Did you get any of the same red flags from the Fallweather staff?"

"The one we spoke to didn't send up any red flags, but they must have at least three or four employees who'd all have access."

"Along with other managers." Tibble sighed, gazing down at the legal pad he'd been jotting notes on. "Let's start there, so we're not all the way back to square one. Leo, Emma, go talk to Bency. See if a second interview scares anything up now that you can question him about the footage." He jerked his chin at the Boston agents. "Paul, Midori, you two go back to Jimmy Conrad's wife and see if she can confirm whether the shirt he wore in the other footage is still at their house. That could prove we have shots from two different nights of footage."

Leo nodded easily enough, but Emma glimpsed the tension in his jaw. When they moved back into the bullpen, she caught his elbow and leaned closer, walking in step with him as they moved back to the elevator. "I haven't seen her since last night. That means she's okay."

He exhaled and punched the elevator call button a little too hard. "I keep thinking about her lying in the hospital. She's asleep. I have to think about her that way. Being asleep means she'll wake up."

"She will." She squeezed his arm. "And we'll be there when she does. Jacinda's text said her condition 'remains stable,' and so does Vance's. And Mia will be out of the hospital by the time we get back."

18

Emma parked in the hotel's garage rather than annoying the Fallweather's valet like Paul had done. As such, she and Leo came up to the front desk from the opposite direction and surprised the concierge behind the computer. His red curls formed a somewhat disheveled halo, and the forced smile on his face put Emma back a step.

Something happened. Maybe Bency leaned on him, or maybe it was someone else. Only one way to find out.

"Front desk duty today?" Emma leaned on the counter. "You do a little bit of everything, huh?"

Elliot's smile faltered a touch. He glanced around the lobby. "They got me cross-trained on the front desk, but Fridays are a nightmare here. If you have more questions for me, they'll have to wait."

Leo stepped up beside Emma. "No, not at all. We were just hoping to talk to Mr. Bency again. Is he on duty?"

Elliot signaled for an approaching woman to give him just a second. "He was supposed to be, but Rodney Carlson is on duty instead. You want me to call him?"

"Please." Emma waited for Elliot to speak into a handheld

walkie-talkie. She and Leo backed up from the desk and waved at the next customer to take their place. As Emma did her best to observe Elliot's behavior, Leo leaned in and spoke under his breath. "Any, ah, sightings right now?"

Emma shook her head, not bothering to answer. The space in the lobby where the Romanian ghost had previously stood wailing was now empty but for a couple of teenagers staring at their phones. From where she stood, Emma had no reason to suspect either of being a ghost.

She was about to suggest they sit down to wait when a harried-looking man in a suit came rushing out of an elevator, his eyes immediately landing on them. Black and with short braids lining his head, he virtually flew over to them.

"Agents Last and Ambrose? I'm Rodney Carlson, manager on duty today. Call me Rodney." He stepped close enough that nobody else would hear, even from a few feet away. "Do you need to get back into Mr. Conrad's hotel room? We've left it as is."

Emma flashed her badge so that only he'd see it. Clearly, discretion mattered to the man, just as it had to Bency. They had no reason yet to tread on his good graces. "Actually, we were hoping to talk to the manager we spoke to yesterday, Dirk Bency, but perhaps you can help us."

Rodney's lips dipped into the fastest of frowns, but he nodded. "Well, I'm willing to try, at least. I'm not normally here, you understand, so Dirk knows this place a lot better than I do."

"You're not normally here?" Leo lowered his voice still further. "Mind us asking why you're here today, then?"

"I work for the parent company that owns the Fallweather. I'm typically at the Greenwalk, over by Logan. We have a larger management staff over there, so sometimes they shift one of us over here if a manager calls out sick.

That's what happened today." He shrugged. "Dirk called out sick. I got called in."

Out sick. Talk about convenient.

"In that case, could we just speak to whoever's in charge of security?"

Rodney nodded and turned to lead the way toward the elevators. "No problem. You may have already met him since I believe Steven said he's the normal afternoon-evening guard on duty during the week?"

"Steven Nassar?" Emma stepped into the elevator, snatching the name from her memory of the notes she'd reviewed on the drive over.

Leo nodded. "Yes, we met him yesterday."

On the ride up to the next floor, Rodney's walkie-talkie went off, and he lifted it to his ear to receive a flood of panicked Spanish. His eyes went a touch wider.

Emma tilted her head. "Problem?"

He waved her off. "Just normal hotel headaches. A guest smuggled in a Labrador who's in the process of destroying a hotel room, and the housekeeper is afraid of dogs."

Leo bobbed his head as the elevator door opened. "Not quite a dead body, but good luck."

"Indeed." Rodney held his arm across the elevator door for them to step out, then pointed up without getting out. "Do you two mind, since you know where you're going? Steven or Elliot can call me down if you need anything else."

Emma waved him off with a smile. "Go help your housekeeper."

"I wouldn't mind having a problem like that once in a while." Leo led the way down the hall toward the security office. "Talk about a change of pace."

"You'd charm the dog in a half second and be bored." Emma's joke was rewarded with a low laugh that eased the ache in her heart. It was good to see her partner in a lighter mood.

At the doorway to the security office, they found Steven leaning back in his chair and idly viewing the array of monitors with his feet up on the desk. The empty wrapper of a sub sandwich sat spread out on his lap, and he had a soda bottle in one hand.

Emma knocked lightly on the door. "Mr. Nassar? Sorry to bother you again."

He twisted his head around to see them, and she was reminded of how very tall he was. His surprised smile still didn't offer up any red flags for her, though. Physically, yes, he absolutely could've tossed someone off the upper roof. But it was hard to picture this lanky man with crumbs on his shirt doing so.

"Come on in. Agents Last and Ambrose, right?" He brushed off his shirt, crumpled his trash and tossed it, and turned to face them. "What can I do ya for?"

Emma took the same seat she'd occupied before, aiming to come across as casual. "We were just hoping to view additional footage from the day of Jimmy Conrad's murder. Could you pull up him coming through the lobby for us?"

Nassar raised an eyebrow, but to his credit, he didn't argue. Instead, he turned to his computer and typed in some commands, taking them back to the lobby on Wednesday. Sure enough, Conrad moved through the lobby just as they'd seen previously, waving to the concierge as he went. Wearing the same shirt as the one they'd found in the hotel suite, the paisley one.

"Could you leave that up on this monitor and bring up the footage of him going into his hotel room?" Leo leaned in, waiting as Nassar did as asked.

"There ya go. I thought we sent this with—"

"Just take a look." Emma pointed between the two monitors, both frozen on Jimmy Conrad. "What do *you* see?"

The man's eyes narrowed on her, but he turned to face the monitors. A second later, he let out a low "shit" beneath his breath. "What the hell?" He leaned closer to his computer, examining the data requests he'd put in, then sat back in his seat to stare.

"Different shirts." Emma pointed needlessly between the cameras. "The one he entered the lobby in is the one we found in his suite."

Nassar nodded, and Emma noticed his pale skin had gone even a shade whiter. "I remember Dirk saying there was no luggage in the room. No change of clothes." He looked back at the image of Conrad coming into the lobby. "Not that he had any on him, obviously. Shit. I don't know what happened."

"Can you tell us who'd be able to tamper with the footage?" Leo pointed to the computer. "Who'd be able to log in and also have the know-how to make changes?"

The security guard turned to face them, frowning. "I mean, we don't make a habit of tampering with the footage. That's not something—"

Emma held up a hand, stopping him. "Nobody's accusing you or saying this is normal. Just tell us who'd be able to do so."

"I...guess maybe the other security guards, but realistically, I don't even know how to do it." He turned back to the computer and took the cursor over to the data files on the left of the screen, running through them. He pulled up a shot of an elderly couple getting onto the elevator and began showing them drop-down menus. "See, I can freeze the footage, speed it up, put it in slow motion, whatever. And I can jump between cameras. I can also download it. But you're talking about…switching cameras? Or swapping out days or times, I guess?"

Nassar blew out a hard breath and moused up to the menus controlling playback. The available options matched the ones he'd listed off for them. He searched for other options.

Finally, he turned away from his workstation and shook his head. "I got nothing. No idea how this happened."

Emma believed him too. He looked positively flummoxed. "Okay, so if you don't know how to do it, what about other security guards? Or management?"

He shrugged. "The other security guards have the same access I do. They might know more, but I've worked here the longest. I'll get you their names. Tony's the only one who's been on duty since you two came in before, and he's only worked here a few weeks." Steven hesitated there, stopping, and Leo shut the door behind him, clearly wanting to make sure they had privacy.

"And what aren't you telling us about Tony?" Leo waved the security guard on. "We'll take his last name too."

"Oh, yeah, right. Uh, it's Kingsolver. But you're barking up the wrong tree. Tony's, uh…" Nassar glanced at the door, going a little pink in the face. "He got the job because his dad owns the restaurant downstairs. And I don't mean to talk shit about a coworker, but the kid's not gonna last here. I had to teach him how to sign into the system five times before he remembered how, for crying out loud. If you think he's got the chops to do something I can't do…"

The security guard shook his head with disdain, and Emma mentally filed their interview with Tony under "last priority."

"Okay," she pushed on, "so who else can access the system? Management?"

"Management's all got access." Nassar swiveled back to

the monitors and pulled a clipboard from beside of the computer. The top page had eight names on it, with phone numbers listed beside each one.

The first three, including Dirk Bency, were identified as managers with an *MGR* notation beside the name. Those were followed by five security guards, identified by a *SEC* notation.

Nassar's name appeared among those, but Emma didn't spot Rodney Carlson on the list.

"I assume the hotel's parent company would have information for stand-in personnel, like Rodney."

The security guard nodded. "I'm sure they do. Should I call them and ask for it?"

Emma was already pulling her phone out of her pocket. "My money's on Bency first. Any objections to me calling?" Leo gestured for her to go ahead as Nassar's eyes widened.

She reached for the paper and read off Bency's number, typing it into her phone with her thumb.

Leo pointed to the list. "Make us a copy of that?"

"We also need access to your security system itself," Emma added. "Since it appears the footage has been tampered with, we need to see who might have hacked into your system."

Nassar's eyes widened. "I-I'm not sure if I can do that. I'll need to speak to Mr. Bency."

Emma was already typing the warrant request into her phone. "Don't bother. We'll get a warrant." She wanted to zip this investigation up nice and tight.

"Okay. I can give you this, though." Nassar pulled the sheet off the clipboard and slid past Emma, opening the door and stepping out of the office a second later.

With the warrant request initiated, she pressed send on her call to Bency. It went straight to voicemail, and she hung up. "No answer."

Leo's mouth tightened. "Seems like all signs are pointing back to Bency, though we may have to consider other managers first."

Nassar peeked in, holding the paper up. "Uh, you two need privacy, or—"

"No, it's fine." Emma waved him in as Leo accepted the page he'd copied. "Could you get us Dirk Bency's address before we head out?"

The security guard's eyes went a touch wider, but he sat down to get the additional information. Leo spoke low as he did. "You want to head over to Bency's now, or…?"

Emma considered the question, gazing down at her phone and the printout. They had no shortage of leads now, but while they were at the Fallweather, there was one other thing she'd taken Bency's word on, and now doubted.

"He's the one who told us that other door to the roof doesn't get any use." She licked her lip, thinking back to all he'd told them that hadn't been verified. "While we're here…"

"I agree." Leo met Nassar's gaze as he stood to hand them the address. "You mind taking us up to the roof while we're here?"

"Uh…can I call Rodney?" The guard blushed, gesturing back at the monitors. "'Less it's an emergency, I'm not supposed to leave the monitors. How about I call him and have him meet you by the roof stairwell on the top floor?"

Emma nodded for him to go ahead. "That'd be great, thanks. We'll head up there."

She followed Leo out and texted Midori as she did.

Bency called out sick. You and Paul want to stop by his place?

Emma added his address to the text, then hit send.

In the elevator, Leo glanced over the printout they'd been given and shook his head. "This is a lot of potential suspects, but it sounds like Bency's the most reasonable one. I know we didn't read him as a killer—"

"But he certainly seemed like he was hiding something." The elevator dinged open just as Emma's phone buzzed with a reply.

We're over at the Conrad Manor still, so you guys are closer, but we can hit Bency's if you need us to. Not sure how long it'll be. We just convinced the missus to go through her husband's shirts, and she's getting the butler to do it, but apparently, he's got a whole walk-in closet of them.

Emma held back a groan, wishing she were more surprised at the idea of a politician having a whole closet of shirts. She held the message up so Leo could read it as they moved down the hall toward the stairs. "Shall I tell her we'll do it once we're done here?"

"Might as well." Leo reached the end of the hall and determined that the door was locked. Sighing, he leaned on the wall across from the stairwell door. "So how long, in your expert opinion, do you think it takes to calm down a housekeeper and evict a Labrador?"

Emma grinned. "Look at it this way. If Rodney brings up the Labrador with him, we'll just have the pooch break down that door for us. Sounds like he's capable of it."

19

On the rooftop, with flecks of cushion stuffing dotting his suit jacket, Rodney Carlson led them over to the locked door.

"Dog was a holy terror. I'll be hearing about that one for months." He swiped at his shoulder, knocking aside a small wad of stuffing.

"What do you know about this door?" Emma moved up to it and bent, eyeing the lock. Despite the rust along some of the door's edges, the lock looked serviceable enough.

"Nothing." Rodney shrugged, frowning at it. "I've only been up on this roof once."

"When was that?"

"Two years ago. The parent corporation hosted a party for new hires at all four of their Boston hotels. I don't even remember seeing this door, but they had the lounge area behind us screened off with all those ferns." He pointed to the edge of the roof where Jimmy Conrad had been killed.

The ferns stood sentinel around the same three lounge chairs. Emma could still pick out the dark patch of gravel where Conrad's blood had been spilled.

She was about to ask Rodney if he had a master key when

the air grew tight around her and filled with cold. Emma shivered as she looked at Leo, whose expression went slack on seeing hers. She mouthed, *Gimme a minute*, and he nodded.

"Hey, Rodney, you know Boston better than me." Leo gestured out at the skyline, eyes still on Emma. "Mind walking me over to the chair we think Jimmy was hanging out in? Maybe you'll see something in the city he should've been focused on. Anything that stands out to you."

Rodney walked away, Leo following. Emma's lungs went lighter with relief. Goose bumps rose on her skin with the deepening cold of the Other, but they didn't touch the rush of emotion warming her heart.

Leo believed her. One-hundred-and-ten percent, he believed her and just covered for her.

Don't bask in it now, Emma girl. Figure out what you're feeling first.

Emma focused on the door, crouching before the lock. The cold of the Other was as numbing as the worst D.C. winter mornings she'd experienced, but she forced herself to remain steady and still. The cold thickened as she rested a hand on the gravel. One way or another, they were going to have to get into this—

A hand slid through the door, an inch from her foot, and Emma yelped and fell back on her ass.

Hurriedly, she scurried backward as a ghost began crawling through the door, inch by inch. She came to her senses as the full arm came into view, and Leo's voice echoed out across the roof.

"You okay? Emma! You okay?"

"Yeah!" She breathed deep, fighting for calm, and looked toward the men to wave them off. "Just lost my balance! Must be shaky after all the caffeine I had today!"

Even from across the roof, Emma could see Rodney's

frown, but Leo had his attention back on the skyline an instant later.

She turned back to the ghost.

The girl's whole front half was through the door now, crawling slowly with her head to the ground. Emma couldn't see her face, but from the look of her hair and slim build, she appeared similar to the other ghosts Emma had glimpsed. And she was muttering foreign phrases like them too.

Wearing a camisole and panties, on all fours like she was, this ghost looked even more pitiful than the others. Emma bit back the cold, shivering, and tried to focus on the syllables she was hearing.

"New dee-no. Vuh-rue-gun-suh new dee-no." The girl repeated the words as she swayed, struggling forward and moaning in pain between the iterations.

Carefully, Emma brought her phone out and recited the sounds, recording her own voice and mimicking the ghost's language as best she could. The same accent as before tinged the words. She had no doubt they were Romanian.

The girl came to a stop a few feet from Emma, her head hanging before she began a slow crawl back to the door. The same words kept echoing from her lips, but Emma no longer had the heart to listen to them.

Especially now that she knew this was likely a girl who'd been pulled from some small Romanian town, treated like cargo, and shipped to the United States by sex traffickers. Even if Emma didn't know the exact meaning of the words, the pain in them was undeniable.

Cringing, Emma pushed herself to her feet and turned toward Leo and Rodney, allowing the cold of the Other to fade behind her. She didn't know who that girl was, but she would get justice for her. Somehow.

Across the roof, the two men pivoted to face her as she

approached. Rodney's smile was open. Leo offered a cautionary smile, and she simply nodded at him before addressing the manager. "I think we need to get that door unlocked."

20

With the sun beginning to set in the background, Rodney tried yet another key on the old rings he'd retrieved from the managerial offices downstairs. Much as Emma had been tempted to call a locksmith or try her own skills at it, this was likely faster.

Even as Rodney worked, another ghostly hand flowed through the door, this one gripping the doorframe and struggling outward. The ghost girl's hair hung in her face, and snot and drool painted her skin, slick even in the Other. She moaned, clutching her middle, and Emma wished she could cover the ghost's nudity, to give her a semblance of comfort even in death.

The girl fell forward. Emma watched her out of the corner of her eye. Leo and Rodney remained focused on the door, one key after another hitting useless obstacles. But that same phrase as earlier echoed up from this girl's voice, as well.

"New dee-no. Vuh-rue-gun-suh new dee-no."

With the cold of the Other seeping into her body as the ghost came closer, Emma pulled out her phone and began experimenting with her translator app.

Now that she had the language, her experiments with spelling moved along faster, and she hit pay dirt in only a minute. As she did, the cold dissipated, and the ghost faded back into the door.

Emma stared down at her phone, processing the words before calling Leo over. "Another ghost, on top of the earlier one. Both saying the same things." She held the phone up in front of him.

The Romanian spelling she'd hit on showed, *Nu din nou. Vă rugăm să nu din nou.*

And the English. *Not again. Please, don't again.*

Leo's jaw clenched, and he lifted one hand to run it through his hair without saying anything. Even in the dimming light, however, nerves vibrated off him with more urgency. "We need to—"

"Got it!" Rodney's cry all but echoed off the rooftop. "Got the key that fits."

Emma hurried over and accepted the key from him. She waved him aside as she reached for her weapon. "We don't know what we might find in here. Please go back to the lounge area, to a covered position."

He nodded, backing away step by step. "I'll get behind the bar." He took a huddled position, peeking out at Emma as she and Leo prepared to open the door.

Placing the key in the lock, and with Leo on the hinge side of the door with his gun at compressed ready, Emma drew her weapon. "Opening on three."

She turned the key, then nodded to indicate the count. On three, Emma gripped the handle and swung the door out, stepping back and to the side so that she and Leo each had a clear line of fire into the space.

Despite the rusted exterior, the door swung on oiled hinges until it reached its full arc, banging against the exterior wall with a metallic clang.

Emma pivoted around the doorjamb and peered into the space. The last rays of sunlight cast weakly into the stairwell. She fumbled for a light switch. Bare, fluorescent bulbs cast shadows down an unpainted cement staircase with a heavy-duty pipe railing.

Leo stepped up beside her and frowned. "You hear that?"

She leaned over the top rail, fighting back her mostly dormant skittishness of heights. Muffled sounds of pots and pans echoed upward. "The kitchen."

Emma led the way, hurrying downward, even as Rodney promised he'd wait for them above. Two flights turned into four, then ten, with the kitchen noises becoming louder all the time. Each door they passed had a crash bar on it and opened to a hallway of rooms. When they finally came to a steel door marked with the sounds of an active kitchen behind it, she holstered her weapon and pushed the crash bar.

The door squealed open, revealing white-coated cooks and aproned dishwashers trading armfuls of trays, pans, and mixing bowls. Knives clattered against cutting surfaces amid shouts to "fire three salmon!" and calls for more salad and bread.

Emma and Leo's brief intrusion went unnoticed, and they backed into the stairwell. She pulled the door fully closed and looked up the flights they'd descended. "Hard to imagine anyone using the kitchen as a route to bring sex workers into the hotel. It's such a busy place."

"Unless everyone in there is either part of the operation or knows better than to open their mouths about it. Hell, maybe the activity provides decent cover." He pointed up the shadowy stairwell. "Did you notice this, though?"

Following Leo's outstretched hand, Emma spotted an open doorway tucked behind the last flight of stairs they'd come down. She went to it and peered in, using her phone's flashlight to illuminate the space.

A flight of stairs continued downward. "What is this, basement access? A root cellar?"

"Could be, but does it look like people come in and out of here all the time? The floor shows signs of passage, but also a lot of dust. You wouldn't get that if cooks were constantly hauling boxes of potatoes back and forth."

Emma followed Leo downward, both of them with their weapons out again.

When they got to the bottom, two full flights of stairs lower than the kitchen floor, they were presented with two doors. A steel door with a small window stood beneath a flickering exit sign on the left. To their right, a solid metal door stood propped open by a cinder block.

Peering through the inset window on the door to the left, Leo scoffed. "Well, that's one question answered."

"What?" Emma squeezed in next to him.

"See for yourself." Leo moved aside, and Emma looked through the window. The door opened onto a sub-street staircase that rose some dozen or so stairs to take users up to street level. "I guess this might've been an exit or a back way to get garbage out, but I wouldn't call it convenient."

Emma stepped back, nodding. "I think we'll set off a fire alarm if we pop this thing open, but I don't see a point anyway."

When she pressed the other door open, she couldn't see anything beyond a few feet. She fumbled at the flat, cinder block wall to the side of the doorway, finally finding a light switch. A bare bulb overhead glowed with light, along with a string of bare bulbs that stretched into the distance.

Freezing, Emma just stood and stared, with Leo at her back doing the same. Ahead of them stretched a long, narrow hallway running underground. All cinder block and lit by bare bulbs, but for the dusty, puddle-strewn floor stretching into the distance. Even for a maintenance hallway, the place felt abandoned, with tube wiring running along the ceiling and corroded piping lashed haphazardly to the walls.

Finally, she found her voice to whisper, "Let's prop this door open and see where the hell it goes."

Leo shoved the cinder block into place, and Emma closed the door gently on it.

When she backed away, Leo examined the interior side of the door. "Looks like it's set to lock automatically. And I don't think we want to drag Rodney down all those stairs to change the mechanism over."

Emma gave the block a doubtful look. "This'll hold. Nobody's coming after us."

Nobody alive anyway.

"All right, then. Let's go." Leo set out at a fast jog, moving down the hallway with Emma on his heels. It was easy enough as travel went. Every step echoed, so there was no point in keeping quiet, and with no doors or windows outward, caution would've been pointless.

They stopped only once, when Emma caught sight of a word or a name scratched into the wall. "*Ajutor…*" She pulled up her translation app but had no signal. "We're too far underground, even deeper than the case with Mr. Leeches."

"Don't remind me. My knee still hurts from when he kicked me."

Emma snapped a photo of the word scrawled on the tunnel wall. "I'd bet anything this is Romanian."

Leo's lips tightened. "We'll look it up later." With that, he turned and kept going. Emma shoved her phone back into her pocket and followed.

Soon enough, she lost track of any estimate she might've attempted in terms of distance. When they finally saw an ending to the tunnel, Leo slowed to a careful walk, and he and Emma each kept one hand close to their guns. The steel door ahead of them had an inset window, but the sight was less than threatening.

Spread out on the other side of the door was an average city parking garage. Decently lit, with cars stretching in both directions. An empty loading space sat in front of the door, marked off with white lines. Leo twisted the door handle, and it popped open.

They stepped into the garage, and Emma glanced at the back side of the door. A crash bar allowed entrance to the tunnel, but the door was marked with *No Exit* and *Emergency Access Only* signs that she imagined would keep 'most anyone back.

Across the garage, over the roofs of polished sedans and SUVs, Emma spied the elevator. She and Leo made a beeline for it and thumbed the call button. With a grinding sound, the car arrived, and the doors opened. Emma slid inside.

"Let's check the location."

The interior signage read, *Eighth Street Parking Garage*. Grimacing, Leo typed the information into his phone. "We're at least three blocks from the Fallweather. I'm letting Rodney know he can stop waiting for us on the roof. We're coming back another way."

21

Emma nodded and punched the button for street level. "Good thinking. And let him know it might be a bit before we get back at all. We need to find out if anyone employed here knows about that door and the tunnel."

The elevator clunked to a halt, and the door groaned open to the first level of the parking garage. Emma led the way through a maze of cars to a small attendant's booth along the back wall. She flashed her badge, and the lone man in the booth straightened up in his chair. He wore a jacket and tie over a white button-down shirt.

"How can I help you?"

Emma made note of the man's name on his blazer, *Chris Jiang*. "Mr. Jiang, we just came through the door marked 'No Exit' on sub-floor three. You know the one?"

He blinked, mouth opening without replying.

"The door has a crash bar on the front and leads into a tunnel that connects to the basement of the Fallweather Hotel."

"Oh, yeah. I know the door you mean. Come on in. And

call me Chris, please." He backed up, allowing them entrance into the tiny office.

Emma and Leo crowded in front of the man's desk, and he stood across from them, not bothering to sit. He leaned his hands on the back of his chair, frowning at them. "Long as I've worked here, and that's four years, that door's been a mystery to me. Never understood why it was still operable since it's no good as a fire exit. People could get trapped in that tunnel, you know?"

Leo pointed to a row of security monitors spread along the back wall. "Any of your cameras show that door? Could we see what you've got from Wednesday night if so?"

The man shrugged but gestured for them to pull up seats. "We keep the monitor views on the corners where accidents are more likely to happen, and we don't really pay attention otherwise. Did something happen?"

"We're hoping you can help us answer that question."

He nodded fast. "Sure thing. Gimme a second." He fiddled with the different views, cycling through various numbers until the door they'd come through showed in a lower corner of the monitor, clear as could be.

A blank screen showed up on the monitor, but the screen appeared dirty. Emma's heart flinched at the sight of it, which reminded her all too well of the footage they'd seen at the port. "Is that—"

"Hold your horses. Looks like the obvious camera down there got painted over black." Chris scribbled on a notepad he'd pulled out of a drawer. "Just markin' it down so I don't forget to report it. You'd be amazed how often that fuckin' happens. Mostly just skateboarders who want to use the damn ramps to try to break their legs."

"I thought you don't pay attention unless there's an accident."

"Well, yeah. That's just it. If a skateboarder's coming down the ramp and a car's coming up, who do you think's gonna come out on top?" Chris clucked his tongue. "Accidents shut us down until they're cleared. That's lost revenue."

Leo shifted on his feet, betraying his impatience, but the guard kept writing before he went back to the camera feeds. And then, finally, they got a view of their door.

"There ya go. Ain't nobody gonna find this beauty, skateboarder or otherwise. This footage is from one of the hidden cameras we installed a few years ago when the mayor had that stick up his ass about neighborhood drug deals. Supervisor wanted us to add in all this high-priced gear to catch every little thing, but do ya think they gave us the budget? We got two of them installed, instead of the ten we were supposed to." The man grunted. "That's Masshole politics for ya. You say Wednesday?"

"Please." Emma glanced at the calendar. "The seventh, say around four o'clock on. We're looking for movement on that door."

"Whatever you say." Chris paged them back to the requested time, then began fast-forwarding. Various vehicles passed by, but the floor was mostly empty by seven. "See, quiet night really. I don't even think…" The security guard paused and stared at the screen, mouth open in surprise.

At seven thirty p.m., a large black van pulled up just before the door, and Emma waved at him to go back to normal speed.

The van put on its hazard lights. A man in a hat that shaded his face from view got out of the driver's seat and seemed to peer around the area, waiting.

"Checking to make sure the coast is clear." Leo leaned closer, waiting alongside Emma.

When a few more seconds had passed, he went to the back of the van and yanked open the cargo doors. He reached in and yanked a scantily clad woman out by the elbow.

Their man in the hat shoved the first woman toward the door. She carried stiletto heels under her arm but pressed the push bar in and moved into the tunnel, where she stood aside to hold it open. One by one, four more women exited the van, followed by another man.

"None of them look old enough to be doing what I'm pretty sure they're doing." Chris's breath sounded choked, and Emma looked up to see that the man's face had gone pale with shock.

"Sit down, Chris, please." She stood up, pushing him into her own chair despite the fact that her own knees felt weak.

A glance back to the frozen monitor didn't help. One of the teenage-looking girls stood huddled in the doorway. She appeared to be pleading with the second man who'd exited the van. He held up a hand at face level, clearly threatening to backhand her, and she hurried past him into the hallway, following the other girls into the dark.

The man in the hat drove the van off camera, presumably to park in a legitimate spot. He returned to follow them all into the hallway that led to the Fallweather.

Chris let out a little sob. "I got a niece their age."

Leo had written down the license plate and already had his phone to his ear to call it in.

Emma turned back to Chris. "If you want to help us, what I need you to do is copy all this footage. Can you do that for me? And then fast-forward into the night for us and see when that man comes back out for the van." She touched his shoulder lightly. "You don't have to watch what happens after that. Just mark down the time and copy out the next hour or so of footage for me. Okay?"

His jaw shifted, tense, and his eyes went a little narrow, but he nodded. "Yeah. I can do that. Right now."

"Good man. Thank you." Emma swallowed down her own emotion, which was agitated in part by the sorrow wrapping itself around the parking garage attendant.

But in another second, Chris moved back to the monitors, focusing on the computer controls rather than the screens. Emma put her business card down beside him. She tapped one finger over her email address, and he nodded.

That done, she hurried to Leo, who'd moved back into the garage to get some privacy for his call. He grimaced after a few seconds, shaking his head as he said, "Thank you," and ended the call. "Plate number's fake. No record of it with Massachusetts DMV."

Emma sighed. "No surprise there." She glanced back at Chris, thinking through their options. "Okay, so we need forensics on that door and tunnel. How about you call Tibble, and I'll check in with Midori and Paul? See if they've got anything."

Leo nodded. "And as soon as we get all that going, we hunt down Bency."

Emma punched in Tibble's number, lifting her phone to her ear. "He's somewhere, and he has to know something about this."

Tibble answered, and she began running through what they'd found over the course of the evening. Within seconds, she had him yelling instructions at agents on his end of the line to get forensics and uniforms over to both the hotel and the garage.

"We'd like permission to find Dirk Bency. If you're—"

"Reasons," Tibble barked. "I need clear reasons for why you think Bency's the best use of your time. Right now, I think we should be coordinating with Boston Vice squads and hauling in every pimp from here to Staten Island."

"We have evidence of what appears to be sex trafficking taking place at the Fallweather, using concealed means of access, well out of the public view." Emma paced up and down between the parked cars. "Our first victim was known to have had sexual partners in his suite at the hotel."

Tibble *mm-hmm*ed. "Cause and circumstances of death are similar enough to victim number two, and we have the political connection between Conrad and Wilhelm. Could this be related to the campaign? Or maybe these guys both pissed off the wrong mafioso. Unless you're suggesting Bency's mobbed up or involved in the trafficking."

"We're thinking he's involved in the trafficking, at least to the extent that he either profited from the murders or was instrumental in making them happen."

"You like him for the job of taking a knife to…for mutilating guys the way our victims got done?" Tibble sounded doubtful.

"That, or he knows who did."

After a brief pause, Tibble coughed. "That adds up to us at least needing to question the guy. Go find the bastard and bring him here. Please."

Emma was about to answer in the affirmative as the man hung up, but she simply offered a small smile to Leo. When it worked in their favor, she found she didn't mind the brusque nature of the Boston unit's SSA. She couldn't have thought of a better way to put the command herself.

22

With SSA Tibble's efforts directed at their discovery in the parking garage, Leo drove them out to Dirk Bency's address, having hopped into the driver's seat before Emma could protest.

Boston's traffic should've been clearer, even on a Friday, but an accident up ahead at a tunnel entrance slowed them down. Leo allowed a sedan to swerve into the narrow space between their rental and a truck that edged forward.

Emma sighed in the passenger seat, drumming her fingers on her leg.

"Listen, Emma…my brain's been on the translations all day. What you've told me about what you can, uh, see."

She shifted in her seat, watching him.

"It's hard to take in."

Understatement of the dang year.

She offered a smile that appeared forced. "Believe it or not, it was hard for *me* to take it in too."

Yeah, he could see that. But she'd had time to accept it by now. He just had to catch up with her.

"I'd just like it all to make sense." He flicked a glance in his rearview mirror, half expecting to see a dead person in the back seat. "So whatever you can tell me to help…I mean, do you see ghosts everywhere? Do they ask you to get messages to people—"

Emma half laughed, half snorted.

Leo's cheeks warmed, and he was suddenly glad for the dimness of the tunnel they'd entered. "Sorry."

"No, I get it." Emma waved a hand at him, staring at the passing lights. "The thing is, everything would be so much easier if ghosts did show up all the time and ask me something as simple as getting a message to someone."

"What do they ask you?"

"That's just it. They don't. Most of the time, they mumble about something that appears important to them, but I can't make heads or tails out of it. To be honest, the ones I've seen on this case have been the most communicative and the clearest of any I've seen."

"Even with the Romanian?"

"Well…yeah. Even with that, because we translated it, and now we have a good idea of what's been happening."

"The problem is, we're not any closer to finding our killer." Leo's answer had been immediate. Maybe harsher than he'd intended, from the way Emma's cheeks reddened. "I mean, they have helped you on cases, right?"

"You remember the circus case?"

He blinked. "Of course. That was our first case together, three months ago."

Emma nodded. "Remember how we found that little girl's underpants in the dumpster and followed that lead?"

"Couldn't forget if I tried." The way rage had boiled up in him when they'd made that discovery…he was lucky he hadn't done something a lot worse than hauling their suspect out of his camper and yelling at him. "But he wasn't our killer. It wasn't a dead end, but—"

"But it wasn't nothing." Emma toyed with a loose thread trailing from her jacket hem. "That's kind of how this stuff goes. I get a ghost pointing a finger or saying something to me about something they've seen. It's like it's translated, though."

Leo glanced over to see that Emma's face was creased in thought. "Translated...do all ghosts speak to you in foreign languages?"

"No. But I don't think we're really meant to communicate with them. Whatever they say, any meaning comes at me sideways, or not at all."

Leo finally turned out of the tunnel, waiting for the GPS to kick back in. He'd memorized the next few turns toward Dirk Bency's home but didn't want to pull over to check the directions. "So they're not usually as helpful as these girls have been."

Emma hunched her shoulders. "Sometimes. But a lot of times no. And sometimes it just hurts."

Leo glanced at her again, slowing the car a touch. Her voice had gone soft again. "Like when?"

"Well, the night I told Mia...it was because of her brother showing up in Little Clementine, as we were wrapping the case. Seeing Ned wasn't easy, and at first, I didn't even know it was him."

"I can't imagine Mia took that well when you told her."

"Imagine her at her maddest and add a few levels." Emma leaned back into the headrest. "She accepted it, though, because Ned told me something I couldn't have known otherwise."

Just like Denae did. Maybe the dead want Emma's friends to trust her, and that's why they tell her these things.

"Do you think he knew? Ned, I mean. Did he know Mia would believe you, and that's why he said what he did?"

She turned to stare out the window, silent for a long

moment. "I don't know, and the answer would be the same if you'd asked about what Denae said to me, but she was the first to be explicit about who I should talk to. Ned just mentioned something from his and Mia's childhood, and I had no idea what it meant until I blurted it out to her."

"And that's when she accepted that you were telling the truth?"

Emma nodded, still with her head turned away. "She was about to put up a wall between us, shoving me away from anything but professional contact."

Leo swallowed down a ball of emotion in his throat, unable to avoid going back to the image he'd had in his head ever since Emma had told him about Denae's ghost speaking to him. Her, standing over him while he still tried to stop the never-ending flow of blood from her bullet wound, watching him trying to save her and being able to do nothing about it. "That sounds like a lot."

The words were completely inadequate, but he had no others.

"Ghosts show up when they want to, and they say what they want to." Emma exhaled, fogging up the side window. "Honestly, we're getting lucky on this case that they're saying exactly what we need to hear."

"Just in a foreign language."

They shared a quick laugh at that.

Leo glanced at the GPS, finally back on track with its all-powerful satellites, and noticed they were nearing their destination.

He slowed for the upcoming turn, which would bring them onto Bency's street.

Unlike the Conrads' neighborhood, the suburb of Boston they'd entered at least felt more down-to-earth. Wealthy, without doubt, but not unreasonably so. Out of the price range of a federal agent, yeah, but not the average suit.

Emma pointed ahead to a looming shape on the left. "Bency's address is an apartment number. Maybe up there?"

Sure enough, the complex matched their address, and Leo pulled into a large, circular drive that ran through a maze of three-story buildings. Neat, coal-gray trim accented white siding and black roofs, and the sidewalks and roads were so well-lit, Leo had no trouble navigating to the fourth building down.

He parked next to a Corvette, ignoring the *Residents Only* sign placed prominently on the nearby lawn.

Emma shouldered her bag and headed toward a glass-doored lobby entrance. Inside, a narrow staircase rose from beside a bank of mailboxes. She pointed to the numbers at the bottom of the stairwell. "Looks like he's on the second floor."

Following behind her, Leo gave a little more attention to the premises.

When they got upstairs to an actual hall of apartments, most of the doors sported welcome mats. The hallway was wide enough for the residents to make each threshold their own without cluttering up the space. A few had tasteful little decorations nearby—potted plants and such—which suggested crime wasn't something these folks worried about. In a city, living in an apartment complex like this wouldn't be cheap. "Is our Bency married?"

Emma shook her head as she moved out of the stairwell. "Not on record. Maybe he's got a roommate. We're looking for two C…there." She raised her fist and waited to knock until Leo gave her a nod. "Mr. Bency, this is Agent—"

The door moved under her fist, inching inward.

"Reasonable suspicion," Leo exhaled. "In we go." He drew his weapon alongside Emma and held his gun muzzle-down, pointed to the carpet. Emma placed her palm flat on the door.

"This is the FBI. Does anyone inside require assistance? We're coming in."

Nodding to Leo, she pushed it open all the way.

Inside, papers were strewn across the floor ahead of them. An open kitchen sat to their left. Most of the drawers and cabinets hung open, with an assortment of junk and protein-powder containers littering the counter. On the right, couch cushions had been ripped open, and an expensive flat-screen TV lay cracked on the floor.

Leo advanced toward the television, eyeing a hallway that extended off the living room area. "Mr. Bency. This is the FBI. Are you here?"

Behind him, Emma made a noise. He turned to see her using her weapon to push aside a sheaf of papers on the floor beside the overturned dining table.

He stepped up beside her and saw the knife immediately, with a thick band of blood dried along its edge. "I'd bet even money that's from one of our victims."

Emma nodded toward the hall splitting off from the open living area. The first door they came to led to a small bathroom, and the second to what would've been a second bedroom. Dirk Bency had kitted out the space into a snazzy home gym. "Equipment looks pretty top-of-the-line." She moved across the room to open the one extra door and froze.

Leo settled his hand on her shoulder. "Emma, you okay? Is there a…ghost here?"

She drew in a deep breath, and he felt her relax as she shook her head. "No. Not the kind I've been seeing anyway. Just memories." She pointed at an exercise mat rolled up and tucked inside the closet. "Same color as the one Oren always used at his studio."

She closed the door and led the way to the open bedroom door at the end of the hall. The en suite bathroom had also been tossed. A walk-in closet door hung open, with most of the hangers empty. Drawers had been pulled open and ransacked. "Someone packed in a hurry."

"Hurried enough to leave their knife." Leo moved across the room, stepping over discarded laundry, and nudged open the bathroom door. "Medicine cabinet's been emptied. No toothbrush in the holder. Our guy's gone."

"Hello? Hello!"

Leo backed out of the room and went back down the hall, following the voice to the front door. A gray-haired man with a poodle on a leash stood in the doorway, frowning around the room at the mess. He jolted a touch at the sight of Leo's gun, but relaxed when Leo lowered the weapon and flashed his badge.

As he approached, the old man gestured at the television. "A burglar do this? What the hell's happening to this city?"

Leo moved close enough that the man—and his dog—couldn't actually come any farther inside. "We're not sure what happened right now, sir. Do you know the man who lives here?"

The man frowned at Leo's badge, staring. "Not well, no. He in some kinda trouble? I saw him rush outta here wicked fast this afternoon. Lugging two big suitcases. Maybe something happened here and scared him off? Should I be worried? I live right across the hall."

"There's no apparent reason for you to be concerned." Carefully, Leo stepped sideways and blocked the man's view as he craned his neck to look into the apartment.

"You sure?"

Holstering his weapon, Leo took out his phone and opened the Notes app. "Can I get your name, sir?"

"Me? I guess you need it since I'm a witness?"

"Just standard procedure, sir."

With a shake of his head, the man complied. "City's going

downhill. My name's Morris Canter, and you can quote me on that. About the city, and my name too."

Leo tapped the man's name into his notes as Emma came up beside him. "You mentioned you didn't know the occupant of this unit well?"

Morris crouched to pet his poodle, then stood. He looked back and forth between them and confirmed his earlier statement. "Never exchanged more than two words with the guy. 'Hello' and 'goodbye.'"

"When was 'goodbye' exchanged? Was that this afternoon, when he rushed out of here with his suitcases?"

Morris nodded.

Leo noted that as well. "What time was that?"

"I'd just come back from walking Pudge here and getting my milk from the grocery down the street. Around three o'clock."

"And did you speak with this unit's occupant?"

"Nah, I didn't waste any breath trying to talk to him today. I doubt he'd have heard me anyway. He had those ear things...what do you call 'em? Ear buddies?"

"Earbuds?"

Morris laughed. "Yeah, them things. Had 'em in and was talking, like he was on the phone with someone. Didn't see a phone in his hand, but these days, that doesn't mean anything."

Taking down the information, Leo thanked Morris and asked him to leave the scene so they could continue their investigation undisturbed.

"Come on, Pudge." Morris pulled on his poodle's leash, backing into the hall. Leo shut the door.

"I called the scene in. Midori and Paul are going to head over here, and Tibble's sending forensics now." Emma swept her gaze over the apartment, sighing. "He has several hours on us and no car listed with the DMV."

"Not unusual in Boston." Leo moved back to the knife and gave it a closer look. The blood had turned mostly black, with cracks forming along the edge of the blade. "Judging by the coloration, I'd say this blood is at least eight hours old. I don't think it ended up on the knife today."

"So maybe Wilhelm and his unlucky chauffeur were his last victims?" Emma moved over to the window and glanced out. "Uniforms are pulling up now. What say we leave them on guard duty and go back over to the hotel? See about getting a peek into Dirk's office? If he's got an office computer, it might link us up to whatever travel plans he's got."

Leo nodded, even though it was hard to imagine them getting that lucky. "Let's clear it with Tibble and move fast. Maybe we'll catch up to this guy yet."

Before he kills anyone else.

23

Emma flagged down Rodney Carlson as soon as they entered the hotel. He hurried around the check-in desk to meet them in the lobby. "I didn't expect you back so soon. Everything okay?"

"Can we speak over here?" Leo gestured him to a set of chairs off to the side, away from a nearby group of patrons. "Has Dirk Bency been in touch with you at any point today?"

Rodney's eyes went wide. "Haven't heard a peep from the man. They sent me over from the Greenwalk to cover for him, like I said. He in trouble?"

"We're hoping to get into his office. Would that be possible?"

He gestured toward the elevators. "If it'll help you out, it's no problem. You're welcome to find whatever you can."

Back on the second floor, Rodney opened the door to a small, neutral-toned office without a shred of decor. The only touch of personality was a huge map of Boston that hung on the wall behind Bency's desk, which took up the majority of the room and faced the door. File folders sat atop the desk, and Rodney gestured to them. "I just put these here earlier. Finished background checks on a couple of potential employees he interviewed earlier this week."

"We'll look around, thanks." Leo moved over to the file cabinet against the left wall. "You'll be downstairs?"

Rodney ran a hand over his braids. "I'll probably be there all night. If you need me, just pick up the phone and dial pound-zero. That'll connect you to the front desk."

He disappeared a second later, and Emma settled herself behind the desk. After slipping on a pair of gloves, she opened the pencil drawer, looking for where Bency might have kept his passcodes written down. Instead, she found a tabloid paper with a picture of Jimmy Conrad on the front page and a notebook held to the tabloid with a binder clip.

She separated the two and flipped open the notebook.

"Leo? I think we have something."

He closed the file drawer he'd been sifting through and came around the desk.

Emma drew a finger down the first page in the notebook, which had the initials *JC* at the top. The page showed a list of dates alongside notes that included a set of numbers and what looked to be women's measurements and other physical attributes. "Am I seeing what I think I'm seeing? Redhead, blond…"

Taking the notebook, Leo flipped the page and found a different set of initials at the top. "*WF*. No idea who that might be, but it seems clear Bency's been tracking more than just Jimmy Conrad's escapades in the hotel." He ran his finger down the column of numbers. "I'd bet these are room numbers, since the one for April seventh shows the suite he was in, ten twenty-three."

Emma scanned the list. "Do you think Bency was keeping track of this for blackmail or because he's the one bringing the girls in?"

"Since the notebook was clipped to that paper, I'd say

blackmail is the most likely answer." Leo picked up the tabloid and showed Emma the headline, which read, "Mayoral Candidate's Husband a Cheating Philanderer!"

He flipped to the article and scoffed. "If that's a picture of two people having sex, it could be anyone. It's so blurry, I'm not even sure those are people."

Emma waved her hand over an article on the next page. "They could be space aliens, if this is to be believed. Even if Bency was building a blackmail scheme, he couldn't possibly be thinking this is a reliable source. He might have a bunch of numbers and hair colors jotted down, but that doesn't prove anything."

"Maybe Bency's behind the girls coming in, and the tabloid article spooked him."

"Perhaps he killed Conrad for putting his operation in jeopardy?" Emma scrunched her face. "He'd be an idiot if he thought a murder like that wouldn't be worse for his operation. Now I'm less convinced he's the killer, though it looks more and more likely that he's involved in some way."

Leo closed the tabloid on the desk and picked up the notebook. "This is our best bet." He thumbed through at least five pages. "Only, we'll need a warrant to access guest records here, to check names against these initials."

"Rodney said Bency was on the up-and-up as far as he knew. And the only one who hinted at a sex scandal involving Jimmy Conrad is our concierge."

"You saw his house." Leo jerked his chin at the tabloid. "Conrad or his wife, the actual mayoral candidate, could afford to bury whatever dirty laundry they might have."

Emma's phone buzzed, and Tibble's name showed on the screen.

"Emma here, Walter. Leo's right beside me." She put the phone on speaker.

"Just calling to let you know we got a rush job on that

knife at Bency's apartment. DNA from the blood came back positive for Mark Wilhelm, so it's time to kick this search into high gear."

She met Leo's gaze. "That's great to hear. Leo and I found something in Bency's office at the Fallweather too. It looks like a logbook of Conrad and other people using the hotel's top floor as a brothel."

"Excellent work. I'm having a warrant sent over to the hotel as we speak, and we have a BOLO out for our guy now."

"You want us back at the office after this?"

"No. Get done there, and then get some sleep. Meet Paul at the hotel bright and early tomorrow, assuming nothing on the case breaks tonight. I'll let you know if it does."

Tibble hung up on that note. Emma twisted to stare up at the map of Boston on the wall.

It almost seemed to taunt her. Somewhere in one of those little grid spaces, Bency was hiding from them. The fact that they knew it but had no idea where to start looking was maddening.

24

Dirk Bency sat freezing at the side of the dock, staring off over the horizon from a bench that smelled like spoiled shrimp. Beside him, his two suitcases sat accusing him. Cursing him.

Horror at what he had done coiled in his stomach alongside the spaghetti he choked down before fleeing his apartment.

He had called Rosco, begging to get on the next ship going back.

The man laughed. Laughed and told him he had "been in America too long," and it had made him "think life is like a Hollywood movie."

"I am totally screwed." Dirk glanced over his shoulder, half expecting those FBI agents to be trotting up to arrest him. The port lay quiet. Middle of the night on a Friday was not exactly peak shipping time. "They will find out what I did, and I will spend the rest of my life in a shitty American prison."

He closed his eyes, picturing himself in an orange jumpsuit. Then he saw himself working out on a rusted bench in a prison yard and wanted to vomit. Compared to his equipment at home, where he could never go again, it was a nightmare.

"And all for money. Shit. Grandad is rolling in his grave."

Dirk should have known better than to make such a stupid deal with Jimmy Conrad. He kept track of the guys who used the top floor. He messed with the security footage, to make sure their "dates" could come and go without being recorded. He was gonna force Jimmy's hand, get him to pay for his own safety somewhere.

Hell, a ticket back to the old country, to visit Grandad's grave like I always promised my parents...

The whole thing spiraled out of control. Jimmy was dead, and Mark Wilhelm, too, plus his driver. Dirk heard about it from the guys at the port.

Whoever was out there cutting off dicks, they did not care about the people standing on the sidelines.

Except that is not you. You are up to your balls in this.

The money just made it so easy…

Jimmy's grinning face flashed in his memory. Offering him an envelope full of cash like he had stumbled into some fucking gangster movie. Hell, the first time it happened, he expected Scorsese to come around the corner and yell, "Cut!"

What a joke.

Before that, Dirk had been flat-out disgusted by Jimmy Conrad and the whole arrangement.

But the money he dropped on you…when was the last time you saw anything like that, and for doing what? Sitting on your hands and turning a blind eye.

The horizon still showed the same ship approaching the port at a snail's pace. He hoped he would not freeze to death by the time it came in.

He would pay the captain whatever he asked if it meant

leaving Boston. All of Jimmy's money could go right back into the hands of the people it came from for all he cared.

Just as long as it meant he got to keep his prick and keep breathing.

He was lucky he had even made it to the port. Nobody could get on an airplane in America without ID.

Even rideshares required him to show his name and his face.

He had to take the frickin' bus to get to where he was.

At least a hat and a medical mask were not out of the ordinary. Dirk could keep himself disguised.

He just had to figure out a way to get the captain to let him on board. He had never been involved in this part of the operation and only knew about it because of the guys at the port. Once in a while, that cop, Fontaine, would check in and sample the wares that came in on these ships.

Dirk figured him being a cop would mean that Fontaine was working undercover, but the guy was ready to talk about anything and everything related to the operation and said it was "the best thing that's happened" since he put on the badge.

Jimmy and his pals were paying the cops too. They were paying everybody in this city.

He shrugged himself deeper into his coat and glanced backward, but the port still seemed empty. If anyone was coming up behind him, he would hear them. The area behind the bench was all gravel, then a road and stacks of shipping containers.

Endless shipping containers surrounded him at the back, and endless ocean confronted him from the front. Everything was endless, his pain and guilt included.

The ship was pulling into the port. Its lights casting shadows along the dock as it drew in, slow and massive, like some giant spear puncturing the city.

Looking at the enormous vessel, Dirk realized just how much of a fool he had been.

Like the captain is going to let me get on board, even with one of these suitcases being half full of cash. He will probably have his guys stuff me into a shipping container that "falls" off the ship in the middle of the ocean.

I am sunk. Locked in a cell or dead, no matter where I go.

A sound from behind him drew his attention. He twisted at the crunch of footsteps in the gravel and squinted into the dark. A figure emerged from the shadows, a knife gleaming in the starlight at his side. Dirk's pulse skittered.

"I am guessing money will not stop you, huh?"

The figure stayed half-hidden in the dark as he spoke. "No. Your crime is too great, and the only price you can pay is in blood."

Dirk's heart climbed into his throat.

25

Dirk Bency looked no more respectable than the last time I had seen him, racing from his apartment and talking to someone named Rosco. I did not know who that was, but I could guess.

Rosco is the man who brings the girls over from Romania. He will be receiving a special kind of treatment once I take care of the people paying him to do his filthy work.

But first, I had to deal with the coward in front of me.

After I told him he was about to die, he only stared forward, over the water.

"You do not want to run?"

"What good will that do?" His voice reminded me of a man in my town, one who had been caught stealing from his neighbors. He had been sent away, exiled to live wherever he could find people to take him in.

Should I do that for Bency? Allow him to live, after everything he's done? No, he has earned no such mercy from me.

I lifted my knife but paused when he spoke once more.

"I know I have earned this, but I swear I never touched the girls. I am not like Jimmy and the others."

"Yet you allowed them to touch the girls, to use them. And you took money from them to keep your mouth shut. Do you expect mercy?"

"I do not expect anything. I just want it to be over." He hugged his arms around himself.

"You did earn this, Dirk Bency, and you know it." I stepped closer and rested my hand on his shoulder. "For that, you will die intact."

Even as he opened his mouth to likely beg me to reconsider, I brought my knife down and stabbed into his chest. He grabbed weakly for my arm, as if the urge to fight had somehow found its way into his heart alongside my blade.

A little gurgle escaped his throat on the end of a groan, blood bubbling up out of his chest as well as out of his mouth.

I pulled the knife free, wiping it on his overpriced coat before tucking it back into its sheath on my belt.

I stepped around the bench and crouched to stare into his dying eyes. He gurgled and choked on his own blood. "I did not come here, all the way from Romania, to show mercy to rich, corrupt Americans. I came to do the justice their law enforcement never will."

The pathetic man lifted a hand toward my face, like he was reaching for a lifeline. "I am Rom…Romanian. I am…like your brother—"

I clamped a hand over his mouth as blood welled up over his lips. "If you are like my brother," I pressed my weight against my hand, forcing his head back so he looked into my eyes, "then why did you help the men who steal and sell and kill *our* sisters?"

He spasmed beneath me but did not answer.

The light faded from his eyes, and he went still. I had only intended on killing the four men who built this operation and profited from it, the ones Daniela had told me about in her letter. Wilhelm's driver and now this waste of humanity, a fellow countryman no less, made two ancillary kills.

But that number could have been a dozen, and I would not have cared. I knew the men collecting and transporting my country's daughters were also Romanian. I would kill all of them, and any others, no matter their origin.

I had no problem killing anyone who enabled the cruelty being done against innocent girls like Cristina.

Quickly, I opened his suitcases, grabbing the first piece of clothing I could find, a black silk shirt. Taking that, and a heavier shirt beneath it, I wrapped Bency's body so I could carry him without making a disaster of my own clothing.

I picked him up over my shoulder and stalked back the way I had come. I passed between the shipping containers, watchful and listening for any sound of the cops who patrolled the port area at night.

They had last been on the other side of the harbormaster's building, and I knew the arriving ship would occupy their attention for a little while.

Ahead of me, a dumpster stood at the end of an aisle between stacked containers. I had passed it on my way in and knew it would make a perfect resting place for Dirk Bency's body.

He could lie and rot while the FBI searched for him.

Two men on my list were down, but two remained, still breathing, still profiting from the horrors being carried out this very minute.

That ship coming into port no doubt had more young women and girls in the hold, and I could do nothing to stop their transfer to the pimps and gangsters who would sell them off like trinkets on a shelf.

To stop the operation entirely, I needed to cut off the head from where that money flowed. Conrad and Wilhelm were a good start. Wheeler and Field would have to die soon, and then, I could concentrate on disrupting the shipping itself.

With the money stopped, no more ships would come in, not until the criminals running the operation could find new funding. That would make them vulnerable. When I showed up with a promise of more cash than they could dream of, they would welcome me with open arms.

Money has corrupted their moral sense, so I will use it to blind them to threats.

They will never see me coming.

I would need to get information from Wheeler, or perhaps Field, maybe both, and that meant I would need time to plan my attacks on both men.

The more distraction I could create with Dirk Bency, the better. His apartment had likely been searched by now. The knife recovered and a DNA test performed.

America's agents would be hunting for him, so I would make him that much harder to find.

At the dumpster, I threw the body in first, then climbed in and covered him with garbage.

Another quick trip back to the bench, and I had his suitcases buried along with him, except for the pile of money he had stuffed into one.

That went into my pockets and a plastic bag pulled from the trash. The money would serve me well when I went to seduce the traffickers responsible for Cristina's fate.

Daniela had not told me who they were, probably because she never heard their names. But she told me where she and Cristina had been taken, and the name of the ship they had traveled on.

She was always the observant one, always looking out for danger and making sure she and Cristina were safe in the village. But they were both very young, and the promise of employment, with money and a place to live in the city, was too much for either to resist.

My sister would not see the suffering I intended for the men who caused her torment and death. But Daniela would.

I checked over Bency's resting place, ensuring he and his belongings were not visible. With any luck, the trash collector would fail to see either the body or the suitcases.

Cristina would be avenged. Daniela and her friends would be on their way back to Romania, the Fates willing. And I would be able to rest.

When my phone rang, I was already out of the port, moving back toward a bus stop closer to downtown.

"Did you do it?" Daniela's voice wavered on the line, softer even than usual. "I hated him so much."

"I did. Thanks to you." I itched to say more—to tell her I would come to get her out of her nightmare tonight—but there were still other things to do. And I could not keep her safe while also avenging my sister. "I would not have known he would make a good distraction for those agents if you had not said anything."

"Yeah." She muttered something on her end, and I cringed. Likely, she was moving locations to avoid being overheard speaking on a phone. Being *caught*. "Guess we were both lucky Jimmy couldn't keep his mouth shut. I'm just glad Bency's gone. I couldn't stand him. Always so prim and proper while he was collecting money hand over fist."

I turned down a side street. "I still have some work to do. Soon, everything will be finished. You will be safe, Daniela, I promise."

"I gotta go."

She hung up without giving me time to say anything else, and I stuffed the phone back into my pocket. Making sure my coat covered my knife, I picked up the pace. The mission would be over soon enough.

26

Emma waved down Paul as soon as he entered the Fallweather. Stubble on his face suggested he and Midori had been held up at Dirk Bency's apartment a lot later than desired, but she couldn't find much sympathy. She and Leo had searched every corner of the man's computer and files at the hotel the night before and had still come up with nothing.

Making yet another pass at reviewing the hotel lobby footage from the night of Jimmy Conrad's murder was a shot in the dark. They knew multiple girls had been brought in through that parking garage, courtesy of the hidden camera system Boston Transit had in place.

So who else was "buying" that night, and why didn't any of the women show up on the hotel cameras?

They were hoping Paul would recognize some other guests from the lobby footage, to give them an idea of who the other johns might be. Jimmy Conrad was so high-profile, it seemed likely that the other clients would've been high-profile too. Paul had previously worked for Boston PD and provided security at donor events where Conrad's crowd was in attendance.

If he spotted familiar faces, they'd have a lead on the trafficking operation as well as a potential next target, or accomplice, depending on how the cookie crumbled.

"Another day, another dollar." Paul met up with her and kept right on walking toward the hotel elevator. "You look raring to go."

Emma forced a smile. "Just anxious to get somewhere on this case."

"Fair." Paul loosened his tie and glanced at his watch while they waited for the elevator. "'Least we might find something here. I know Leo and Midori are hell-bent on pounding doors to track this guy down, but gimme surveillance footage over the sidewalk beat any day."

"Long as the footage gives us something. Two camera systems surrounding this case have been tampered with, that we know of."

Emma stepped into the elevator and pressed two, just as anxious as Paul to get things going. When they reached the security office, they found a new guard on duty, but he vacated his chair and disappeared with barely more than a wave.

Emma gestured for Paul to take the seat. "We're here because of your eyes, so you go ahead."

He dropped into the seat and fiddled with the computer settings, taking them back to the night Conrad had been murdered. "I admit, having a chance to see some Boston elite get their comeuppance wouldn't bother me much, bad as that may be to say. Not that any guy deserves getting his—" The agent cut himself off with a quick glance at Emma, apparently remembering he wasn't with one of his longtime drinking buddies, and shrugged in apology. "Sorry. Point is, the powerful run this city. I don't love it."

Emma nodded at the monitor as the footage came up. "No apologies necessary. Let's just see what you see."

They scrolled through the hours of five to seven that night without Paul keying in on any familiar faces, but in the fifteen minutes or so before Jimmy Conrad was due to walk onto their footage, Paul froze the screen. "There, see this guy? That's Bert Wheeler. Lifelong Bostonian just like me, and someone who graces the high-society get-togethers with his good friend Jimmy. Or rather, he did."

Emma jotted down his name. Wheeler looked like a sloppy version of Conrad. Gray-haired and heavyset, maybe in his early sixties, but not wearing the decades well. As Paul kept scrolling, she called down to the front desk to see whether Wheeler had a room the night of Conrad's murder, but there was no record of him.

Her next call was to Tibble.

"Paul recognized a man named Bert Wheeler. Sounds like he's a buddy of Conrad's. You want us to head to his home and check him out once we finish here?"

Tibble said something to someone else on his end of the line. "Yeah, I'll get someone to send over his address. I've seen the guy around, but I couldn't tell you what he does for a living. Money sort. No surprise he was friends with Conrad. High-up circles and all."

"Any luck tracking Bency down yet?"

"Not yet. Midori and Leo are banging on doors while I try to track down his family. No cell phone was found at the apartment, but he must have turned it off. Any luck, he'll turn it on, and we'll be on him."

"Fingers crossed."

Emma hung up after confirming receipt of Wheeler's address. She recognized the street name as one near the Conrads' mansion, which meant they were in for another view of wealth and privilege once they got out of the cramped security office.

Meanwhile, Paul kept scrolling to no effect and finally tapped on the time stamp when he hit the nine thirty mark. "Seems like anyone coming in to get his jollies off would be here by now. You ready to call it and get over to this schmuck Wheeler's house?"

Emma stood, stretched, and fought down a yawn. "Thought you'd never ask."

Plus, the sooner they got out of the Fallweather, the less she had to worry about seeing more ghosts of girls who had yet to escape the scene of their torment.

27

Bert Wheeler's mansion didn't disappoint. Emma pulled up the stone-paved driveway and parked beside a neon-green pickup truck that couldn't have been more out of place if it had been tied to a sleigh of reindeer. She pointed to it as Paul got out of the car across from her. "What the hell is that monstrosity?"

"The Wheelers have a couple of twin frat boys who like their toys. They make the society pages too." He passed by her and headed to the front porch, which was literally lined with white Romanesque columns. "Think they get their jollies off like their dad or stick with coeds?"

Emma cringed, wishing not for the first time that she and Leo had stuck together. The Boston agent might be good at what he did, but she wasn't sure how Midori put up with him. "Let's just see what they say about that night in the hotel first, okay?"

Paul rapped on the door, then rang the bell when nobody answered immediately. He leaned closer to Emma. "Somebody's here. Place like this, there's a servant or two on duty at all times. Wheelers are old money. Grandfather was a railway tycoon, and between investments and ties to local politics, they're set for infinity."

"Ties to politics as in ties to Wilhelm or to Conrad's wife?" Emma forced a smile for the benefit of a suited man who peered through the bay window.

"Wilhelm. Big funder for his last few campaigns. They make headlines with their yacht parties and—"

The door opened before them, quiet as a feather, and the man Emma had glimpsed through the window stood staring them down. She flashed her badge just as Paul did.

The butler—a gray-mustached man—narrowed his eyes at their badges. "Mr. Wheeler is indisposed at the moment. I can leave him your cards—"

"We're investigating a murder, buddy." Paul began to step forward, crowding the butler in the door, but the man blanched and held up a hand. The agent stopped just short of planting the hand on his chest.

"I understand your business is urgent." The butler grimaced. "Please don't say anything more. I'll go and retrieve Mr. Wheeler. He's out back playing tennis."

In another second, the butler had stepped back and all but slammed the door in their faces. Emma felt her smile going a touch more thin-lipped. "Not good enough to be shown inside, are we?"

Paul raised his arms, gesturing to the breadth of the mansion. "You see this place? What, I'd guess ten bedrooms and ten bathrooms, plus a theater and a frickin' moon room for stargazing or seducing lovelies? Their damn toilets are probably gold-plated."

Emma found she didn't particularly mind waiting out front. She'd had about enough luxury for a while, thanks to the Conrads' piano room with those perfect little silver trays of coffee.

The door opened up again sooner than she'd expected,

and Wheeler stood before them in a tight white polo shirt and tennis shorts that would've been considered short in Tom Selleck's heyday.

"You asking for me?" He shifted his beady eyes between them, red-faced, and Emma and Paul both flashed their badges once again.

"We're here because of your friend Jimmy Conrad's recent murder, and more recently, the murder of Mark Wilhelm." Emma pocketed her badge, noting that Wheeler also wasn't inviting them inside. "Anything you can tell us? They have enemies you know of?"

"I can tell you they're dead." Wheeler fidgeted, one of his hands twitching at his side as if seeking out a nonexistent pocket to hide in. Finally, he settled for leaning against the doorframe. "As for enemies, men of means always have enemies. Comes with the money. I hope you catch the bastard who killed them, but that's all I got for ya."

"And what about the night of Jimmy's death, Bert?" Paul lowered his voice, taking a small step forward. "You were at the Fallweather that night too. We have footage of you in the lobby. Your pal was with a girl who definitely wasn't his wife. What about you?"

Wheeler's mouth gaped open. He snapped his jaw shut, opened it again as if to speak, and once again thought better of it.

"We know you were there, Mr. Wheeler." Emma stepped up beside Paul, holding the investor's gaze. "Let's cut to the chase. We need to know why."

He's about as red-faced as a lobster, Emma girl. Don't press too hard, or he'll have a heart attack on you.

"I was…we were…" He stopped, and his Adam's apple bobbed with a hard swallow. "Fine. Nothing illegal about having a party, is there? So we had one, and yeah, there were girls there. Our wives knew, too, so don't try to get all blackmaily about it, all right?"

He let the door open a bit wider, showing more of a marble entryway and a crystal chandelier playing off shadows in the light.

"The 'girls' were of legal age, right? Sex workers?" Paul spoke so casually, the question might've been about car insurance for the monster of a truck outside, but Wheeler's face still went a touch more red. His hand searched for that pocket again, too, betraying every nerve he had.

"Legal age, yeah. For damn sure. Were they pros? I don't know. I didn't pay 'em, and I didn't ask any questions. Just enjoyed myself, but I guess maybe they could've been." His shoulders hunched, and he leaned forward. "I didn't know, all right? We done now?"

Emma forced a smile that didn't make it to her eyes, working to disarm him further. "Were they trafficking victims or sex workers, Bert?"

A sneer curled Wheeler's lips for just a second before he pulled it back. "Am I under arrest?"

"We're questioning you about your experiences with a murder victim on the night he was murdered." Emma channeled charm into her voice, knowing she sounded about as conniving as a news reporter. "Is there some reason you should be under arrest?"

"I…I…you don't know what you're talking about," Wheeler spluttered, looking back and forth between the two of them as he drew himself up taller. "I'm not saying anything else without my lawyer present."

"All right, Bert, calm down." Paul pulled out a card and held it out for the investor's sweaty hand. "But you call us if you think you know who might've killed your buddies. And we may be in touch regardless."

Bert Wheeler fisted the card, stepped all the way back inside, and slammed the door.

Emma watched the door for a moment longer before following Paul back to the vehicle. "He knows plenty he's not telling us."

Paul nodded, sighing. "This city's dirtier than a pigeon in the subway. You thinking what I am?"

"Dude's sketchy as hell, and we hang around to see if we can follow him anywhere more useful than this mansion?"

Paul coughed through a laugh. "Ya read my mind. Let's get back out on the street. Mansion next door looks empty and has a for sale sign. We'll park there and wait with eyes on this place until the fucker leads us somewhere useful."

28

Leo turned down the main road leading to the port, almost glad for the news that Bency's body had been found.

Beside him, Midori texted back and forth with Tibble and sipped from her coffee. She glanced up to see how close they were. "Not that I wanted to be heading to a new crime scene, but…"

"I get it." Leo frowned as he pulled to a stop at a light. "Door knocking gets old when it gets you nowhere. Are we meeting Paul and Emma here?"

"They're sitting on a guy Paul spotted on the Fallweather's security footage, Bert Wheeler. Tibble said to call them if we need backup."

"On a body dump in a low-traffic area?" Leo hit the gas again when the light turned green, anxious to be there already. "Not likely."

Conley Terminal hadn't changed a bit since they'd been there the day before, but their crime scene wasn't so obvious this time. A pair of stevedores flagged them down at the entrance gate. One of the men gestured for Leo to lower the window. "You the Feds?"

Leo flashed his badge, as did Midori.

"Right on. Your scene's on the other side of the port." He proceeded to give rapid-fire instructions, including several mentions of "shipping containers." By the time he'd finished, Leo wasn't sure if they needed to go left, right, or stay where they were and let the crime scene come to them.

"Mind saying all that again but slower? And let me get my phone set to record first."

The guy rolled his eyes and waved his hand in a circle, as if to encourage Leo to speed things along. "Yeah, go on, go on. Get your phone up."

Leo did and held it out while the stevedore recited his instructions a second time. He kept his eyes on Leo's and wore a shit-eating grin as he rattled off the turns and landmarks.

"Thanks," Leo said when the man was done. "I appreciate the careful attention to detail."

"Sure thing, buddy."

"One more question. Do you know if any of these containers have a point of origin in Romania?"

The stevedore laughed out loud and slapped his partner on the shoulder. "Oh, sure. But you'd have to get that from the harbormaster."

Leo thanked him, and the man turned to his partner, aiming a thumb at Leo over his shoulder. "This fucking guy…"

Ignoring the jab, he got them moving, playing back the recorded directions to their crime scene.

Within minutes, they'd navigated the endless containers and straightaways and were coming up on a line of five squat dumpsters backed up against a nine-foot chain-link fence that signaled the edge of the port's property. A forensic van sat nearby, with the dumpsters roped off by crime scene tape.

Midori was out first, flagging down a man in a biohazard

suit who'd just climbed out of a dumpster. Leo detoured to a shaken-looking man in coveralls. He held a construction helmet in his lap and sat cross-legged on the ground. Two port cops stood nearby.

As Leo approached, one of the port cops gestured to the man in coveralls. "Got your guy who found him right here, you wanna talk to him."

The cop sounded so casual, Leo didn't bother answering. He instead walked up to the stevedore and squatted in front of him. "Sir? You found our body?"

The man scrubbed an oil-stained hand down his cheek, still looking at his own helmet rather than Leo. "Yeah. Yeah, I did."

Leo waited for him to continue, but the man's hands were literally shaking with nerves. "Sir, what can you tell me? Did you see something suspicious that led you to him?"

"Nah. Nothing like that, man." He took a breath, and seemed to require a force of will to finally set his helmet to the side and look Leo in the eye.

His lips were raw from being bitten, and his eyes appeared haunted. Skittish from what he'd seen.

"I just came out to dump the trash. Saw something on the side of the dumpster. I thought it was oil, but…you work in my job, you know what oil looks like on *any* surface. Wasn't oil."

The man shrugged, out of words. Leo pulled a card from his pocket and pressed it into his hand. "Thanks for checking out your suspicions. Someone else might not have. You need anything?"

"Nah. Just…maybe to go home. That okay now? I was on the overnight." He clasped his hands, his knuckles white. "I'd like to see the wife, if it's all the same to you folks."

Leo nodded, standing and reaching down to give the man a hand up. "Just make sure the officers here have your name and number. Then go get some rest, and call if you think of anything I should know."

"Right, yeah." The man glanced over toward the dumpster, shook himself visibly, and then turned away to speak to the officers.

Leo moved over to where Midori stood, still talking to the tech.

"They found two suitcases full of clothes in with the body. Ready to take a look?"

At his go-ahead, she gripped onto one side of the dumpster and looked over the rim. Leo did the same on the opposite side in order to get a glimpse of their guy.

The body belonged to Dirk Bency without a doubt. His muscular figure had been shoved into the trash, in a contorted posture. Rigor appeared to have set in throughout, with his face frozen in a rigid grimace and his limbs locked in a bizarre akimbo position.

"Body was found about an hour ago, so time of death has to be at least eight, maybe ten hours prior?"

Midori's face was blank, but she nodded her agreement. "Somewhere in there, yeah."

Blood spread out on Bency's chest and stained his lips and chin, but it was the man's empty-eyed expression that stilled Leo's heartbeat.

Just like Denae. Staring off into nothing. Lifeless.

Leo choked on the air coming into his lungs, fighting for breath for reasons that had nothing to do with the stench coming off the trash.

Jacinda would've let you know if anything changed. And Emma would've told you if she'd seen her again. She's still there, and you'll see her when you get back.

Forcing himself to focus on Bency's body, he aimed a finger at the bloodied shirt he wore. "Looks like this kill is closer to Wilhelm's driver than to our other victims."

"No mutilation to be seen, but we need to get him out of there to be sure." Midori lowered herself back to the ground. "What I find interesting is the placement."

"You mean his position, or that he's in a dumpster?"

"The second one. Wilhelm's driver was left in plain view in the parking lot, and the car was found near Wilhelm's body, which was in a different location." Midori gestured in the direction of the parking lot. "That tells me the driver was a kill of necessity, in the moment, but not part of his mission."

"The mission being to bring down a trafficking ring that we think Conrad and Wilhelm are part of. They bore the Roman numerals and the same mutilation."

She nodded. "Exactly. Those feel like obvious statements, the mutilation indicating they played a larger role in our unsub's view of things."

"You think Bency fits into the mission as a bit player?" Leo tilted his head toward Bency's body hidden within the dumpster. "Someone working the hotel side of the operation. Maybe he was behind the camera footage getting swapped out."

"Could be. Or he could be the trafficker's liaison."

"But if our killer knew that, wouldn't Bency be wearing a Roman numeral and missing an ounce of flesh as well?" Leo waved at the dumpster. "His shirt isn't ripped open, and he still has his pants on."

"Maybe he got interrupted before he could finish the job."

A forensic tech came up and pointed at the dumpster. "Can I get to work on him? The M.E. says he can put a rush on the autopsy."

"Yeah, do what you need to."

Turning away from the dumpster, Leo walked to the edge of the area so that his back was to Midori and all the cops and techs. There, he pointedly stepped back around the side of the line of dumpsters and finally allowed himself to bend over, hands on his knees, and tried his best not to throw up on his own shoes.

Denae's face sat in his mind. Lifeless. Having her image come to him like that, so suddenly, when he'd been clinging to the edge of a dumpster and looking down at a sea of trash…

It wasn't right. He shouldn't have pictured her there.

Just like she shouldn't have been almost killed.

He pawed at his coat pocket for this phone and called Emma. The call connected and rang twice. Emma's voice was breathless when she picked up. "Leo? You okay?"

"Yeah." He shifted on his feet, wondering just how good her instincts were and if she'd catch him in the lie. "We found Bency's body along with some suitcases. At the port."

"Shit. Any sign of the killer?"

"Not yet, but—"

"Leo, I'm sorry, I gotta go. The guy we've been sitting on just started moving. Talk later?"

Leo's throat clenched, but Emma's focus was enough to bring him back to the immediacy of the case. Away from thoughts of Denae. "Go. Call if you need us."

She clicked off, and Leo breathed deeply and exhaled before he turned back to the heart of their crime scene. Their two prime suspects were dead. And they still had a vigilante murderer to catch.

29

Emma slouched in her seat, her head below the level of the headrest as Paul maneuvered through traffic. Three cars ahead, Bert Wheeler changed lanes *again*, his bright-orange Lamborghini an eyesore for sure, but one that made him easier to tail. "I can see where his sons got their taste."

Paul barked a laugh, moving into the fast lane to keep up as Bert hit the gas to swerve around a minivan via the bicycle lane. He jumped a few digits up in speed after that. "You ain't kiddin'. It could be full-on dark out here, and we'd still be able to see him. And did you notice those hubcaps? Neon purple. Egads."

Emma blinked. "Egads?"

"You want me to go back to dick jokes?" Paul leered at her in jest, and she knew well enough to see he was harmless by now.

"I'm good, thanks. Just keep your eyes on our suspect."

"Your wish is my command." Paul hit the gas again, and Emma stayed low. If Wheeler was smart enough or calm enough to look for a tail—and she doubted he was—then he'd only see one person in the car and discount them as the two agents who'd darkened his door earlier.

But when he turned onto the highway, Emma read his intentions loud and clear. She pointed to a sign just as they sped by it. *Conley Terminal, five miles.*

"You gotta be kiddin' me." Paul grunted and shifted four lanes over, speeding ahead and past the Lamborghini. "Hold onto your heels, and I'll get us there before him."

Emma almost doubted her instincts as Paul sped them ahead and then took the exit ramp for the port, leaving Wheeler beeping his horn at a moving van going the speed limit.

Within minutes, they'd arrived, Paul having navigated traffic with chirps of his siren. As before, her badge opened up the port gate for them without delay. Once again, she was reminded that Wilhelm and their killer had gotten in somehow. And now they could add Bert Wheeler to the list. One more potential oddity in a case full of them.

And maybe it was just rich men flaunting their money to people who could be swayed by it, but just in case not, it deserved a check.

We're not lacking leads, that's for sure. They're stacking up faster than bodies.

When they'd parked in the visitor lot in the port, right beside Leo and Midori's SUV, they didn't have to wait long to be proven right.

Bert Wheeler pulled into the port entrance and came to a screeching halt, revving his engine on the little road while he waited for the gate to rise. As soon as it had cleared the hood of his car, he sped toward the lot where Wilhelm's driver was found and onto the road running alongside the harbormaster's office.

Paul let out a string of curses. "How the hell does a rich

schmuck in a car that looks like a giant jelly bean rate access to Conley Terminal? He doesn't own the place."

Emma gripped the passenger's side door handle. "He shouldn't be able to get in at all. Not since 9/11 tightened down security on every airport and shipping terminal in the country."

Watching Wheeler drive up the road abutting the dock and the adjacent shipping containers, Emma and Paul left their own vehicle. They had no cover between them and Wheeler's position, but he was so focused, it didn't matter. He jumped out of his car and stalked down the dock, shouting, "Darrow! Hey, Darrow! Over here!"

Emma glanced at Paul. "Darrow's one of the cops who found Mark Wilhelm and Harold Simpson the morning after they were killed."

"And our guy knows him by name?" Paul whistled under his breath. "Let's see what they have to say.

Paul broke into a light jog and skirted away from the path Wheeler had taken.

Following a line of shipping containers that sat alongside the dock, the agent maneuvered to a position that would let him see Wheeler. Emma followed behind him along the dock until a pair of Massport officers came into view.

Careful to stay out of sight between stacked containers, Emma and Paul peered out to observe the man they'd tailed.

Wheeler stood face-to-face with the black-haired cop Emma had met before, Officer Darrow.

They were talking, and from the look of things, the conversation was a heated one. Wheeler flung his hands out to the side and waved his arms about, but he kept his voice low enough that Emma couldn't pick up anything he was saying.

For his part, Darrow looked bored, the way he stood with his hands on his hips and his cap tilted back on his head.

Beside him, the other Massport cop fidgeted in discomfort, keeping silent.

"That's not Fontaine, the guy who was with Darrow the other day."

"Whoever he is, I'd say he's not too happy about Wheeler's surprise visit. Darrow, on the other hand, looks like he's ready to offer the guy a beer. Wish I could hear what they're saying."

"We're not gonna hear them from here." Emma shook her head, pointing back to the car. "How about you head back to the car and keep him from leaving the port? I'll stay here just in case they raise the volume."

Paul nodded without a word and took off at a trot. Emma monitored the quiet discussion, but aside from the one officer looking more and more nervous, nothing changed.

Finally, Wheeler's voice erupted in anger. "You assholes don't know who you're dealing with, you get me? You understand?"

Darrow held up his hands in surrender, backing up a step, and the other cop followed his lead. They both kept their mouths shut after that, and Wheeler pivoted to head back to his car.

Emma let him pass her hiding place, then checked to see where Darrow and the other cop had gone. They were nowhere in sight, so she stepped out and casually tailed Wheeler.

When they reached the last line of containers, she let him go ahead and shove himself into the Lamborghini. Then she stepped out into full view and followed in the dust of the expensive vehicle as it did a U-turn and headed back toward the exit.

She had to hold in a laugh as Wheeler slammed on the brakes. Paul's SUV blocked the street leading to the gate.

Emma caught up just as Wheeler's door slammed open.

He looked from Paul—standing by the driver's side door—to Emma walking up behind him, his red face going a dangerous shade of crimson. Sweat soaked his collar and the top of his button-down.

"What the hell! Did you two follow me? I can make one call and have your badges!" The man marched up to Paul, coming to within a foot of him before putting his hands on his waist. "Move. Now! Or I'll make that call!"

Emma hurried up behind him. "You can try it, but I don't think you'll have any luck. Now, you want to tell us what you were talking to those port cops about?"

"You frickin' bitch." Wheeler drew himself up taller, but Emma only stepped closer. "What the hell do you think you're doing, comin' into my town, and talkin' about—"

"Watch it, Wheeler." Paul spoke low, but his voice had the desired effect. Their investor shut his mouth. "There are lives at stake, and you're obstructing our investigation. You want to start insulting Feds and picking fights, this isn't gonna come out the way you want it to."

Wheeler glowered at him but took a decided step back. "Whatever you say, Mr. Federal Agent. But if you think I'm saying another thing to you without my lawyer, you've got another think coming. Now, am I free to go, or do you two want to arrest me?"

Emma was so, so tempted to haul him into the station. And she could see in Paul's face that he was thinking the same thing. "One question, Mr. Wheeler. How often do you visit the Fallweather Hotel?"

"The Fallweather? Who the fuck knows and why should I tell you?"

"Do you know a man named Dirk Bency?"

"Yeah, so what? He works at the Fallweather. I go there sometimes."

"When was the last time you saw Dirk?"

"Couldn't say." His angry snarl went slack for a moment, and he looked back and forth between them. "Wait up, you asking me if I know Dirk and saw him because he's a suspect or because he's dead?"

Paul stepped a little closer, sliding a hand toward his sidearm. "We're just asking, Wheeler. When's the last time you saw Dirk Bency?"

"Fuck you. And that's the only answer you'll get from me without my lawyer present, so can I go now?"

Without another word, Paul got back in his SUV and turned the vehicle on.

But Emma stepped into Wheeler's path as he made a move for his candy-colored compensation. "Mr. Wheeler, you are free to go. But understand that your friends have been meeting the sharp end of a knife. If I were you, I'd want us to catch this killer sooner than later. Keep that in mind." She extended her card. "Call us if you have a change of heart."

Wheeler spit on the ground at his own feet and snarled at her. "Keep the greeting card."

Emma stepped aside, and he got into his car. She didn't bother offering a wave as he drove by.

She headed back toward the labyrinth of shipping containers, hoping they would have better luck talking to Darrow and his new partner.

30

Emma waited for Paul to park, then led the way to the harbormaster's office, where a Massport sergeant, with her brown hair worn in a tight bun, was monitoring work on the security system. Paul stepped aside to let a technician—weighed down with a tool belt and carrying spools of cable—exit the building. Once the door was closed, Emma displayed her badge for the sergeant, whose name tape read, *Carruthers*.

"Agents Last and Branner, FBI. We'd like to talk with Officer Darrow if we could. This is about the body that was discovered."

"I'm Sergeant Jane Carruthers. Pleasure to make your acquaintance. Give me a minute to call Darrow back from his rounds."

She thumbed her shoulder mic and exchanged a few words with the officer. "He'll be here in two shakes. Mind waiting for him outside? That tech's coming back to rewire the entire office, and he might need some elbow room." She gestured at the tiny space.

They stepped out the door, again making room for the tech, now carrying different spools of cable. Emma held the door open for the man, and he nodded his thanks, hefting his burden.

"Grabbed the wrong ones from the truck."

Moments later, Darrow and the other officer he'd been with approached from the maze of shipping containers. Emma pulled out her badge and kept it visible as the officers continued in her and Paul's direction. They were still across the roadway, but she kept her voice low.

"Darrow's nervous. He keeps looking side to side, like a car's going to come from out of nowhere and hit him."

Paul chuckled. "Whereas the kid with him could win the prize for most eager beaver."

The two Massport officers were near enough now, and Emma held her badge up.

"Officer Darrow, thanks for talking with us again." She held out her hand to the other one, who shook it. "And Officer…?"

"Danny O'Halloran." He swept back his dirty-blond hair after shaking her hand, and she revised his age lower. The young cop couldn't be past his mid-twenties. "What can we do you for?"

"We saw you two speaking with Bert Wheeler." Paul tucked away his badge, glancing back and forth between them, but Emma kept her gaze on Darrow.

The cop fidgeted, looking over his shoulder at the harbormaster's office. "Guy's paranoid. Wanted to know what happened to Wilhelm and thinks we been hiding details from the media."

"He looked pretty PO'd for a guy who's just feeling a little paranoid." Paul pointed back to the entrance gate. "And the way he zoomed in and out of here, I'd say there's a hell of a lot more he's getting emotional about."

"That's entirely possible, but I'm not gonna speculate about what gets under a rich guy's skin." Darrow shrugged, but the gesture seemed forced, calculated. "Wheeler had a bug up his ass, and I told him to shoo, fly, shoo."

O'Halloran had the grace to flush in reaction. "He, uh… said he couldn't blame us for hiding news, ya know? Can't go leaking details about a crime. That's Academy one-oh-one. Wheeler was real freaked out, though, and kept saying how he wanted to know 'the score.'"

Darrow tugged at his belt as Emma and Paul kept watching him. "Was that all you wanted to talk to us about? Because me and the FNG here have a job to do."

The younger cop gave a nervous laugh and tucked his thumbs into his own belt.

FNG. Fucking New Guy, right. O'Halloran's a rookie, which means he might not be aware of everything going on at Conley Terminal.

Emma aimed a finger at the harbormaster's office. "We see the security system here is getting an upgrade. Did you have any luck retrieving the footage from Wilhelm's murder?"

"No." Darrow's gaze remained firmly set between her and Paul, observing nothing even as sweat dampened his forehead. "Seems like it's gone for good. No footage from last night and that guy you found today either. Shit luck, huh?"

O'Halloran paled, and he darted a quick look at his partner. "Hey, um…"

The other cop gave O'Halloran a side-eye, and the young rookie backed up a step, meeting Emma's eyes as she zeroed in on him. She spoke to Paul without taking her eyes off the young pup. "Agent Branner, maybe you could walk down the dock with Darrow and see if he can remember anything else Bert Wheeler might have said. I'd like to take a walk with Officer O'Halloran here."

Darrow opened his mouth to protest, but Paul caught his arm and turned him around, talking over him.

Emma relaxed into a smile. "Walk with me, Officer?"

He nodded, and though Darrow seemed to be trying to catch his eye, O'Halloran avoided the other man's gaze and turned with Emma.

"I get the sense you know more than Darrow wanted to share." Emma waited, wondering if he'd answer, but he only hunched his head and shoulders a touch. "We have four dead bodies right now, Danny. Whatever you're hiding—"

"I need this job." He stopped in his tracks with a sigh, then turned to face her.

She waited, softening her expression as she nodded for him to continue.

"You're right, there's more to tell, but seriously, I need this job. My girlfriend just lost hers, and if I don't have—"

She held up a hand to stop him. "I realize I might be asking you to make some enemies, based on the way Darrow acted back there."

O'Halloran flinched. "He's supposed to be my training officer."

Well, that "supposed to be" speaks volumes, doesn't it?

"Danny, I'll be up front with you. I can't make any guarantees. I'll talk to Sergeant Carruthers on your behalf, but I need you to cooperate. If you're not involved and have information that can help me, you'll stay out of trouble. But only if you cooperate."

The cop cursed under his breath, staring at the ground. "Sergeant's clean. If you could talk to her for me, that'd help."

Emma waited for him to look up, then nodded. "Okay, so let's start there. Tell me what you know. Maybe start with how you felt the need to confirm your sergeant's clean."

At his prodding, the officer blushed, but then he gestured off to a trailer beside the harbormaster's building. "You should come with me."

Emma fell in step with him, shooting a quick glance over

her shoulder to make sure Branner was keeping Darrow busy. She saw no sign of either of them.

"Thing is," Danny sped up, seeming to feel the same urgency she did, "I had no idea they were this corrupt until I was on the job. After that? I went along with it because I need the job. Figured I could distance myself from Darrow and his shit after I was off the training beat."

"Does that mean you saw the footage?"

Danny's step faltered, but he nodded. "Yeah, I saw it. Don't know if it'll help you at all, but I can show it to you. Darrow and Fontaine kept a copy before they messed with the cameras."

"And what about footage of last night's murder?"

"Yeah, that too."

The officer went up the stairs to the little trailer and held the door open for her. Emma kept one hand near her sidearm and gave a quick glance back the way they'd come. Still no sign of Branner or Darrow.

She motioned for Danny to go in ahead of her and stayed in the doorway. To Emma's right, the trailer held a bank of lockers with a bench in front of it. Danny went to a small desk against the opposite wall. A single workstation had been set up there.

"It'll take a minute to boot up. This thing's older than dirt." He slapped the yellowed monitor. Once he had it up and running, he motioned Emma to join him. With another glance around the port, looking for Branner and Darrow, she went inside.

The officer moved with more confidence than he had previously. His fingers banged out commands on the keyboard, and in minutes, he'd pulled up footage that showed Mark Wilhelm on the dock with two cops from Thursday, April eighth.

Emma leaned in as O'Halloran began talking again.

"Fontaine and Darrow have this idea they'll be able to blackmail somebody with this, but since that guy," he aimed a finger at Wilhelm on the screen, "is deadsville, I don't know who they're planning to roll."

Emma reached over and zoomed in the video, taking care to avoid even blinking as Mark Wilhelm pulled an envelope from his jacket and passed it to Darrow. The cop opened it up, flipped through its contents, and tucked it into his jacket.

With a heavy sigh, Danny sank back in his chair. "Gotta be a handoff, and if you saw the kinda lettuce Fontaine keeps in his wallet…this ain't the first time."

"Do you know what the payoff's for?"

"I heard Darrow say something about girls, but figured it was him and Fontaine talking about going to a strip club after a shift. They invited me along one time, but I begged off. I got a girl at home, and I'm hoping one day we'll have enough to get married. I don't need to be watching…all that."

"I understand." Emma perched on the desk, leaning closer to the monitor. "What about the murder? Wilhelm and his driver were both killed that night."

Danny blanched. "I'd rather not see that again. The guys were laughing over it earlier."

"You don't have to watch." Emma gestured to the computer when he still seemed to hesitate. "Please, this is important."

He gulped a breath, then began typing. When the camera view changed, she saw a figure leaned over a black car, blocking the driver's side door. In another moment, an arm came down, and she realized they were watching the chauffeur being stabbed to death.

"There's our killer." She spoke at a near whisper.

"If I'd thought you could get an identity off this, I swear I would've called it in."

Emma only half listened as she leaned forward to focus

on the killer, but she feared the officer was right. Excited as she was to have the murderer on camera, dragging Harold Simpson out of the car and then killing him, his face was completely obscured by the camera angle. "He stood with his back to the camera on purpose. So we couldn't get a view of his face."

He wore all black and didn't make any movements that could distinguish him from any other man of a similar size and build.

We have something, though. It's not enough to start pointing fingers, but it's a starting point. And that's more than we've had on him yet.

The perpetrator was large, but then again, they'd guessed that based on the way he'd overpowered multiple victims, tossing one from a roof.

On screen, he maneuvered the body under the back of the car, then moved back to the driver's seat and slipped inside.

He leaned across the passenger seat, disappearing from view momentarily before sitting upright and settling the driver's cap firmly on his head. Emma grunted out loud in disgust.

Wilhelm approached and stood by the back door for a moment, apparently hollering at the man he believed was his driver. After a moment, he yanked open the door and got in. The car drove out of view, and she looked at O'Halloran, but he only shrugged helplessly.

"We have cameras all over the port, but not where they ended up when he killed Wilhelm."

Emma's eyes went back to the monitor, which Danny had frozen on the car leaving the lot. This was better than nothing.

She passed him her card. "Send me all this right now. I need to call my supervisory agent. You probably don't need me to tell you this, but you should keep your head down.

Maybe call off sick and get yourself home. If Fontaine and Darrow are dirty, you could've just put a target on your back."

The young cop nodded, getting to work immediately, and she stood and paced over to the trailer door so she could watch the area outside. Just as she dialed Tibble, Darrow and Paul appeared from behind two containers, strolling her way.

That was just fine. They had what they needed now, and Emma wouldn't mind having another word with Darrow about exactly what he'd been doing with Wilhelm and his buddies. She wouldn't mind that one bit.

31

Bert Wheeler sped forward into his four-car garage even before the door finished rising. He'd nearly sideswiped his oldest son's new pickup but couldn't find it in himself to care. Their kid getting home from a birthday cruise to find his new ride scratched would've been the least of their worries.

As it was, he shoved himself out of his Lambo and plucked his phone out of a pocket in one motion. It had been all he could do to keep from calling Rosco on the drive home and getting so worked up that he could've caused a frickin' wreck.

Though, maybe that would've been better.

A murderer was after him, and even if he managed to escape that psycho's claws, the jig might very well be up. The fucking Feds asked him questions. And those Massport shitheads couldn't be trusted to keep their mouths shut.

Darrow even had the balls to say they had "a fail-safe" and that he could make my life real interesting if I held back on the payments. Fuck, payments were Mark's job, not mine.

Jimmy and Mark had trusted the two dirty cops, but

where had that gotten them? And where the hell was Rosco? The line kept ringing and ringing.

Bert hung up and hit the call button again, slapping the phone to his face as he paced the garage.

If the operation got busted, he and Shane would lose everything. If they even survived, that was.

Whole damn trafficking setup was Jimmy's idea from the get-go. With him and Mark gone, if the Feds bust it open, me and Shane'll take the fall. And it would be a pretty fucking steep fall.

Bert pulled the phone away from his ear when the call dropped. This was not the damn time. He hung up and hit the number again before punching his fist into the garage door button and then rubbing his knuckles on his pants.

Margie said he'd break the damn thing one of these days. Then he'd be sleeping in the guest room on top of fearing for his life. But the door appeared to still be working.

Rosco's accented growl finally came through after the fourth ring. "What do you want?"

"We got people showing up dead, and you can't even pick up your phone?" Bert swiped his hand across his forehead, leaving the garage behind and stalking inside to his fridge. He pulled out a can of beer and cracked it but didn't take a pull. "The Feds were at my door. They came to my house. They showed up at Conley and guess what. Bency probably got knifed too. The damn Feds were up in my shit about 'did I know him' and 'when was the last time I saw him.' You wanted to stay in charge of the girls, well, now you better stay in fucking charge. Get them out of the city. Somewhere safe."

The other man remained silent for a second. "We have appointments coming, men expecting—"

"Did you hear me? I know English isn't your first language, Rosco, so I'll speak slowly." Bert slammed his beer on the counter, splattering liquid and foam everywhere. "Get. Them. Out. Before we all get found out!"

"Fine. Call me when business starts again." Rosco hung up, leaving Bert staring at the mess he'd just made. Rather than cleaning it up, he picked up the beer and slammed it down into the sink, leaving foamy liquid splattered around the countertop and on the cabinet doors.

Let Margie yell. She's about to see what stress is all about after all these years of me takin' care of her like a spoiled housecat.

He swiped his beer-slicked hands on a dish towel before grabbing his phone again to dial Shane Field.

The man picked up on the first ring. "Bert, thank fuck. Have you heard anything? What's happening?"

Bert coughed a laugh, leaning back against the sink. "Have I heard? Yeah, I'm fucking deaf from all I've heard. I had the FBI at my door a little while ago, and they've been haunting the fucking port. Not to mention that they seem to think I might've killed Jimmy and Mark, which means they obviously haven't caught the bastard who did. And Bency's probably dead too. They were asking me questions about him like he was either a suspect or a victim."

Shane cursed under his breath, and the sound of a game that had been on in the background went down a notch. "I've been freakin' out. I don't know what we're gonna do. If Jimmy and Mark went down, somebody knows, and that means they probably know about us." The phone crackled, as though Shane had rubbed his hand over his mouth. "No way we're not in a shit ton of danger. And it's not like we can go to the cops. Not even those two chuckleheads at Conley can help us."

"Or the Feds." Bert paced out of the kitchen, trying to breathe deep and get his thoughts together. Maybe he'd come clean with Margie. Find out what she thought. She'd gotten him out of trouble before with her quick thinking, even if she was a spoiled bitch. "But we gotta do something and—"

Bert froze at the entrance to his living room. His wife of thirty-odd years lounged on the couch, head tilted back to show the world that her throat had been slit. Blood drenched her dress and pooled in the puckered stitches of their custom-designed couch on each side of her.

"He's here." Bert's voice was choked, his throat throbbing with fear. "Shane, fuck, the killer's here. Margie's dead."

"What?"

Margie stared dead-eyed into the depths of the ceiling, and Bert knew he needed to run. Needed to run for his car faster than he'd ever run before, hit the Pike, and keep going until this guy couldn't find him without searching every county in the States.

Shane was screaming into the phone as he spun on his heel to do just that, but a black figured loomed right in front of him, stopping him in his path.

The man's gloved fist caught him in the neck and flung him backward onto the carpet at the feet of his dead wife. A small puddle of her blood saturated the ass of his pants while he held his throat on instinct, scratching his attacker's gloved hands and fighting for breath.

But the man who towered over him was strong. Bert aimed a knee into his gut. All that did was force the man to press his full weight onto Bert's body. He was trapped under him.

With a massive paw wrapped around Bert's neck, his attacker yanked his shirt from his pants with his free hand.

Lungs burning, Bert tried to fight his attacker off, swinging a wild punch that hit nothing but air. That earned him a fist to the gut that drained his lungs and stole the fight from him.

The man muttered something in Romanian.

Just like the girls! He's probably somebody's daddy or brother, shit!

"Stop. Please stop." Bert choked between gasping for air. "I'm not the guy…the guy who takes the girls. I can get you to him. I can—"

The man lifted a knee and sank all his weight onto Bert's stomach, crushing something inside that crunched and sent a violent stabbing pain through his abdomen. He cried out and swatted at the attacker.

The guy dodged his hands as if they were an annoying bug and, with a sudden motion, forced Bert's shirt into his mouth.

"Shut your sinning mouth. I need to show you what you are made of." The killer pressed a knife to his throat and held the blade there. Bert instinctively grabbed the attacker's hand that held the knife, but he froze as the blade cut into his skin.

The knife came away from his neck, but the attacker's other hand came around in a flash and clubbed him in the head, sending stars across his vision. He rolled to the side, screaming in pain from his crushed ribs.

Getting his hands under him, Bert pushed up from the bloody carpet, still dazed. Despite the pain, he had to escape. To get anywhere but there, lying at his dead wife's feet.

A hand gripped his pants, and he felt the blade being worked into his belt. With a jerk, the man tore the blade through the leather and began yanking his pants and boxers down.

"Shit, no! Shit…no!" *I'm not dying like Jimmy and Mark. No, no, no!*

With renewed strength and panic driving him, Bert threw himself forward, away from his attacker. Even with his pants bunched around his knees, he crawled as fast as he could. He made it around the couch and was heading for the closet where he kept his gun.

All I gotta do is get there, then this son of a bitch will find out what I'm made of.

A heavy laugh filled his ears, and he was crushed to the floor as the man landed on his back. "You will pay, just like your friends."

Bert squirmed and fought, but the killer was stronger. He pulled him backward with an arm around his throat and dragged him in front of Margie.

Her blank eyes stared at the ceiling as the knife came around and rested against the top of his prick.

When the blade sliced down, blood arced from his groin like a fountain. It landed in the puddle at Margie's feet. Pain seared through his loins, so dizzying that Bert couldn't even scream.

Instinct forced his hands to his mangled crotch, but the killer pushed him down. Then he knelt beside him again and rolled him over, and Bert was almost grateful to see the knife coming down in quick slashes on his chest, marking a Roman numeral three.

Shane'll be number four, and then it'll all be over.

The killer raised his knife again. Bert closed his eyes. When the knife fell, it went straight through his throat.

32

I stared at the bodies and thought how beautiful it was that they should be found together like this. Him, the pig, lying dead at her feet, while she stared at the ceiling, as if calling for help from Heaven.

These two deserve no grace. They lived as pigs and earned their slaughter.

Looking at the wife again, I had a second thought. I reached out with a gloved hand and closed her eyes.

Once she had seen me enter the house, her fate as collateral damage had been sealed. But she had known nothing of her husband's crimes. Her protests were genuine when I accused her of profiting from the sale of my country's daughters.

"If Bert is doing that, he can rot in hell for it! I swear I know nothing about it. Please!"

She had begged for her life, but I could not let her live, not after seeing me.

I had made her death fast, thinking I could at least give her that much dignity. Still, she had lived off her husband's depravity, in her fine house and fancy cars, so I had no cause for guilt.

If the butler or the sons had been home, I would have killed them too.

Fewer pigs to carry on their father's teachings.

Looking at the dead man now, I felt real satisfaction in seeing the bloody vacancy between his legs. The tool of his crimes had been taken from him before his final breath, and no more would he rape and torture.

This ruined man at my feet was an offense to humanity, just like his friends. I kicked his little piece of severed meat, sending it into the puddle of blood beside him.

Wheeler's phone buzzed on the ground, and I picked it up. Four missed calls from Rosco.

I hoped he was afraid by now. I hoped he knew I was coming for him. He would have to, since Dirk Bency's body had been found. I had wanted him to stay hidden longer and probably should have thrown him in the water with something heavy to drag him down.

But that could have been heard, and I had already risked too much by returning to the port after killing Wilhelm and his driver there.

Still, Shane Field and Rosco had to be shaking in their shoes. Maybe displaying Wheeler's body would build their fear even higher, torturing them with thoughts of what I held in store for them both.

On that thought, I leaned down and took hold of the old lecher's ankles.

The body trailed blood across his carpet and hardwood floor. I yanked him harder as an added indignity. The motion caused an extra gout of blood to spit from his groin.

More blood poured from his neck as I took him out the front door, past the pillars, and down the brick stairs. Skin tore from his back as I dragged him over the stepping stones and into the front yard. I wished it were not gated and mostly out of view, even though this was better for me.

On the lawn, I dropped him and arranged his arms spread out like an eagle, as they said. Now he could be on display for his neighbors who might pause at his wrought iron fencing.

I had no need to be discreet any longer. My work was nearly done.

Soon, I will return home with Daniela and as many of the girls as she can bring to safety.

I stared at the dead man. "This is for Cristina, Bert Wheeler."

Moisture trickled down my face. Maybe the man's blood, or maybe some last tears cried for my sweet sister.

I thought I had cried my final tears after getting Daniela's letter, telling me what had happened to Cristina.

She tried to escape one night, and they beat her, savagely, until she could no longer see, her eyes were so swollen. And still, she tried to get free. Half blind, she ran from them the next chance she got.

Rosco and his men had killed her for it, in front of the other girls. In front of Daniela.

With Bert Wheeler deposited in the dirt where he belonged, I ventured back into the garage. I had taken a bus for the first part of my journey today, but using the keys, which the good wife had given me, only made sense. Her luxury sedan would blend in as I got out of the neighborhood, then I could abandon it before anyone realized it had gone missing.

The street was nearly empty at this time of the afternoon, so I did not hesitate to pull my phone out when it buzzed with a text. Daniela again, of course.

Rosco says Feds are onto them. We are getting moved outside the city.

Cristina's face flashed to mind, as I imagined a group of girls being herded like cattle. Out of some warehouse and into a van, on to some other warehouse or even another shipping container.

My fists balled on the wheel as soon as I put the phone down.

The dominoes were falling, one by one.

At a stoplight, I texted Daniela back. *I have to finish this before I am caught.*

Promising her that we would still finish our vengeance, and she would be safe.

Each time I communicated with her, the memories bombarded me, but I needed to honor them as well. Her telling me that my sister had been killed for an act of bravery—as vengeance for having tried to go to the authorities—meant one thing to me. It showed me, without doubt, that my sister had been strong until the end. A fighter.

The fact that her childhood friend cared so much about her still, that she would help me avenge her rather than putting herself first in a bid to escape, only spoke more to the impact my sister had had on this world.

And I would continue to be strong for her until my mission was complete.

33

Boston's afternoon traffic conspired to send Emma onto the sidewalk on more than one occasion. No matter how many times Paul honked his horn and chirped his siren in the Bureau vehicle ahead of them, pedestrians and vehicles alike seemed bent on ignoring the fact that federal agents were attempting to race across town.

Both to save the trafficker's undeserving ass *and* to take him into custody.

"Easy, Emma." Leo gripped the grab bar as she swerved sideways into a small space in the middle lane. "We'll get there when we get there."

"How can you be so chill right now?" She groaned and slammed one hand on the wheel in irritation as Paul braked for a taxi blazing through a yellow light. "He could be killing Bert Wheeler while we're stuck in traffic."

Leo didn't reply except to shrug and stare out the windshield.

"Hey, Earth to Ambrose. Everything okay?"

"Yeah. I'm good. Just," he squeezed the grab bar tighter, "just nervous. We're working a case that involves dirty cops.

It makes me anxious to think that's possible, you know? Cops taking bribes to look the other way. I know it happens, but now I'm face-to-face with it."

"That's why I want to get to Wheeler before the killer does. I want to rub it in his face. That we have police testimony against him." She inched through the intersection.

"You told Tibble about Danny O'Halloran?"

"Yep, when I had him on the phone. He looped in Massport Internal Affairs and put in a call to the Inspector General's office as well. Fontaine and Darrow will be arrested, and Danny's getting a protective detail assigned to his address."

"He'll be a solid witness to go along with the footage we got of Wilhelm, but there's still a killer on the loose. This is a mess of bad guys we're dealing with." Leo sighed and fidgeted with his seat belt.

Emma glanced over and read the frustration on his face. Something was eating at him.

The traffic finally eased enough for them to move ahead, and Emma took the opportunity, swerving around a slower vehicle, which earned her another mild curse from Leo.

Whatever's going on, you're not making things better. Slow your roll, Emma girl, for his sake.

She drove more conservatively than she ever had, taking corners at reasonable speeds instead of squealing the tires. When the turn for Bert Wheeler's neighborhood finally showed itself ahead, Emma followed Paul as he zoomed into the bus lane and sped forward.

Minutes later, they were in the Wheelers' neighborhood.

At first, the house appeared the same as it had when she and Paul paid Bert Wheeler a visit, but when Emma pulled into the drive just behind her Boston counterparts, her stomach sank. The door to the stately home yawned, and a white shape in the middle of the yard could only be one thing.

Bert Wheeler. Dead and waiting.

Paul and Midori ran for the house, leaving Leo and Emma to assess the body.

They exited the SUV and approached.

A ghost stood over him, an older woman with perfectly coifed hair, wearing tailored clothes. As the cold of the Other drenched Emma with each step forward, the woman's words became clearer. "I didn't know. I swear I didn't know."

A separate chill from the Other stole up Emma's spine, and she knew, inside the house, Midori and Paul would find the body of Bert Wheeler's wife.

Emma moved opposite the ghost and stared down at the body. Leo was already lifting his phone to call Tibble as she held up three fingers to mirror the mark on Bert's chest.

Wonder how many he's planning for, because he's counting targets, no question.

Uniforms had also been called in for backup, on the assumption that they'd be taking Bert Wheeler into custody. As they pulled up behind the two Bureau vehicles, Emma held up a hand and yelled, "Bring a sheet!"

One of them kept on running over as if he hadn't heard, apparently anxious to see the body, but the other doubled back and grabbed a sheet from his trunk. Emma intercepted him as he approached, took the fabric, and motioned to the uniform who'd been staring down at the mutilated body like a fascinated kid.

They draped the body and stood back. "We'll keep an eye on him until the coroner arrives." Emma glanced back at Leo. "Time to go inside?"

He nodded, already walking alongside the trail of blood that led up the walkway and the stairs into the home. Inside, they both heard Midori and Paul clearing the floor above and stopped for only a second to take in Margaret Wheeler's corpse. Together, they moved deeper into the house with their guns drawn.

Leo gestured toward the kitchen and whispered, "Place like this has to have a cellar."

It did…but it didn't take long to clear it. Wheeler had kitted the space out with pool table, home theater, and minibar. Unless the killer had managed to hollow out the leather sectional and hide inside it—without leaving any signs—the space was clear. They got back to the main floor just as Midori and Paul were coming back down the stairs.

"No sign of anyone upstairs." Paul stopped himself from putting his hand on the banister. "We'll see what forensics says."

Midori nodded, frowning. "You saw the wife?"

"And cleared the man cave downstairs." Emma led the way back toward the front room as Paul called dispatch to report the presence of a second expired victim on scene. "I think we can assume she was an unplanned kill, just like Wilhelm's driver and Bency."

The victims were just where they'd left them, and not another ghost to be seen. Helpful or otherwise. But Leo bent near the puddle of blood left by Wheeler's body. "You see this?"

Emma bent down beside him. "A phone. Must be Wheeler's—"

"Four missed calls." Leo pointed, his finger hovering over the screen. "Somebody was pretty desperate to get in touch with this guy. Guy named 'Rosco' ring a bell for anyone?"

Paul grunted. "Sounds like another rich asshole just teeing up to go dickless—"

"Shut it, Paul." Midori bit her lower lip, staring at the phone. "Someone that antsy could be helpful." She lifted her gaze and zeroed in on Leo. "You don't have any accent, and

Wheeler didn't have much of one for a Boston guy. How you feel about pulling a ruse?"

Emma shrugged. It couldn't hurt. "But what about—"

"Paul couldn't get through a call without a joke. It's gotta be Leo."

When he didn't argue, Midori shot off a quick text to Tibble. And when he okayed it, Emma handed her partner a glove.

Leo bent over the phone and touched one finger to it, sliding the green sign to redial before he put it on speaker. "Yeah?"

"Wheeler, where in hell have you been? It is done, but you better be right!" The man sounded breathless, too panicked to bother asking who he was speaking to. "We moved the girls somewhere safe."

"Safe where?" Leo did his best to sound antsy himself, as if he'd ordered the man to make the move.

"Storage place in Beverly. My friend says he will let us stay."

Leo met Emma's eyes, asking a question by lifting his brow. She mouthed, *How long?*

"Okay. For how long, Rosco? How long can you stay there?"

The caller paused, and for a moment, Emma worried they'd blown their ruse, but muffled voices came through the phone, and Rosco answered a moment later. "Few days, he says. I trust him."

"Well, I don't. Where in Beverly? I need to make sure it's safe. Not take the word of some guy I don't know." Leo's voice was gruffer than usual, and Emma hoped it wouldn't tip off Rosco.

She'd hoped in vain.

The man barked into the phone. "Who the fuck is this? If

you're Bert, drive your little orange penis car out here. You a Fed, go and fuck off."

Rosco hung up, and Leo blew out a long exhale. He met Emma's gaze first, an irritated glower just visible before he deflated. "I shouldn't have tried for more info. Dammit!"

Midori stepped forward and clapped him on the arm. "You did awesome, Ambrose. Better than Paul would have done."

The other Boston agent smirked and gave Leo a light punch in the shoulder. "You did good. Maybe we oughta hit the bar after this is done and get you in touch with your inner Masshole."

A bit of weight left Emma's own shoulders. "At least we know a general location for them. We can zero in on every storage unit in Beverly and close the net around these guys." *And maybe get some innocent girls out.* "Let's get to it."

34

Emma sped them down the road toward the highway. She'd been tempted to let Leo drive, because going back to Beverly meant passing Salem again.

If her body reacted as it had before, she had no business being behind the wheel. But their killer could be stalking his fourth victim, and they needed to move faster than Grandpa Ambrose would get them there.

The weird thing was that Leo hadn't even asked to drive as they left Wheeler's place.

"Leo, if there's something you need to say, please do. Is it about the ghosts? I still haven't seen Denae again, I promise." Emma glanced at Leo. "She's fine."

He barely mumbled his acknowledgment.

"Leo?"

"I told you I believe you, and I'm fine with it. I am."

"So what's eating you alive, then?"

He massaged his forehead as if he had a headache. "I keep thinking about Denae. I'm ready to go back," he dropped his hand and stared out the windshield, "to see her again. Be there when she…"

"Jacinda said she'd tell us the instant anything changes for Denae. Or for Mia or Vance."

He *mm-hmm*ed.

Emma hesitated before saying anything else, eyeing the signs guiding them toward Beverly and wondering if she'd once again be freezing to death within a few more miles of travel.

Here goes nothing, Emma girl.

Hoping to clear her mind, and his, she filled Leo in on the ghost he hadn't heard about yet. "Margie Wheeler was back there, proclaiming she had no idea her husband was involved in the trafficking operation."

Expression barely changing, he only nodded as he took everything in. The thought that came to her next wasn't one she meant to say out loud, but she did anyway. "It's nice to be able to share all this with you."

She shifted in the seat and monitored the road, waiting for any hint that the Other might take her in its grip again. If that happened, she wanted to be prepared, ready to pull over and stop so Leo could take over driving.

Or just fight through it. Because you know that's what you'd rather do.

He remained silent for just a second longer than made her comfortable before speaking, but his voice was easy when he did. "I've been meaning to ask…have you seen… anyone else around…I mean, anyone I knew?" Between the pauses, he spoke fast, the words tumbling out.

"You mean your parents or your grandfather?"

Their phones buzzed. A ball of emotion threatened to spill from Emma's throat, but she swallowed it down as Leo swiped his phone screen to answer. "SSA Tibble, you have me and Emma." He put the phone on speaker. "What's up?"

"Local PD rolled up on a delivery van pulling into a storage unit in Beverly. Officers caught a glimpse of girls being moved from the van, one guy on a phone call. He hung up and trashed the phone before loading the girls back in."

Emma hit the gas, jumping the car forward. "Are they on the run?"

"No, though I don't know if it's better." Tibble grunted as a horn blasted from his end of the call. "Officers blocked the van's exit, and some of them got killed in thanks. It's a standoff. Units on scene are receiving heavy fire from automatic weapons."

Emma's heartbeat thudded with dread. Their phones chimed with a text, and Tibble confirmed he'd sent it. "That's the address. Head straight there and keep your heads on a swivel. Vests on when you arrive." Tibble hung up without saying anything more.

"So much for sneaking up on them." Leo sighed. "They must've been prepared to run, and those cops caught the fire we started."

"Don't say that." Emma glimpsed a sign for Salem and tried to compartmentalize the fear building in her chest. She wanted to pick their conversation back up, to tell him she hadn't seen his parents or anyone else connected to him, but she couldn't finish the thought.

The Other descended on her like a frozen curtain, wrapping her in its grip and sending a violent shiver through her body.

She swerved in the lane, barely able to control the vehicle and dimly aware of Leo yelling at her. He'd leaned across the console, trying to steady them with his hands over hers on the wheel.

"Fight it, Emma! You have to fight it, stay in control!"

She wanted so much to pull her arms around herself, to collapse in her seat and shrink away from the clutching fingers of ice and chill that stabbed at her.

Like a hailstorm, the chill pelted her skin, piercing her clothing and sinking into her heart.

Still, she gripped the wheel, Leo's hands covering her own. The car rocked side to side in the lane, and for a split second, Emma feared she had lost, that whatever aspect of the Other had ahold of her, it wouldn't let go until she was dead.

Leo's hands crushed hers on the wheel as he struggled against her shaking and seizing. An involuntary spasm coursed through her.

"I…c-c-c-can't…can't control…so c-c-c-cold. C-c-c-cold."

"Emma, please! Please, stay in control. Fight whatever it is. Fight it, and take your foot off the gas. I'll get us off the road. Let me help."

He gripped the wheel between her hands, and she registered his attempt at pushing her arms away with his elbows. Emma focused on her right leg, tensing the muscles to pull her foot up from the accelerator.

Her toes cramped, curling in her boots, and she stopped fighting the urge to dig her chin into the top of her jacket to shrink into herself. The cold was a living beast, trying to tear her apart and freeze her breath in her lungs, and the howling she heard in the distance set something loose in her chest.

The ball of emotion she'd held back earlier released itself from her throat in a pained groan that lasted longer than her breath should have allowed.

Beside her, Leo continued to chant his plea for her to let go, to let him take the wheel. She dropped one hand, and it felt like it was moving through icy, rushing water. Her fingers clutched at nothing as shivers raced up and down her arms and legs.

"Hold on, Emma. We'll be past it soon. Just hold on. I'm getting us off the road at the first exit."

Emma couldn't speak. She couldn't even nod. Her body

freezing, her temperature dropping, her teeth chattering, she curled into herself as she went colder and colder. And then, slowly, as the car sped past the last fringes of Salem, the icy grip released her, piece by piece.

Her breathing came easier, her fingers and toes uncurled.

She straightened up and shook it off, placing her hands on the wheel as Leo backed off, settling into his seat beside her.

"Are you okay?"

Emma stretched her neck and re-gripped the wheel. She applied pressure to the accelerator and got them moving at speed again. "I'm good. Thank you for…for covering for me."

He ran a hand down his face. "I'd say anytime, but I really don't need that to happen again. Ever. If it's all right with you, I'll drive us back to the airport when this is over."

She rested back into the seat, briefly letting herself accept that maybe she shouldn't always be the one behind the wheel.

The thought vanished as fast as it appeared. "When this is over, Leo, we'll want to get back to the airport ASAP. We can take the long way around to avoid Salem, and I'll still get us there with time to spare."

He allowed a slight chuckle and tapped the back of his hand against her shoulder. "Okay, Speed Demon."

As the shivers faded away, Emma wondered if going around Salem the long way would be enough. Even though the physical cold had fully departed, the icy feeling in her bones lingered, as if it had become part of her.

35

Kornher's Corner Storage loomed ahead of them, a dismal, gray, two-story structure with very few windows. Up and down the block, black-and-whites were parked with their lights flashing.

Emma passed them and pulled up behind Paul and Midori's SUV. The other agents had beaten them by several minutes, given what had happened, yet again, as they'd driven through Salem.

Barricades had already been established at the entrance to the storage facility and on every corner of the block.

No shots were being fired at the moment, but two bullet-riddled patrol cars in the street sat as a mute testament to Boston PD's losses.

Emma was out of the car before Leo, and she quickly strapped on her vest, double-checking the fit around her underarms. Thoughts of Denae filled her head, alongside a desperate wish for her and Leo's safety. She shook herself to focus on the crisis in front of them and joined Leo at the back of the vehicle, where Paul and Midori were checking their own protective gear.

"Do we have a plan to approach?"

Paul circled a finger in the air and headed back to his and Midori's vehicle. He pulled out a tablet and tapped on the screen.

"We got two gates to this place. One here at the front and another along the back. That one's a rolling gate in the chain-link fence, unlike the heavier one up here. Both are big enough for SWAT vehicles, and we should be hearing the bird coming in soon."

The helicopter's chop could be heard moments later as Paul detailed the plan to enter the storage facility.

"We'll move in with the SWAT truck leading the way. They'll use flash-bangs once they breach the buildings."

Emma examined the image on Paul's tablet, asking him to zoom in on areas so she could assess their plan of entry and where the best routes of cover and retreat would lie.

The storage business had two buildings, opposite each other across a central drive that led from the front gate to the chain-link gate at the back of the property. "Traffickers are in the building on the right?"

Paul nodded. "Two entrances on the ground floor out front, a one-person door and the roll-up garage door. There's another one-person at the back of the building closest to the other gate."

Leaning in to examine the tablet, Leo asked about the second floor. "I'm assuming there's an elevator inside?"

"Yeah, and it's big enough to handle a stacked pallet. Staircase on the back of the building accesses a fire door for the top floor, but it's an emergency exit only."

"We don't have a key?"

"On-site managers said they only took over last year and were never given a key to that door. Could be bullshit, but that's neither here nor there. We know the traffickers drove their van in through this door," he indicated the position on his tablet, "and buttoned up after they shot two of Boston's finest. I would not be surprised if we have very few surviving witnesses from among the traffickers, but that's mostly due to how trigger happy those guys are." Paul's mouth twisted. "They're not going down without a fight."

"And they're armed with automatic weapons."

Paul nodded and continued to describe his plan of approach. As the ranking local agent, he'd been given temporary supervisory authority. Emma did her best to listen, but the cold of the Other encased her, almost as if drawing her closer to the fence surrounding the storage facility.

A ghost emerged from the nearest building and crouched on the other side of the fence, as if hiding from the chaos. She'd been a young girl, maybe sixteen when she died, and wore torn jeans and a t-shirt. Blood trailed from a wound to her scalp. As Emma got closer, she glimpsed angry bruises along her arms, jaw, and collarbone.

Her eyes were two swollen masses of bloody tissue.

She was beaten to death.

"Soar-uh me-uh." The girl's ghost sobbed. "Soar-uh me-uh."

Emma pulled out her phone, nodding along as Paul continued poking at his tablet and briefing them.

She opened her translator app and repeated the ghost's phrase, careful to match the pronunciation.

"*Sora mea*," she read out loud, staring at the app. *My sister.* Emma's heart chilled even beyond the cold of the Other, but the ghost was already gone. She forced herself to hurry forward and catch up with Leo, who, along with Paul and Midori, was forming up behind a SWAT van that idled at the storage facility's entrance.

"You saw something right there," he said without preamble, stepping aside with her.

This time, he didn't even flinch as she recapped what she'd just seen and felt. Maybe whatever was bugging him had been related to her ghosts. And maybe he'd worked through it during the briefing.

Either way, the change in his mood toward her meant a lot, even in the face of the suffering she'd just witnessed.

We can't rescue her, Emma girl. But maybe we can save her sister.

36

Emma, Leo, and the rest of the raiding force were preparing to enter when Tibble rolled up. He tore out of his vehicle and joined them, buckling his vest on with one hand and slapping a helmet over his head with the other. "Sorry. Damn traffic doesn't quit in this town."

Emma was glad of the distraction, because it meant Paul had to bring his SSA up to speed. That gave her a chance to get the rest of the plan from Leo, since the ghost had interrupted her.

"It's pretty simple. We're going in from the back with Boston PD and two hostage rescue agents. Tibble, Paul, and Midori will enter from the front with SWAT. Additional units will stay in reserve, ready to move in when called."

"And it's flash-bangs on entry, clearing as we go."

He nodded. "Ready to join our crew?"

They formed up with the two police officers and hostage rescue team agents who would lead their breach operation at the back of the building.

She and Leo huddled with them as the group examined the facility layout on another tablet.

The lead HRT agent identified their path into the building. "We'll enter at the back door and should be facing a bank of storage lockers. These'll be like closets, running left to right. We want to go right, to the closer corner, then follow the wall along this set of storage units to the next corner. From there, we breach these double doors. They open into the larger units, and that's where we expect the hostiles and hostages to be."

Leo paused the briefing with a raised hand. "Can we get thermal imaging to identify who's where? How many?"

The agent shook his head. "No can do. Bird's up there," he aimed a finger at the helicopter circling the area, "but that roof is corrugated aluminum. Thermal can't penetrate it."

Emma and Leo remained silent for the rest of the briefing. The HRT agents would breach and throw in flashbangs. Emma and Leo would then take point position and follow the exterior wall to the right, with the HRT agents bringing up the rear.

The cops would remain outside in case any hostiles attempted to flee in that direction. They'd also be there to collect hostages whi might use the door to escape.

Paramedics were standing by, with two ambulances on the street and four available just minutes away.

Emma and Leo entered the fenced perimeter with the others, using the SWAT van for cover. Once they'd passed the roll-up garage door, they sprinted along the building, toward the back corner. Tibble and the other agents had stacked around the entrances at the front of the building.

His first move would be to announce their presence and make another formal request for the shooters and traffickers to surrender.

Emma had her doubts. Ever since they'd entered that fence, her ears had been ringing with the cries of every ghost she'd seen on the case so far, especially the last one who'd been wailing for her sister. She forced herself to listen for the human voices she needed to hear instead.

At the back of the building, Emma and the others waited for Tibble's announcement. A call came over the radio that he was ready, and a moment later, his amplified voice echoed across the sky.

"This is Supervisory Special Agent Tibble of the FBI. You are surrounded. Come out now, with your hands in the air. Place all weapons on the ground."

His statements were met with muffled shouting and sporadic gunfire.

"Guess that's our cue." Emma nodded at the agents holding breaching gear and flash-bangs at the ready.

One of them used a Halligan bar to snap the door open. The other flung in two flash-bang grenades and slammed the door closed in its frame to protect the team from the effects. The explosions came seconds later, and he yanked the door back open.

Emma took point, rushing inside with Leo at her back.

He edged into her peripheral vision at her left, his weapon trained down the hall in that direction. "Clear this side."

"Clear on mine too."

The HRT agents entered and formed up beside Leo, motioning for them to move forward. With quiet, even steps, Emma advanced, weapon raised and eyes sighted on the corner ahead.

She passed each storage locker, expecting the door to swing wide, revealing a shooter or hostage. When they came close to the corner, Emma held a hand up to stop the team. Leo's hand settled on her left shoulder. He squeezed to signal they were ready.

Listening for motion ahead, she waited. Hearing nothing, Emma tapped Leo's hand, resumed her grip on her pistol, and pivoted around the corner, feeling the team surge around with her.

She'd almost thought they'd join up with Tibble and the other agents without meeting resistance, but she'd been wrong.

A large man stood directly in front of them, his eyes wide and his gun held to the head of a pretty young woman who couldn't be older than eighteen. Emma held her gun steady. The man sneered at them, tightening his grip across the hostage's chest as he backed up a step.

His gun muzzle ground into her temple as he pulled her with him, covering more of his body with her form. "You are allowing me to go free. With her."

Tears streamed from the girl's wide eyes as she tugged on his arm, trying to get free. His hold was too strong for her to break. She said something that sounded Romanian, but Emma didn't know the words.

Her captor dragged her backward, and her bare heels left bloody marks on the concrete floor. She screamed, and he clutched her to him.

Without even thinking, Emma spoke the last Romanian words she'd heard.

"Sora mea. Sora mea."

The man halted, staring wild-eyed at Emma. The girl raised her foot and slammed it down on the brute's toes. He roared and lifted the gun to bring it down on her head.

Emma lunged forward and knocked his weapon aside with her left hand on his wrist. He fired, and the shot punched through the corrugated metal roof. The girl continued to stomp and kick while Emma grappled with him, keeping his gun aimed up and bringing her other elbow under his chin to knock his head back.

The girl stumbled forward and out of his arms as the man

fell against the wall. He brought his gun around, and Emma took her shot, firing twice at his chest.

He fell sideways, and the gun clattered to the floor.

She checked him for a pulse to confirm he was dead before turning back to the others. One HRT agent directed the hostage back down the hallway.

"To the door. Cops will meet you outside. Go."

She didn't need any more encouragement and raced around the corner to the exit.

Emma took a deep breath that came out in a sudden rush. From deeper within the facility, automatic weapon fire erupted in a deafening volley.

37

Emma took off with the others on her heels. She paused at the next corner, waiting for Leo's hand to slap her shoulder, before pivoting around with her weapon forward. The corridor was empty, and the double doors stood open ahead of them. Gunfire and shouting echoed heavily against the metallic roof and roll-up doors.

Emma did another pivot so she could see through the doorway, careful not to extend her weapon or body into the space. Gunfire continued to come in short bursts.

Through the doors, she saw the backs of a dozen traffickers as well as four bodies lying on the floor. None of the traffickers faced her. In the depths of a storage unit, young women and a few teenage girls gaped at her, pleading looks on all their faces. She motioned them back.

Beyond the traffickers, SWAT members took what shots they could from around riot shields.

The HRT agents moved alongside Emma. One signaled for her to hold position while they moved forward, holding a flash-bang ready. The lead agent radioed to Tibble's team so they could prepare for the grenade's effect.

He raised three fingers and dropped them, one at a time, before throwing the grenade through the double doors.

Emma peeled away, pressing her hands over her ears. The grenade exploded with a thunderclap that would've sent stars across her vision and likely had her stumbling to the floor, dazed, had she not.

As it was, she only had a mild ringing in her ears and could see just fine. The HRT agent radioed to Tibble's element, who were advancing from the other side. "Friendlies coming through. Hold fire."

Taking the lead, Emma and Leo swept through with the HRT agents behind them. They went to secure two traffickers who'd managed to avoid the full effects of the flash-bangs, having taken refuge in the storage unit with the women.

Seeing themselves surrounded and cornered, the remaining traffickers lowered their weapons and raised their hands.

Emma and Leo covered the ones who'd survived. They knelt behind the barricade they'd erected using pallets and boxes taken from an open unit beside them.

Working in pairs with members of Tibble's team, Emma and Leo zip-tied each trafficker's wrists together and hauled them to the roll-up door that led outside. The van they'd come in was riddled with bullet holes and sat on three flat tires.

Of the nearly a dozen traffickers who had been on-site, only five survived the battle unscathed. Two had minor injuries.

The women hiding in the storage unit, all thirty-four of them, were escorted out by HRT to the waiting paramedics. Emma followed along, helping one young woman who clutched her bloody arm with her hand. The rest appeared unharmed, aside from angry bruises and the terror of their ordeal.

Emma passed off the hostage she'd helped to a paramedic, then moved through the scene outside in a half daze herself.

Who does this? What kind of person treats another human being as a product to be shipped, bought, sold, and abused at will?

The surviving traffickers sat in a line outside the storage facility, monitored by cops and a few SWAT agents.

Midori approached Emma with a wry grin. "Paul got shot." She put up a hand. "I'm not happy about that, but it wasn't fatal. He just wanted me to tell you his 'junk' is intact."

The laugh that burst from Emma's chest was as honest as any she'd let loose in recent memory. But her humor faded as she took in the mass of shivering, terrified young women and girls being cared for by paramedics. "Did any of the traffickers give up their contacts here or know who's behind the murders?"

"No. At least, not any who we've talked to. Unless you speak fluent Romanian, you're not getting anything out of these guys."

Emma looked up and down the line of handcuffed traffickers. "Which one of you is Rosco?"

He has to be alive, Emma girl. That kind of scum is the first to duck and run for cover.

None of the men answered, even when a SWAT member walked up and down prodding their feet with his boots, repeating the question.

A shout from behind her had Emma turning toward the paramedics. The first young woman Emma had helped rescue on entering the storage building was shouting in Romanian and pointing a finger at the trafficker in the middle of the line.

Emma waved for the paramedic to bring the woman closer, but she stormed forward on her own.

"That man. The one in the blue turtleneck. That is the piece of shit, Rosco."

Emma stared at the man who'd been pointed out. His lip twitched, but that was all as two SWAT agents stepped in to yank him up by his arms and walk him away from the group.

Leo emerged from the facility and joined Emma. "Is that our guy?"

"Seems like it. She fingered him for us." Emma motioned toward the woman, who'd been taken back to the area where paramedics were bandaging injuries and providing blankets to the trafficking victims. "Ready to see what Rosco knows?"

Leo smiled and held out a hand. "Lead the way."

The agents had Rosco seated by himself across the driveway from where the fighting had occurred. Emma crouched in front of him, meeting his eyes. "What can you tell us about the people in charge of this operation?"

He only stared.

Leo pointed back toward the women. "You're going to spend the rest of your life in prison for your role in this. Nobody is going to bail you out."

The man remained unmoved and silent.

Emma was ready to try again when SSA Tibble stalked over. "This our lead sicko?"

Rosco spit at his feet, but Tibble merely stepped back. "Spit don't do much compared to your fancy guns, does it?" He scrubbed his foot over the saliva. "But your people shot down two cops and wounded three of my agents. Two counts of murder and three for attempted murder of law enforcement officers means this sunlight you're enjoying right now," he aimed a finger skyward, "might be the last you ever see."

Tibble folded his arms with a huff and looked at Emma and Leo.

"You already tell him Bert Wheeler's dead?"

Rosco flinched visibly, and Emma leaned into the advantage. "We forgot that part, didn't we? The whole thing's over, Rosco. This is Leo. He's the one you last spoke to about *keeping the girls safe*."

The trafficker's cheeks reddened. "I figured that. Why did you think we were waiting for you?" He looked between the three of them, licking his lips, and glanced to the girls. "I take care of girls." A smirk curled his lips. "Just hired help, doing what I am paid for."

Leo grimaced. "And that's an excuse? That you're following orders? Sounds like Eichmann's defense. Which means you're a worthless piece of shit." He kicked the side of Rosco's boot, getting his attention once more. "Tell us about the operation. What happened, where, and when."

The man's lips tightened, and Emma coughed. "Now, Rosco. We're losing patience."

Rosco sat back, twisting his arms against the zip ties, but there was no getting out of them. Finally, he relented. "Always at the Fallweather Hotel. Since…for several years. One or two nights a week, rich men get to party with girls, drugs, whatever they want. They pay, we bring girls. I only brought girls and waited for the men to be done with them."

Leo turned away in disgust, his whole face puckered with anger, but Emma crouched in front of him. "Who's running the show, Rosco? Who's in charge?"

The trafficker shrugged, actually managing to look disinterested. "I always deal with Conrad and Wilhelm. They are in charge until they are dead."

Tibble grunted. "Obviously someone outside the organization caught wind of things and has been killing off the guys in charge. Any idea who might've found out?"

Rosco glared at them, then finally turned his gaze toward the women who sat in groups near the open storage unit. "Ask the rat who gave me away. I heard her talking on the phone yesterday. She mentioned a stupider-than-stupid girl we used to have. Cristina." Rosco spat on the floor again. "I went after her and took the phone, but she had already smashed it. She is one of our best girls. So I couldn't make her pay too much. Just a little slap is all she got. You understand."

Emma clenched her fists, fighting the urge to show Rosco just how much she understood. The group of hostages remained huddled together, but the woman who had pointed out Rosco rose to her feet as Emma approached.

Before she could call out, the woman broke from the huddle and ran. She was stopped immediately by a line of SWAT agents. When she turned back to Emma, tears streaked her cheeks, but her lips were set in a defiant line. Emma met her gaze, her breath catching at the ferocity she found there.

She's a survivor and means to remain one.

38

Waiting for Daniela to call had become a chore, but I could not help giving her more time. In front of me, the marina stretched out like a maze. Wooden walkways led between row after row of gleaming white boats, each of them bearing a ridiculous and romanticized name.

The longer I looked at them, the colder and harder the bench beneath me became.

I was so close to finishing my mission, but I also wanted to know Daniela and the others were safe. That the Feds had found them and stopped that side of the operation.

My phone rang earlier, but she hung up before speaking. That could mean she had been found out, or it could mean she had run out of time for the call. If the men who acted as muscle for the operation caught her with the phone, she could even have been killed.

I thumbed my phone, thinking about calling her. If she had not been saved, calling her would likely get her caught. And if the Feds had found her and rescued her...if I called and she was with them, I could be found out.

It has been decided, then. I am out of time.

I hurled the phone out into the dregs of the harbor. It splashed with barely a whisper, and I found myself smiling.

At last, I would be done.

Perhaps, I would be caught…*probably*, I would be caught. But I would go down as a hero to my country, my friends, and my family. And I would do so only after accomplishing my mission. Justice would have been served.

For Cristina, and for everyone like her who had suffered because these rich men wanted to treat the women of my country like cattle.

Luckily, I had already tracked Shane Field to his beloved yacht club. It was only a matter of sneaking aboard and delivering my final message to the wealthy and corrupt in this city.

Your sins will come back to you, and you will know the suffering you have caused.

39

Emma and Leo let the young woman get settled before asking her anything. They'd moved to the back of an ambulance, where a paramedic was treating the soles of her bare feet.

"Am I in trouble?" She peered between them. "I told you who was Rosco. I should be free."

"You're absolutely not in trouble." Emma kept her voice low but serious.

In another situation like this, she might've aimed for gentle, but they already knew this young woman with a giant bruise on her cheek was a fighter. Glitter in her hair and perfect makeup notwithstanding, the woman sitting in front of them wasn't someone she'd condescend to. Not after what she'd been through.

"We only want to make sure everyone is safe and get to the bottom of what's been happening. It sounds like you can help us with that. Let's start with your name."

"Daniela. I suppose you are talking of the murders. Of Jimmy and his friends." She glared over Leo's shoulder, where the captured traffickers were being herded into a van for transport. "I hated them. I am glad they are dead. I do not want to go to prison…but they deserved to die."

Leo nodded, lips pursed. "I don't blame you for feeling that way, Daniela. We believe you know the person responsible for the murders. Is that true?"

The woman's face hardened, and she dropped her hands to her sides. "I am saying nothing without a lawyer. I do not know who is killing anybody. But if he killed Jimmy Conrad and the others, then he is a hero. Look at me. Look at us!" She waved a hand toward the group of women they'd rescued. "A hero protects the vulnerable."

"There is a very clear line between heroism and murder."

"It is for Cristina. For his sister. She tried to escape, and they beat her, so bad she could not see. Still, she tried to run, and they killed her for that. To be an example." She looked at Emma, lifting her chin. "That is why I knew I could trust you in there. When you said those words to me. I thought you were just like all the cops at the port, the ones who let Rosco get away with this. But you said, 'Sora mea,' and I knew you meant it. How did you know to say those words?"

With Daniela, Leo, and the paramedic looking at her, Emma struggled to come up with a reply. Leo must've intuited this, because he quickly redirected the conversation.

"Daniela, you clearly know who he is, so tell us. Please."

She remained determined, her back ramrod straight, lips sealed, and hands balled into fists.

Emma leaned in, speaking quietly. "I know you have been through hell, and nobody will fault you for wanting to see the people who did this suffer. But if you don't help us, you will be implicated in the trafficking and the murders."

Daniela jerked away from Emma, a look of disgust warping her features. "I did not help any of them steal me and the other women. I did not punch my best friend in the face until her eyes were closed with bruises and blood. I did not do anything except survive in this hell they made for me."

"And nobody here is disputing that, but if you had a line of communication to the suspect, you could have asked him to bring the authorities to your location. Did you?"

Daniela stared at her, dumbstruck, as if the thought had never occurred to her. Emma took that as a sign she'd been communicating with the killer more for updates on his progress and possibly to feed him information about his targets.

"If you never asked him to call the cops, to tell them where you were being held, but instead helped him—"

"He only killed the ones who deserved it! The ones who made it all happen, who paid Rosco to take us and keep us hidden. If I go to jail, too, that is okay with me. They deserved whatever he did to them." She ran her hands through her hair, sinking her fingers into the dark tresses. "I would do it myself if I could. And I told you. The cops are against us! They helped our captors."

Leo put up a hand to stop her when it seemed clear Daniela had a lot more to say. Her breath came in heaving gasps, her face a mask of righteous anger built up over months of torment.

"We know he's already killed two people who weren't involved in the trafficking operation. Mark Wilhelm's driver and Bert Wheeler's wife. Neither of them knew of or was involved in this. They were collateral damage in your friend's one-man war." Emma narrowed her gaze at Daniela. "You'll be considered an accessory after the fact for their deaths as well."

Daniela shook her head, but the tightness with which she gripped her hair betrayed her nerves. "Adrian would never do that."

We got a first name now. That's a start.

"Daniela, look at me." Leo waited, and when she did, honest sympathy bled from his expression. "We're telling you the truth. Innocent people *have died*. Adrian is a ruthless killer who is not going to stop until he feels he's completed this mission of revenge for what was done to you."

Emma stepped in, knowing they needed to lean into Daniela's desire to protect Adrian. "We understand why you want to protect him. He's on a dangerous path of revenge, and it's only a matter of time before things get worse. We need to stop this before more lives are lost, including his. Can you help us save Adrian's life?"

The young woman swallowed, twisting her hair back and forth. Finally, she wilted against the ambulance wall and stared at the pavement. "When I was sixteen, men came to my village."

"This was in Romania." Emma spoke gently, only wanting to prod her forward.

Daniela nodded. "We were poor. The men…promised good jobs. My best friend, his sister, Cristina Albescu, she and I went with them."

Emma opened her Notes app and typed in the name, confirming the spelling with Daniela.

The woman met her gaze head-on, the fierce defiance from earlier adding color to her cheeks. "Your suspect, my friend, is Cristina's older brother. Adrian. She was killed trying to escape…trying to go to your police, who were taking money to help this happen."

Leo muttered something about tragedy and saints protecting them, but Emma swallowed down half a million curses and pushed on. "Daniela, who is Adrian going after next?"

She frowned and twisted her hands in her lap. "He only had two targets left, and then he was going to take us back to

Romania. We would use the ship that brought us here in the first place. He would force the captain to take us."

"The targets, Daniela. The longer you take to tell us, the more likely you are to be implicated as an accessory to murder. No matter what has been done to you, that charge will come down because of the vicious and horrific nature of Adrian's acts."

She blanched and set her hands by her side. Sensing she might leap up and try to run, Emma closed the gap between her and Leo.

Daniela finally nodded. "One was Rosco. He should have been first, but he would be the last, when Adrian came to get us. The other is a rich asshole, like Jimmy and Mark and Bert. He is corrupt just like them. He deserves to die."

"His name, Daniela." Emma reached out and gripped her shoulder, near to begging. "Please."

For a moment, Emma thought she'd refuse, but Daniela raised her chin. "His name is Shane Field, and he is probably already dead."

A breath shot from Emma's lungs. "Thank you, Daniela. For your and Adrian's sakes, let's hope he isn't."

She called over two cops, who were standing at the entrance to the storage facility. They walked Daniela back to join the other trafficking survivors, while Emma and Leo made a beeline for Tibble.

"She gave us a name." Emma waved her phone with the Notes app open on the screen. "Shane Field. Jimmy Conrad's wife mentioned that her husband was often on a yacht belonging to a friend named Shane. That's got to be our guy."

Tibble frowned, already typing into his phone. "Most expensive yacht club is the Boston Yacht Haven, forty-five minutes from here. Take Yankee Division west to Highway 1. That'll be faster than going through Salem."

For a moment, Emma feared he had found out. She

flashed a look at Leo, who lifted a shoulder. Tibble had continued divesting himself of his vest and helmet and was getting into a vehicle with Midori. "I'll confirm that's where Field keeps his midlife crisis. If he's got a private slip somewhere else, I'll head there with Midori. We'll catch him, one way or another."

Emma turned on her heel, running to catch up with Leo, who'd already headed for their vehicle. She raced forward and beat him to the driver's side door.

They didn't have time to waste, and she wasn't letting the Other get in the way this time.

Even though she understood what drove Adrian Albescu to kill, they had to stop him.

40

I had been up and down the docks, checking one slip after another before I came upon such a large yacht that I could not even see onto the deck above. And then I saw the name.

Romanian Princess.

My throat tightened. The bastard was making fun of my country's daughters, destroying their dignity even at the level of parading his criminal sins and the source of his wealth for anyone who would look.

I moved to the gangplank with a small landing at the top positioned alongside the yacht. Moving up at a crouch, I reached the landing and turned to scan the deck for crew or guards. Part of me had prepared for multiple obstacles between me and my target, Shane Field, but the yacht seemed nearly deserted.

The muted sound of a television carried on the air. Once I stepped onto the boat, I moved sideways along the rail until I could see the man himself. Watching news on his television, not paying the slightest attention to his surroundings, even though he must have known I was searching for him.

Ever an arrogant fool.

Field picked up his phone and held it to his ear. He nearly yelled into it. "You're supposed to be here! You and your guys. Now! We need to leave frickin' yesterday. Get here, or I swear you'll be sorry and never work on another yacht again, you piece of shit!"

Waiting for his people. Too stupid to even have an escape vehicle he can take care of himself.

Peering back to the surrounding yachts, I listened for anyone. Nobody had been on the ships I had passed leading to this one, and from my current height, the closest person I saw was at least twenty meters away in the parking lot.

A lifeboat strung to the side of the yacht contained a stow with rope, just as expected. I grabbed it, fingering the long coil, and turned back to Field. He was as I had seen him before, seated in front of his giant television, ignorant of his own fate now lurking on his deck.

Leaving the rope beside the lifeboat, I edged around the cabin, out of his sight line. His back was to me as I reached the door. It seemed too much to hope for, to find it unlocked, but Shane Field was an idiot of the worst kind.

Not only confident but parading through his life as if he were immortal.

In one movement, I opened the door and sped forward. He stood from his chair and whirled on me, grabbing at a gun in his waistband. He pulled it free, but I was already there, latching onto his wrist and wrenching the weapon from his grip with my other hand.

I held onto him, squeezing and twisting his arm around.

Watching the man's eyes bug out, I backed him up with one hand on his wrist and the other aiming his own gun at his face. He wheezed a cry, tears rising from the pain I inflicted.

"Please. Please. I haven't done anything."

I laughed. After all this time, all these years spent in serious pursuit of revenge…I laughed.

"This is going to be fun. For me, Shane Field. For you, not so much."

Shane sobbed, and I shoved him to the ground, yanking down on his wrist even as I twisted harder, forcing his shoulder out of the socket.

"I can get you money!" He screamed as I twisted his arm farther behind him. "Please. If you want the girls, they're yours. Whatever you want!"

In answer, I flung his pistol to the side, across the little cabin. I unsheathed my knife and bent down to show it to him in the corner of his eye.

Shane kept blubbering his offers to me until I released his wrist, stepped around his whimpering form, and backhanded him across the face.

His sobbing took over, and his words became unintelligible as he cowered before me.

This is it. Once I am done, once I kill this imbecile, my mission will be over. Daniela and I will take the girls home. We will be free.

But that would only be true if my message reached the people who might support the next Rosco. Any joy I felt from killing Jimmy Conrad, Mark Wilhelm, and Bert Wheeler would pale against what I was about to do to Shane Field.

I had undertaken this mission on Cristina's behalf. I owed it to her, and to my people, to ensure none of us had to endure such torment again.

So I would enjoy this kill, and I would make it a statement that could not be ignored.

"Take off all your clothes." I stood, allowing the knife to dangle from my hand.

Shane remained curled on the floor, sobbing.

"I said, take off your clothes!" I kicked him in his stomach, hard, and he coughed. Slowly, he rose to his knees and tried to unbutton his shirt. But with his dislocated shoulder, he only had one hand, so I knocked it away and used my knife to start a cut in the fabric at his collar.

He pulled back from me, so I placed my knife under his eye. He froze, and I gripped his shirt where I'd made the cut, tearing it down the middle. Buttons popped loose and flew to the side. He tried to back away from me again, and I surged forward, pushing him over onto his back.

If he had been more cooperative, I might have made less of a mess. But Field proved himself utterly useless, and I was forced to hold him down with my weight and slice his clothing from his body, sometimes adding little cuts to his skin, while maintaining a firm grip around his neck.

All it took was a few little squeezes, and the man understood who was in charge.

I worked fast, and he was finally naked and bleeding from the many places where I had cut him. Slapping his face twice, I thought of my sister, and of Daniela, and all the girls who had been lied to and turned into cattle for these pigs. I punched him in the mouth, again and again, then grabbed the bicep on his good arm, tugged him forward, and aimed him at the door I had come through.

"We are going outside. Move."

He stumbled out and landed in a naked heap on the deck. I grabbed his other arm, the one I had been twisting, and gave him a kick in the stomach to ensure he could not scream yet. He curled around himself, grunting and heaving in a breath.

But I still managed to drag him to where he needed to be.

Forcing him prone, I used the rope I had found to tie his wrists and ankles together. I made sure the knots were tight enough to cut off circulation before I hauled him to the side of the boat.

Once I secured the rope to the railing, I sheathed my knife, picked up the whimpering worm I had caught, and threw him overboard.

He screamed but quickly went quiet as his body slammed into the side of the boat and the wind was knocked from his lungs. I leaned over and gazed down. He wiggled, struggling, but his wrists were secure. Another small laugh broke from my throat as the man screamed and begged for help that would not come in time.

Help was coming, of course. Somebody had to have heard him, so the police would be on their way. Any moment, I guessed. And I would make them watch while I mutilated and killed this man.

I ran down the gangplank and watched Shane dangle a few feet down the dock. With three quick strides, I stood before him, his feet brushing the water below. When I reached out my knife and pricked his manhood, he squealed and jerked to the side, setting himself swinging left to right.

"Good game, Shane Field. You will swing. I will play pin the guilt on the evil motherfucker."

He shrieked again, screaming for someone to help as I lifted my knife and aimed it for his chest.

I would make my mark before anyone arrived.

With the first sting of injury, the man squirmed even more and squealed into the sky, crying. I gripped him by the throat with my other hand.

And I kept cutting.

41

Emma had never liked yacht clubs, not least of all because they were a mess of luxury and arrogance, but because her father had brought her to a fair number of parties hosted at them. For the first time in her life, she was thankful for those very events.

Tibble had texted the slip number for Shane Field's yacht and said he and Midori were on the way with backup.

Sirens blared across the evening sky as Emma and Leo rounded a ship and aimed for Shane's slip, weapons drawn.

The yacht loomed ahead of them, larger than the ones to either side. But the vessel was also the only one to have a naked man hanging from the gunwale. Bit of a dead giveaway.

His arms stretched taut above him as blood streamed from the Roman numeral four incised deep into his chest.

And their killer stood just in front of him. His knife at the ready.

"Greetings, Agents." The killer edged his blade closer to Shane Field, whose eyes bulged. He'd been gagged with a strip of fabric but still managed to whimper incessantly from behind it. "You are here just in time. I am about to show you what real justice looks like."

Emma opened her mouth to debate the man, to say something—anything—that might hold him back, but Leo stepped up first.

"This isn't real justice, Adrian." Leo moved slowly forward, inching ahead of Emma, and she fell back. His voice didn't ring with the charm he usually used to placate suspects, but raw sympathy and pain. "I'm sorry for what happened to your sister, Cristina."

"Do not tell me about my sister!" Adrian's roar echoed around the marina.

"I'm not." Leo stepped forward once more, voice even. He hadn't even faltered. "I promise I'm not. She deserves justice, Adrian, but this is a step too far. Between you and us, the trafficking operation is shut down. Done. Captain Mariz's ship is being impounded, and he and his crew will face extradition for their roles. Daniela and the other women are safe now."

Adrian shook his head, and Emma thought she saw the blade tremble. With anger or some other emotion, she couldn't tell, and the man's face didn't give them any clues. "No. Until the system changes, there will always be rich and powerful men who exploit it. Another ship and another captain will come. The daughters of Romania and other countries will not be safe unless the people who want to steal them know what it will cost."

He reached to the side quickly and took hold of Shane's penis, stretching it out from his body and placing his knife against the organ. The bound man squirmed and tried to scream against the gag in his mouth.

Emma rushed a step forward to stand beside Leo, holding her aim on the killer. "Stop, Adrian. Mutilating and brutally murdering this man will not bring Cristina back or stop human trafficking."

"It will stop him, and others like him will stop when they see what I will do to them."

"What you will do, Adrian? You're going to jail for the murders of five people, two of whom had nothing to do with the trafficking that killed Cristina."

Adrian seemed to choke on air, and when he spoke, Emma realized he'd begun crying. "If I had done nothing, more lives would be stolen. More women raped and killed. None of you would have known the difference. The FBI never would have brought down this operation without me."

His words dissolved into sobs, and he wailed something that might've been an attempt at his sister's name.

"Adrian, that might be true." Leo softened his voice a touch more. "But killing Shane Field won't change anything. It won't bring your sister back, and the trafficking operation that killed her is already done for. Finished for good. Now… you have to let Shane go. If you do, we will make sure he's punished."

"*No.*"

The word had come fast and hard, and Emma knew without question that he was about to use his blade on Field. She had to act *now*.

Emma's mind raced through the numerous scenarios, debated the ethics and consequences, and the decision now rested on her shoulders. It was her last vote, the final call on how to proceed.

Not allowing herself to doubt her sense of hearing, Emma fired once, aiming for and hitting Adrian in the upper chest. He fell back, releasing his grip on Field's genitals and staggering down the dock as Emma raced forward with Leo beside her.

They reached him together as he found his feet and took

a fighter's stance, but he wobbled and dropped to one knee. Keeping her weapon trained on him, Emma motioned for Leo to cuff the killer's hands. He moved in a wide circle around the bleeding man and stepped up with his cuffs in hand.

Adrian seemed to gain a second wind as the metal clasps went around his wrists. He struggled against Leo's grip but could only muster the strength to shout at them. "You will never stop them! They will keep taking girls away and making them into slaves!"

He stood with Leo's assistance and attempted to bring up a leg to kick at Emma. She backed away, holstered her weapon, and helped Leo restrain the man.

Emma was dimly aware of cops and agents swarming the marina. A woman in uniform edged past her and climbed the gangplank to Shane Field's yacht. She and another officer hauled him up to the deck and gave him a blanket for cover.

The man released a string of curses when the gag was removed, but the woman only laughed. "According to someone named Rosco, we should be fitting you for an orange jumpsuit, too, so maybe save it until your lawyer gets here."

On the dock, with a bloody and semiconscious Adrian Albescu between them, Emma and Leo exchanged a look. They'd completed the case, brought the killer down, and even managed to avoid another death. If they played things right, they'd be able to use the piece of shit to bring down the rest of the empire. Or at least a chunk of it.

"Time to get back home, yeah?"

Leo met her eyes, and the fatigue and worry she'd seen him wearing since earlier that afternoon was suddenly back in full force. "Yeah. I'm ready to be back."

Her heart thumped. "Leo, what…?"

"I got a text from Denae's brother. Her family has been

holding a bedside vigil since the last time Denae's heart monitor alarm went off." He drew in a shaky breath. "That night you saw her, in the motel room."

"But she's still alive." Emma gripped Leo's wrist. "She has to be. Jacinda said she'd—"

"She's alive. Yes, she's alive, and her family's living in fear of the moment that might not be true. They want me to be there…if it happens." His voice was thick with the tears he was clearly holding back. "I need to be on that plane yesterday."

"Our flight leaves tomorrow morning. It's the first one out. We'll be there soon, and you'll be with them."

His chin dropped to his chest, and he shook with a single sob. Emma did the only thing she thought might help and wrapped her friend in a hug.

42

Monique sat cross-legged in front of her ritual table, focusing on Emma Last. She anchored her spirit to the cleansed silk cushion that she'd had sitting outside in a patch of lavender all morning. She'd spent the last day and a half preparing her magic, but now she was ready to call upon the Other for guidance.

Carefully, working from true north to true south and back to north again, she spread the herbs she'd collected from her garden across the table. She anchored the table with hematite next and gave a calculated glance to the perimeter of the chalked circle surrounding herself and her magic table. All the crystals were in place, charged with energy from the moon and as ready as they would ever be.

Don't hesitate now. You can't.

She pulled her sacrificial blade from beneath the table and, slow and steady, drew it across her forearm. The ritual words of protection spilled from her lips, and she could only hope they worked. Kept her in hiding, unseen, as she had been all these years.

Not having felt the coldness since yesterday, she still

sensed how close it could be if she allowed it. Like it lingered in her mind.

Moments passed. Then seconds, then minutes.

Slowly, she felt a weightlessness come into her chest. Her connection to the Other opening.

Closing her eyes, she relaxed her mind into that weightlessness, pulling her consciousness inward until she began to feel two presences surrounding her. When her body had gone cooler with the Other, the presences radiating their own energy against hers, she finally opened her eyes to see a figure sharing her space. She didn't recognize him.

The man had died by gunshot. His countenance was calm, like someone who'd lived with the give-and-take of energy all his life and had been comfortable in the spirit realm even before he'd made his first visit. Knowingly or not. His loose exercise pants and light t-shirt were covered in blood. But his eyes sparkled, even through the milky-white haze of the Other.

When he realized she was there, he attempted to speak to her, but the words were muffled.

He remained calm, but his eyes went sorrowful and wide. He pressed his palms together as if centering himself, then stared forward at her as if to broadcast his message. When he spoke this time, she understood him.

"Emma is in danger. You have to help her."

Monique's eyes shut tight as her body went stiff with the veracity of the message. Her mind traveled to another place, to a forest. In the vision, the grown-up Emma was being hunted by an enormous wolf. The young woman looked so much like her mother. Between that, the howl of the wolf, and its intensifying pursuit, Monique's breath nearly stopped.

The chase grew more desperate until Monique couldn't

take it anymore. Her hands jumped to her ears, cutting off the sound as well as the vision, and she breathed out.

Counting down, she escaped from both the sound of the wolf and her connection with the Other.

She pushed back from the circle in horror, but there was no question about what she'd seen and heard.

Somehow, she had to help Emma Last. The promise Monique had made to her mother all those years ago was still in effect, for as long as Monique lived and even beyond, should it come to that.

But the presence of the wolf suggested that the danger might go far deeper than their mutual enemy's hunt for Emma. Monique still didn't allow herself to think the woman's name, lest she call her foe's attention. If that woman was working with the wolf, their combined plans might be far more ambitious than simple revenge.

And we might all be in far more danger than I realized.

43

Leo waited in the hall outside Denae's hospital room beside her younger brother Jamaal. They looked on awkwardly as Jamaal's girlfriend, Hope, clung to Emma and sobbed as Emma spoke quietly to Denae's mother. Leo had already survived that, if barely.

"Leo, it's been so good to meet you. Denae...she loves you. I hope you know that, and thank you for joining us at our vigil."

Hearing those words from her mother had nearly broken him. And when her father had stepped up and told Leo he should join the family for dinner...

The man was in with his daughter now, sitting by her side as monitors beeped and chirped.

She's still alive. She's asleep and may not wake up for a long time...or at all. But she's still alive.

Emma whispered nearly those exact words into Hope's hair, holding her tight as the girl finally calmed. Jamaal swallowed hard. "Her and Denae didn't spend much time together, but the way Hope sees it...Denae's family, too, and seeing her like that..."

Fighting not to break down, Leo clenched his lips and

swallowed a sob. "My and Denae's whole team are here for you and your family if you need us too."

Jamaal nodded. "Thanks for that. Means a lot to Mom and Dad that you agreed to come back to the house later today." He paused, taking a deep breath.

The door to Denae's room burst open, and her father stormed out. "Doctor! Get the doctor!"

Leo's heart flew into his throat, and he moved to enter the room, but Jamaal beat him to it, grabbing at his father's hands.

"Dad! Dad, what's going on?"

The whole family, along with Emma and Hope, surged forward, closing around Denae's father, who had tears running down his cheeks. His eyes were on the ceiling, and he kept yelling for the doctor.

A nurse raced up and shoved her way into the room.

Leo had his hands in front of his mouth. His helplessness tore at his heart. Knowing the only thing he could do was wait...

Denae's father wrapped his arms around his son, then reached one arm out for his wife.

They held together, only moving aside when a woman in a white coat approached.

She squeezed her way past them, and moments later appeared again, waving for everyone to stand away from the door.

Leo's knees sagged, and every moment he'd spend with Denae flashed before his eyes. Her laugh. Her touch. The way she looked at him, those dark eyes filled with what he knew was love.

Was that all gone?

Closing his eyes, he waited for the words that would rip his world in two. A hand came down on his shoulder. He braced himself for the worst. It didn't come.

"She's awake."

The End
To be continued...

Thank you for reading.
All of Emma Last series books can be found on Amazon.

ACKNOWLEDGMENTS

The past few years have been a whirlwind of change, both personally and professionally, and I find myself at a loss for the right words to express my profound gratitude to those who have supported me on this remarkable journey. Yet, I am compelled to try.

To my sons, whose unwavering support has been my bedrock, granting me the time and energy to transform my darkest thoughts into words on paper. Your steadfast belief in me has never faltered, and watching each of you grow, welcoming the wonderful daughters you've brought into our family, has been a source of immense pride and joy.

Embarking on the dual role of both author and publisher has been an exhilarating, albeit challenging, adventure. Transitioning from the solitude of writing to the dynamic world of publishing has opened new horizons for me, and I'm deeply grateful for the opportunity to share my work directly with you, the readers.

I extend my heartfelt thanks to the entire team at Mary Stone Publishing, the same dedicated group who first recognized my potential as an indie author years ago. Your collective efforts, from the editors whose skillful hands have polished my words to the designers, marketers, and support staff who breathe life into these books, have been instrumental in resonating deeply with our readers. Each of you plays a crucial role in this journey, not only nurturing my growth but also ensuring that every story reaches its full potential. Your dedication, creativity, and finesse have been nothing short of invaluable.

However, my deepest gratitude is reserved for you, my beloved readers. You ventured off the beaten path of traditional publishing to embrace my work, investing your most precious asset—your time. It is my sincerest hope that this book has enriched that time, leaving you with memories that linger long after the last page is turned.

With all my love and heartfelt appreciation,
Mary

ABOUT THE AUTHOR

Mary Stone

Nestled in the serene Blue Ridge Mountains of East Tennessee, Mary Stone crafts her stories surrounded by the natural beauty that inspires her. What was once a home filled with the lively energy of her sons has now become a peaceful writer's retreat, shared with cherished pets and the vivid characters of her imagination.

As her sons grew and welcomed wonderful daughters-in-law into the family, Mary's life entered a quieter phase, rich with opportunities for deep creative focus. In this tranquil environment, she weaves tales of courage, resilience, and intrigue, each story a testament to her evolving journey as a writer.

From childhood fears of shadowy figures under the bed to a profound understanding of humanity's real-life villains, Mary's style has been shaped by the realization that the most complex antagonists often hide in plain sight. Her writing is characterized by strong, multifaceted heroines who defy traditional roles, standing as equals among their peers in a world of suspense and danger.

Mary's career has blossomed from being a solitary author to establishing her own publishing house—a significant milestone that marks her growth in the literary world. This expansion is not just a personal achievement but a reflection of her commitment to bring thrilling and thought-provoking stories to a wider audience. As an author and publisher, Mary continues to challenge the conventions of the thriller genre, inviting readers into gripping tales filled with serial killers, astute FBI agents, and intrepid heroines who confront peril with unflinching bravery.

Each new story from Mary's pen—or her publishing house—is a pledge to captivate, thrill, and inspire, continuing the legacy of the imaginative little girl who once found wonder and mystery in the shadows.

Connect with Mary online

- facebook.com/authormarystone
- x.com/MaryStoneAuthor
- goodreads.com/AuthorMaryStone
- bookbub.com/profile/3378576590
- pinterest.com/MaryStoneAuthor
- instagram.com/marystoneauthor

Printed in Great Britain
by Amazon